SONS OF DARKNESS

A NIGHT VIGIL NOVEL: BOOK ONE

GAIL Z. MARTIN

SOL

CONTENTS

SONS OF DARKNESS

A NIGHT VIGIL NOVEL: BOOK ONE

By Gail Z. Martin

For my readers. Because you read, I write.

CHAPTER ONE

THE ABANDONED WAREHOUSE squatted next to a rusting railway spur, the faded paint of its sign almost unreadable against the old brick walls. Too sturdy to knock down, too expensive to gentrify, the decaying building smelled of mold and dust, rats...and blood.

Travis Dominick moved silently through the shadows, intent on his prey. Moonlight and the distant glow of streetlights filtered through the dirty windows and skylights, giving barely enough illumination for him to make his way.

He knew his quarry had gone to ground here. The ghosts told him so, and the vision that woke him in a cold sweat showed him where to look. With raven-dark hair and black clothing, Travis melted into the shadows.

There. He saw the creature's matted brown coat as it eased around one of the pillars supporting the roof. In its beast form, the monster was the size of a large wolf or even a mastiff. But that's where the likeness to any normal canine ended. The *nachzehrer* was a vampire-shifter, a plague-carrier, and it had murdered—and eaten—an entire family. Travis had come to put an end to its killing spree.

He pulled a silver knife from the bandolier across his chest and hurled it. It flew silently and sunk hilt-deep into the creature's hindquarters. The beast gave a howl, not from the injury—which Travis knew wouldn't be lethal—but from the shift the silver forced.

Sinew and slick muscle glistened as the dirty pelt stripped away into bloody ribbons, and the body reshaped itself when bones broke and knit with a disturbing snap and crunch. The monster hunched, no longer on all fours but not yet standing upright.

A burst of gunfire cut into the creature and pockmarked the pillar behind it—fast shots from an automatic weapon. The beast bellowed, bloodied but not seriously hurt.

Then the bullets weren't silver. Fuck. There's a newbie out there who thinks he's Van Helsing.

Travis peered out from where he'd retreated with his back to one of the pillars. The creature shook off the last gory remnants of its fur. In the half-light, Travis made out the thing that had once been human, before it brought plague to its family and stripped their bones clean with the knife-sharp teeth of its changed form.

More shots tore into the monster's head and body, but the creature did not collapse, needing more than steel to slay it. Then, with a burst of speed, it leaped into the shadows, intent on bringing down its assailant.

"Shit," Travis muttered, taking off at a run. *I could have done this the easy way, but no...some Buffy wanna-be has to fuck it all up.*

Travis held a coiled silver whip in his left hand and a Glock with silver bullets in his right. Silver and steel knives of varying sizes filled the bandolier and hung from sheaths strapped to his belt. He had come prepared to destroy the monster. Now, he had to save the idiot who had gone looking for trouble—and found it.

The creature moved fast, leaping for its attacker with its teeth bared and its sharp claws out. A man cursed, and the beast yowled in pain. Travis closed in on the scene, to find a powerfully built, blond man going after the monster with a Ka-Bar in each hand. Every time

Travis moved to line up a shot with the Glock, the combatants pivoted, putting the man squarely in his sights. As annoyed as he was at the interloper, Travis couldn't justify shooting him.

The beast stood half a head taller than its opponent, but whoever the dipshit was who had blundered into Travis's hunt, the guy knew how to fight. Travis might have answered to a different authority for his training, but he'd learned from some of the best, and he recognized the close-quarters moves as elite military, maybe special ops. So perhaps the fight was not as uneven as he had first suspected.

Travis circled, looking for an opening, figuring he and the mystery man could double-team the creature.

"Stay back! I've got this!" the blond man growled, slashing with the knife in his right hand and thrusting with the blade in his left.

Unless those knives were edged with blessed silver, Travis knew the other man could harry the creature all day without ever bringing it down.

"Get out of the way, and I'll finish it," Travis called back. He lashed out with the silver whip, flaying open a deep gash in the monster's back. The beast jerked and turned, recognizing a second threat, but shifted its stance before Travis could get off a shot with the Glock, putting the man between them.

"I told you, I've got—" The reply broke off as the creature put on a press of speed, swiping its powerful clawed hand across the man's shoulder and tossing him effortlessly through the air. The stranger hit one of the support pillars hard, but he staggered to his feet, ready for another round.

"Of all the stupid, asinine, fucking idiots," Travis muttered as he tried to flank the creature, but although the beast remained intent on its injured quarry, it was clever enough not to expose its back to Travis.

The stranger didn't wait for the beast to attack again. He came at it with kicks and punches in a flurry of expertly trained movement that would have had a human opponent down in seconds. The two long knives sank deep into the monster's body, and the thing howled in fury and pain. It lunged, and claws tore into the fighter's shoulder as the beast opened its maw and bared its fangs, lowering its head toward the struggling man's throat.

Intent on fresh blood, the creature made a mistake. Travis dodged into position. He didn't dare shoot into the back of the beast for fear the bullets would go through and hit the man. But three side shots would do nicely—head, chest, and hip.

The monster roared and tossed the man aside. This time, he did not get up. Travis faced the beast, putting a silver bullet between the creature's eyes and through its heart. It fell to its knees, covered in its own blood and that of its would-be attacker, and leveled a baleful glare.

Angry red blisters criss-crossed the monster's pale skin as the blessed silver worked its poison, fighting against the unholy energies that animated the beast. Travis reached for a flask on his belt and sloshed a measure of salted holy water into the creature's ravaged face.

Travis raised a hand in blessing. "In the Name of the Father, and of the Son, and of the Holy Spirit, let there be extinguished in you all power of the devil." He made the sign of the cross. "Through this holy unction may the Lord pardon thee whatever sins or faults thou hast committed."

The *nachzehrer* that had once been a man named Rick Kohrs collapsed in a bloody heap on the floor.

Travis doused the body with lighter fluid and tossed a match, watching the corpse go up in flames, assuring that it would not rise again. He ran to where the stranger lay, fearing what he might find. The man was pale but still breathing, bleeding from deep gashes where the beast had torn into him. Travis ripped strips of cloth from the man's tattered shirt and field dressed the wounds, making it unlikely he would bleed out until Travis could get help.

Sirens wailed in the distance. Travis hefted the unconscious man over his shoulder in a fireman's carry, and dumped him into the back seat of his black Crown Vic, pulling away before the first of the fire trucks reached the scene.

He toggled hands-free dialing, and the call rang through. "Have Matthew standing by. I'm bringing in a casualty."

"You're bringing someone here?" Jon sounded incredulous. "Are you sure—"

"He's not dying, but he's banged up pretty bad," Travis said, trying not to be snappish despite the adrenaline crash. "And before we let go of him, I want to know what the hell he thought he was doing playing monster hunter."

St. Dismas Outreach took up a hard-worn former hotel off Wylie Avenue in the Hill District of Pittsburgh, a down-on-its-luck neighborhood not far from center city. Aptly named for the believing thief on the cross, St. Dismas was—as far as most people were aware—a halfway house, soup kitchen, food bank, and shelter, a last chance outpost for the tired souls who found refuge there. Fewer knew that forays like tonight's battle were equally a part of its vital, if secretive, mission.

Travis pulled the car up to the back door. Matthew and Jon came out to meet him, gentling the wounded stranger onto a stretcher and hustling him into the building before Travis had released his seatbelt. He got out and glanced in both directions. Before they had opened St. Dismas, being in an alley in this part of town in the middle of the night would have been asking for trouble. Travis had been no more willing to put up with human monsters than the kinds of creatures he hunted. It didn't take long for word to spread that hassling the folks at St. Dismas wasn't worth the grief.

Jon met him in the hallway. "What happened?" Jon was Travis's second in command, and one of the few entrusted to the knowledge of Travis's past and his nighttime hunts. They were a study in distinctions. At thirty-three and six-foot-two, Travis was solid, lean muscle, with chin-length black hair and green eyes that were in sharp contrast to the pale coloring of his Irish heritage. Jon was five-ten and forty-something, built like a fireplug, with close-cropped dark hair, wary eyes, and skin the color of espresso. Jon had been an Army chaplain before St. Dismas, and Matthew, who had disappeared with their visitor, had been a medic. Their skills still came in handy on nights like this, far too often for Travis's liking.

Travis recounted the mucked-up hunt as they walked to his small apartment on the third floor. "So you have no idea who this guy is?" Jon asked, pausing at the door.

"Trouble, that's what he is," Travis replied wearily. "And dangerous. He knew how to fight, just not how to fight a *nachzehrer*. Navy SEAL maybe, or one of the other Special Ops."

"I saw the guns and the knives. Impressive."

Travis gave a snort in reply. "And it did him so much good. I need to make sure he learns from his mistake and leaves things alone that he doesn't understand."

"He's gonna know about you when he wakes up, and he'll connect you and St. Dismas—"

"And I know about him, too," Travis replied. "I'll bet my 'day job' is more understanding than his."

Jon chuckled at the understatement. "Yeah. True. All right. I've got the front covered. Go be Batman."

"Hardly. How's the night going?" Travis asked, shifting into work mode.

"Typical. We've got more people than usual for overnight, but that's probably on account of the rain. The soup kitchen was scraping the bottom of the kettles, but we took care of everyone," Jon reported. "Broke up a fight between a couple of guys who were too high to be able to tell us what they were actually arguing about," he added, shaking his head. "You know. The usual." He paused. "On the other hand, the group therapy session with the halfway house residents went really well. So there's that."

St. Dismas served a tough part of town. While the "Steel City" had remade itself with software and technology industries after much of its manufacturing went elsewhere, not everyone could make the leap. Travis often wondered how many of the men who sought refuge here would have been just fine in the days when a millworker could earn enough for a nice house, a decent car, and retirement in Florida. Nothing in their reach paid like that now, or ever would again.

"Good," Travis said, clapping Jon on the shoulder. "Then I'll go see to our new guest. I wouldn't mind having one of those flashy-thingies like in that movie, to make him forget."

"You sure your connections don't have something? They always have the good stuff," Jon joked.

Travis sighed. "I doubt it. If people forgot what they did, why would they need to go to Confession? It would put priests out of jobs, and they can't have that."

Jon left, chuckling, while Travis headed back toward the clinic where his unexpected guest would be recovering. It had taken three years for him to be able to joke about the priesthood, after making his decision to leave behind it and the secret Vatican order of demon-hunters that had nearly cost him his life, his faith, and his sanity. The Sinistram reported to Cardinal Vasylyk, one step away from the Pope himself, and its very name implied its role, the "left hand" of the Holy Father, fighting things too terrible to acknowledge. Those among the Cardinals who did not approve had another name for the elite warrior-priests: *Filios Tenebrarum.* The Sons of Darkness.

Right now, what mattered to Travis was finding out where the hell this stranger had come from, and how it was that the man even knew about threats like the *nachzehrer.* Travis hoped to be able to dissuade their "guest" from going looking for more trouble, but he doubted that would be easy.

He reached the clinic just as Matthew closed the door behind him. "How is he?" Travis asked, worried about the stranger despite being annoyed that the man had put himself in harm's way.

"Banged up, but not too badly," Matthew replied. "He's gonna be sore, and I had to close up the worst of the gashes with stitches, but considering the alternatives, he's a pretty lucky guy."

Travis gave a snort. "What's the saying? That God looks after fools and drunkards?"

He heard a voice shout from behind the door. Matthew gave him a look. "Well, that particular 'fool' is demanding to know what's going on. He wants to talk to the boss man, and that's you."

Travis grimaced and rolled his eyes. "This should be fun," he muttered and shouldered past Matthew to enter the room.

"Who are you, and where the hell am I?"

Travis got his first good look at their houseguest in the harsh light of the clinic. It had been too dark in the warehouse to see much, and the *nachzehrer* had kept his attention occupied elsewhere. The man sitting on the edge of the clinic bed looked to be in his early thirties, with short blond hair and a muscular build that suggested boot camp rather than gym rat. The haircut said "civilian," but the way the man sat, poised to spring at the first sign of threat said "military."

"My name is Travis Dominick, and you're at the St. Dismas Center."

The stranger gave Travis a glare. "The homeless shelter?"

Travis shrugged. "That, and more." He took in the set of the man's chin, and the fire in his blue eyes, anger covering fear. "Who are you?"

The newcomer remained silent long enough that Travis began to doubt he would answer. "Brent Lawson," he said finally. "And don't get me wrong, I appreciate what you did, saving my ass, but why the fuck were you there?"

A side effect of giving up the clerical collar was that people stopped watching their language around him, Travis thought. The upside was that they now treated him like a human being, in all its messy glory. "Why were you?" he countered.

They glared at each other, and Travis was reminded of staring matches back in middle school. Finally, Brent huffed out a breath and looked away. "I tracked that thing to its lair. But I had bad intel, and the weapons I had didn't work."

"I noticed," Travis replied. "A *nachzehrer* is a vampire shifter. You needed silver to kill it, and nothing short of a head shot, decapitation, and then burning would do it."

Brent gave him an appraising look. "And you know this, how?"

"Training," Travis replied with a maddening smile. "But you still haven't told me how you ended up tracking a monster to a warehouse."

"It's what I do," Brent said after a moment. "At least, it's part of what I do." He glanced around. "Looks like you're in the part-time monster hunting business, too."

Having been a full-time hunter with the Sinistram, Travis was quite content to be "part-time," although he couldn't tell Brent that. "You would have died back there."

"I said 'thank you.'" Brent's eyes narrowed.

Travis leaned back against the wall. "You really need to leave this kind of thing to people who've been trained for it."

"Like you, Father Dominick?"

Brent couldn't have known about Travis's past, but the barb still made him wince. "I'm not a priest. Not anymore," he said quietly.

Brent frowned, then managed to look contrite. "Sorry. I thought priests only went monster hunting in the movies."

"And I thought soldiers didn't go freelance."

This time, Brent flinched. "Yeah, well. I'm out now. I have my own detective firm."

"And someone hired you to look into the family's deaths?" Travis guessed.

Brent nodded. "Yeah. A brother from out of town. When I put the pieces together, I knew it wasn't something the cops would ever believe. So I decided to handle it on my own."

Travis tried to unpack that statement because there was as much not said as what Brent admitted. "The cops wouldn't believe a monster killed those people, but you did?"

"Apparently, so did you."

Travis was in no mood to explain his past, and from the look of it, neither was Brent. "So the *nachzehrer* is dead, and the family is avenged," Travis said, trying to defuse the stubborn glint in Brent's gaze. "Now you can go back to busting Worker's Comp fraud and finding cheating spouses. Or tracking mobsters."

"Fuck you," Brent said, sliding down off the table and reaching for his shirt. His face and shoulder were already starting to bruise from where the creature had thrown him around, and despite the stitches, the wounds looked sore and puffy. There were older scars, too. Two that looked like bullet wounds, but others that might have been from knives, teeth, or claws. Travis had similar scars, knew what made marks like that. It lent credence to Brent's claims that he wasn't new at this.

"It's the middle of the night," Travis replied, ignoring the outburst. "You're welcome to stay. Matthew would probably like to check on your stitches in the morning. Those claws can carry taint."

"Not my first rodeo." Brent grimaced as he moved to pull on his shirt. "Thanks for the assist, and the medic. But I need to get home."

"You almost died out there," Travis said, blocking his way.

"And I'm glad you were there," Brent said evenly. "But I've been at this for a while now, and it's like any battle—you win some, you lose some. Every fight might be the last. Goes with the territory."

Travis reached into a pocket of his tactical vest and pulled out a card. "Look, the next time you hear of something like this, how about giving me a call? If I can't talk you out of going after it, maybe we team up? Safety in numbers?"

Brent scowled, staring at the card as if debating whether to accept it, then finally snatched it from Travis's fingers and shoved it into his jeans. "Yeah. Maybe. Depends." He moved around Travis. "I'd give you my card, but why bother? You think you've got it all figured out." With that, Brent walked out and headed down the hallway, to the rear exit and into the night.

Matthew returned to the clinic before Travis could leave. "Did you talk him out of a repeat performance?"

Travis shook his head. "Nope. And I believe him when he said he's done it before. Hell, maybe 'Special Ops' goes after creatures like this, for all we know. Not like they'd tell civilians."

"Then it's out of your hands," Matthew said. "Maybe, with luck, he'll decide it's a bad business, and you'll never run into him again."

Travis stared down the empty corridor at the back door. "I doubt that. I wonder what his story is. No one starts hunting monsters for fun," he said quietly. "They lose someone. It's always personal."

CHAPTER TWO

BRENT LAWSON THRASHED, fighting with all his strength against the creature that held him down. He tore free from the bonds that restrained him, overwhelmed by the smell of sulfur and the smoke that burned his eyes.

Tasting blood, Brent's heart thudded, and his breath came short and fast, sweat plastering his clothes to his body. Another surge and he fell, landing on his hands and knees.

Brent opened his eyes, sure he would see the ruins outside of Mosul, where his career—and his sanity—went up in smoke. Instead, he found himself staring into the carpet on his bedroom floor and trailing the shreds of yet another ruined bedsheet he had torn to pieces.

"Shit," he mumbled, falling back on his ass. He brought his knees up and covered his face with his hands until his breathing slowed and his heart stopped racing. "I'm home. I'm safe. It's over," he chanted silently, repeating the words until the shaking stopped.

Only then did he feel the pain. Adrenaline blocked out the ache of bruised muscles and the burn where stitches closed fresh gashes. The blood seeping down his chest told Brent that he had probably popped a few sutures in his wild struggle against the shadows that haunted his dreams.

"Fuck it all." He staggered to his feet, knowing that he wouldn't be getting any more sleep before dawn. The light in the kitchen guided him; the only thing worse than night terrors was waking in total darkness. Brent turned on the faucet in the sink and ducked his head beneath the cold water, sluicing it over his face and short hair. He came up, dripping like a wet dog, and blotted dry with a hand towel, then grabbed a glass and a bottle of Jack Daniels and sat at the kitchen table.

Outside, an autumn wind rattled the shutters. The old house on Pittsburgh's South Side held both his office and his apartment. A cold draft made him shiver, and his heart spiked again, remembering the slither of icy fingers against his skin in the darkness, on a night not nearly long enough ago.

Enough. Brent sucked in a deep breath and let it out slowly, willing himself to be still, hating the way his hand trembled as he poured a couple of fingers of whiskey into the glass. This wasn't the first time he'd had a one-sided conversation with "Jack," and it wouldn't be the last. Not until he found the fight he couldn't win.

Brent ran a hand through his wet hair, then rubbed his neck. When he finally sipped his drink, the glass was steady. The whiskey burned, and Brent knew it would take the edge off both the dreams and the aching muscles from the fight in the warehouse. Shit, everything had gone wrong so fast.

The dream was still vivid; it always was, even after five years. He could see the ruins of the village fifty klicks from Mosul, with artillery fire lighting up the night. The sulfur mines were burning again, stinking up the air and settling yellow dust over everything. He and his team were part of a unit fighting the insurgents, but there'd been explosions, and they'd gotten cut off from the others. Under fire in hostile territory, they had ducked into the shell of a stone building, hoping to ride it out until the enemy fighters moved on.

Jamison had seen it first, the black shadow that moved all wrong in the moonlight. Hendricks took a shot at it, but the bullet went right through like it was made of mist. The thing took on the form of a woman, tall and statuesque, with red eyes and sharp, white teeth.

She didn't notice them at first. The dark and terrible creature swept into the battle, trailing the fog behind her. Men screamed, and the *rat-tat-tat* of automatic weapons split the air, and then, only silence.

"What do we do, Captain?" Jamison had asked. Hendricks and the others had looked to Brent, expecting him to know how to hold off a monster. They didn't cover ancient Sumerian demons in Basic Training, so it was a damn good thing Brent had played video games.

"Fall back," Brent ordered. They couldn't go far. The creature—whatever she was—prowled the ruins ahead of them, and the firefight was still going strong behind them and on both sides. But they needed a defensible position, and what they had at the moment were three walls and no roof.

He spotted a small house that managed to remain relatively unscathed. It had only one room—all the better for defense—and its occupants had fled, along with most of the other civilians. The glass was gone from all the windows, and its door was torn off the hinges, but it had a roof, and the walls were solid.

"I want salt. Anything you've got that's iron. Whatever will burn —lighter fluid, alcohol, I don't care," Brent ordered. "If you have religious medallions, make sure you're wearing them and have them out. Say a prayer, if you're the praying kind. It can't hurt."

"What is that thing, sir?" Benny, the youngest of the team asked, and while he looked terrified enough to shit himself, he stayed at his post.

"Death," Brent replied, although he did not know how right he was until much later.

How do you fight a demon? He wracked his brain for what he could remember from games and movies. At his command, Jamison laid down thin lines of salt from what they had in their rations and could scavenge from the house where they'd taken shelter. Brent ordered Hendricks to grab any empty bottles he could find as well as the cooking oil from the house and their lighter fluid and begin making Molotov cocktails.

"Pray over the oil," Brent instructed. "Anybody here got a rosary?"

Benny held one up. "Right here, Cap."

"Has it been blessed?"

"My grandma brought it back for me from the Vatican," he said. "They told her it was."

"Dunk it into that bucket of water and swirl it around, then say a prayer over it," Brent said. Outside, the screams and gunfire waned.

"What do you think's up with all the funny marks?" Jamison asked as he finished putting down salt. Brent looked up and followed the soldier's gesture toward the scratches that covered the small building's walls.

Brent had heard that game designers and scriptwriters drew on legend and lore, although he'd always doubted the authenticity of their creations. But now, as he recognized the symbols, he had never felt more vindicated for all his hours leveling up.

"That's why the house is still standing," he said reverently. Some of the scratches looked like intersecting "Vs," what one game called "witch marks." On each wall, a pentacle in a circle was surrounded by four crude drawings. The heads of a horned bull, a lion, a crow, and what looked like an Egyptian pharaoh marked the quarters of the circle, and numbers were scratched into each segment of the pentacle. He glanced around, looking for more charms, and saw crossed twigs wound with yarn dangling in front of each window.

"Sir?" Jamison asked.

"The symbols, the charms, they're all ways to protect against demons," he said, still gobsmacked that he seemed to have stepped out of the real world and into one of his games.

"Demons?" Hendrick echoed. "That's what that...thing...is?"

"Got a better idea?" Jamison challenged his buddy.

"If the marks work, then where're the people who lived here?" Benny asked.

Brent shook his head. "No idea. Maybe they went to get food, and couldn't get back when the fighting started. Or maybe they were forced out. The marks keep out demons, not people."

"Do you hear that?" Jamison asked suddenly. Brent and the others paused, but the night had gone quiet. Brent's eyes widened as he realized that the silence was profound.

"They're not fighting anymore," Hendricks said in a hushed voice.

"Maybe they moved on?" Benny replied, and the hope in his voice broke Brent's heart.

"I don't think so," he said. "We stay here, until daybreak. The demon's power will be weaker once the light comes up."

"How do you know all this demon shit, Cap?" Jamison asked. "You got a priest in the family?"

He could tell them the truth, that what he knew came from playing games and watching TV, and see their fragile faith shatter, or lie and give them something to believe in. "Yeah," he replied. "Something like that."

They hunkered down, waiting out the night. Then the shouts of insurgents rose over the distant thunder of bombs, and Brent waved his men to stay down and have their weapons ready. He glimpsed a group of a dozen fighters who came charging into what was left of the village like they were late for a party. He couldn't make out their faces, but he bet they were young and angry, anxious to prove themselves.

The night grew suddenly cold, and the hair on Brent's arms rose. He gestured for his small band of survivors to stay where they were and remain silent. The wind swept across the wrecked houses and burned-out vehicles, whistling through crevices. A feeling of dread rose in Brent's chest. The insurgents outside, who had at first been jubilant, grew quiet, and then began to shout in terror.

"Mavet! Mavet!"

Boots thudded against the hard ground, followed by gunfire and screams. The last of the men begged and sobbed, then the voices abruptly went silent.

Jamison's eyes were wide, white orbs against his dark skin. Benny clutched the rosary, lips moving silently in prayer. Hendricks gripped a gun, his jaw set in anger. Brent held his breath, hoping the angel of death would pass over them.

The smell of blood, piss, and gunpowder filled the air. Then red eyes appeared at the window, and Brent sprang back with a gasp. Mavet—that was what the insurgents had called the demon—vanished, only to reappear framed in the doorway. Her dark form looked solid, blacker than the night around her. Brent and the others froze, wondering if she would sweep into the house and kill them all, but she did not pass the salt line at the door.

"Throw the bottles!" Brent ordered. Jamison scrambled for the lighter and sent two of the incendiaries through the doorway.

The rag stoppers burned bright as the improvised bombs flew through the entrance and burst apart in a plume of flames just outside the house. They could see Mavet clearly silhouetted against the firelight, saw blood dripping from her fangs. The demon was a primal force that lured its victims with a lethal attraction, like the urge to step too close to the edge of a cliff to see the view.

Benny moved, but Hendricks clamped a hand on his shoulder and shoved him down.

"Nobody's going anywhere until daybreak," Brent ordered.

Throughout the night, Mavet pounded on the roof and on the walls or threw herself at the open windows and doors, but the wardings held. Benny prayed, switching from the Hail Mary to the Our Father and back again. Jamison hummed hymns that Brent recognized from his childhood in South Carolina. Hendricks hurled bottles of holy water and Molotov cocktails, as his curses grew more obscene and creative.

A strange inner coldness filtered through Brent, bringing calm and detachment. He had evaded another demon, years ago, and it cost him his parents and twin brother. If this was the reckoning for that painful grace, Brent was ready to accept his fate, but he had no desire to hasten it.

When the long night finally ended, and the sun rose, the sounds of battle ceased. Mavet had vanished with the darkness, leaving behind the savaged bodies of the insurgents.

They heard a chopper, and Brent could have wept for joy. "Don't say anything about Mavet," he cautioned the others. "They won't believe us. Just say we were pinned down and rode out the firefight. That's an order."

BRENT'S SHRILL ringtone brought him back to the present, leaving Mosul and the demon in the past. "Lawson," he answered, only belatedly checking the number.

"Hey Brent, it's Mark. I catch you at a bad time?" A glance at the clock told Brent it was just after two in the morning.

Brent scrubbed a hand down over his face to drive away the last of the dreams and memories. "No, I'm awake. Whatcha need?" His Southern accent got thicker when he was tired, and the whiskey deepened it.

"Just got in. Been out all night after a bunch of ghouls that got loose." Mark Wojcik's offhanded tone didn't fool Brent. He'd been on those kinds of hunts himself and knew that it took hours for the adrenaline to stop pumping, and for the reality of still being alive to sink in.

"Sounds like fun," Brent replied. Ghouls were fast and vicious, but relatively stupid compared to other creatures, like the *nachzehrer* he and Travis had faced down in the warehouse.

"Hey, I called Simon for some research, and he said you'd been asking about vampires. You need any help? I can be down there in a couple of hours. I know it's late, but I figured I'd better call. Don't do anything stupid. If it's vampires, let me help. You don't tackle those bastards on your own."

Both Mark and Brent relied on a loose network of experts in the occult, and Myrtle Beach-based folklorist and psychic medium Simon Kincaide was both a resource and a friend.

Brent took another sip of whiskey and reminded himself that he was lucky to have friends who gave a damn. Mark usually handled the northwestern corner of the state, near Lake Erie, but on occasion, hunts brought him as far south as Pittsburgh.

"I appreciate it," Brent said, and he meant it. "But we took the son of a bitch down last night."

"We?"

His pride made him hesitate for a moment, then he decided that Mark probably needed to know about the demon-hunting ex-priest. "I went into a warehouse after the bastard, and it turned out to be different from what Simon and I thought it would be. You ever heard of a *nachzehrer?*"

"Can't say I have."

"It's a shifter-vamp. I didn't have the right ammo. Fucker would have got me, but this guy came out of nowhere and blew him away. Next thing I knew, I woke up in the clinic of a homeless shelter downtown. Turns out, the guy's an ex-priest, and he actually seemed offended that I was monster hunting in his territory." Brent managed a harsh laugh.

"Ex-priest?" Mark echoed. "Did he have ninja moves?"

Brent frowned, not sure whether Mark was poking fun. "Actually, kinda."

"Shit," Mark muttered. "That means he probably is—or was— Sinistram. They're trouble."

Brent pinched the bridge of his nose. He'd grown up nominally Methodist, and so the intricacies of Roman Catholicism eluded him. "What's Sinistram? Aren't they the guys you work for?"

"No. I report to the Occulatum. Our priests are advisors and do exorcisms and that kind of thing, but they pay guys like me to do the fighting. The Sinistram, they're badass. If the Occulatum is the Church's version of the FBI, then the Sinistram is Vatican Black Ops. No one's even supposed to know they exist."

Brent knocked back the rest of his whiskey and poured himself another. "So I'm guessing they wouldn't take kindly to rogue agents, like me." His demon hunting was unofficial and very personal.

"Yeah, no. Not so much. You're saying he broke cover to take you back with him?"

"You expected him to leave me there?"

Mark's silence suggested that very thing. "I've only heard whispers about the Sinistram, but they're the kind of guys who shrivel the nuts off the biggest badasses in the room. So watch your step, and don't spread the story around."

"Who am I gonna tell besides you and Simon?" Brent replied. "It's not like I post this stuff on the internet."

"Speaking of Simon," Mark replied, veering the conversation to a new topic, "he wants you to call him—at a decent hour. Said he has a message for you."

A chill went down Brent's spine. Simon Kincaide was a gifted medium and clairvoyant, as well as being a walking encyclopedia of folklore and mythology. If Simon had a "message," then it was almost certainly from the other side of the Veil.

Brent could tell from Mark's voice that the other man had started to wind down from the hunt. "Get some rest," Brent advised. "I'll do my best to steer clear of ninja priests. But if you know of a good place to stock up on silver coated hollow points, text me. I apparently need to up my game."

Mark promised to send him a reliable source for the ammo and ended the call. Brent stared out the kitchen window as he finished his second drink. He was too wired to sleep, even after the whiskey, and it would be hours yet before he could call Simon. Brent's office, Lawson Investigations, didn't open until nine, not that a private investigator got a lot of walk-in business.

With a grunt, he got up and walked to the counter, and started a pot of coffee brewing. Then he grabbed his laptop from the ottoman in the living room and brought it to the kitchen table. Brent spent a couple of hours chasing down details for the two open investigations he had under contract. Those jobs paid the bills, but they weren't what drove him.

He poured another cup and shifted his focus. Brent needed another hunt to occupy his time and keep his mind off old nightmares. By now, he knew what to look for in unsolved murders and cold cases, details that didn't add up, oddities more likely to be supernatural than psychopathic.

Missing person cases were usually a good place to start. Brent settled in, bringing the coffee pot over to minimize distractions, and started combing through reports for anything that seemed odd.

Most folks didn't like to think about how many adults went missing every day. Big cities, small towns, and places in between, people vanished, and a disturbing number were never seen again. Sure, some of those were runaways or people intentionally looking to leave their old life behind, although that was much more difficult now than it used to be, unless you were a CIA operative, or in Witness Protection. Many of those missing individuals would eventually be found, victims of violent crime and trafficking or wandering the streets, homeless and drugged.

Some were never found. When Brent left the Army and went to work for the FBI, he chased his share of serial killers. He knew that some of those psychopaths remained on the loose, evading capture. But the small number of true serial killers weren't prolific enough to account for the rest of the missing people. Brent chalked those disappearances up to a different kind of monster.

He'd spent three years with the FBI, but even then, he couldn't escape run-ins with the demonic. He'd quit rather than risk the lives of his team, and ended up here, in Pittsburgh, taking a job as a beat cop working the night shift until he could get his investigator's license and go out on his own. The PI work paid the bills. Hunting monsters was purely for revenge.

A text message pinged. A glance told him it was his girlfriend, Angela, bored with the night shift at the medical center.

"Slow night. You up?"

"Couldn't sleep. What, no drunks in the ER?" Brent texted back.

Angela worked rotating shifts as a trauma nurse at the University of Pittsburgh Medical Center and usually came off nights with stories of shootings, DUI accidents, and gang fights. She rarely had enough downtime to eat, let alone be bored.

"It's Wednesday. They're waiting for the weekend."

Brent had met Angela when a fight gone wrong with a ghoul had landed him in an ambulance. He'd been able to blame the gashes on a car accident, but the upside was meeting Angela. That she'd stuck around after he finally told her his whole story still amazed him, but Brent wasn't about to question good fortune, because it happened so rarely.

"Just as well you're working. I would have woken you up. Dreams." He didn't need to say more. Angela had woken to his cries and thrashing more than once, and each time, Brent was certain she'd walk out, disgusted by how broken he was. So far, she proved him wrong.

"Wish I'd have been there. I get off at seven. See you later."

"Be careful in the parking lot."

"Always," she replied, adding a couple of hearts and a sultry winking smiley for good measure.

By the time the sun rose, Brent had found half a dozen disappearances that didn't fit any of the usual patterns. That was suspicious, but when he plotted the last known locations on a map and found them all along Interstate 80, and all within the past four months, he knew he was onto something. In each case, witnesses had spotted a large black truck, no plates, and no description of a driver. He sat back, staring at his screen with satisfaction.

"Challenge, accepted."

His ringtone startled him, and Brent glanced at the ID. "Simon. You're up early."

"I've got inventory to put away at the store before we open," Simon replied. He ran Grand Strand Ghost Tours in Myrtle Beach, South Carolina, and his shop also stocked a wide variety of crystals, charms, and amulets as well as other protective supplies.

"I was going to give you a call in a bit. Mark said you had a message for me?" Brent steeled himself, afraid of what Simon would say next.

"Yeah. From Danny."

Brent closed his eyes and took a deep breath. One hand gripped the edge of the table, white-knuckled, and his gut clenched. "Tell me."

"You know he doesn't mean to hurt you," Simon said gently.

"I know. It's just..."

"Yeah," Simon agreed. "I understand." He paused, and Brent guessed that carrying messages from Beyond took a toll on the medium as well. "He worries about you," Simon went on in a quiet voice. "He doesn't blame you."

"Old news."

"He said 'Sherry' and 'coal mine' and 'not the first time.' Does that make sense to you?"

Brent shook his head, even though he knew Simon couldn't see him. That meant Simon also couldn't see the tears that filled his eyes at the thought of Danny reaching out to him from the Other Side. "No. Not at all."

"Danny seemed agitated this time," Simon told him. "He pushed harder with his energy. Gave me a migraine. So it was really important for him to tell you that, and I think he's afraid that you're in danger."

Brent's dry laugh was bitter. "Nothing new about that." Danger, like demons, seemed to haunt Brent. One of these days, his luck wouldn't hold, and he'd finally catch up with Danny.

"If you won't listen for your own sake, or for his, then for hell's sake, do it for mine," Simon said wearily. "I get tired of the headaches."

"Roger that," Brent replied. An awkward silence stretched. "Hey, Simon—thanks. I appreciate it. I do. It just throws me when it happens, you know?"

"He also said to tell you that there's no hurry to join him, so don't take chances."

"That's Danny," Brent agreed. "Always the careful one."

Simon said goodbye, telling him to stop in if he ever made a trip to the beach. Brent stared at the phone after the call ended, ignoring the now-cold coffee in his cup, resolutely refusing to top it off with Jack.

Starting the morning with a message from his dead twin brother pretty much guaranteed that the rest of the day couldn't get any worse.

CHAPTER THREE

———————

"YOU'RE sure the pickup was black?" Travis watched the man's reaction, looking for any sign he was holding back information.

"Yeah, I'm sure." The long-haul truck driver sported more than a day's worth of salt-and-pepper stubble, and his hair held the impression of the band of his gimme cap. "Don't think it had a license plate, either. You'd think the cops would pick up on that."

Travis suspected that whoever was inside the black truck wasn't worried about mortal police. "Anything else that you noticed? Even the smallest thing might matter."

Chuck Davis, the driver, shifted in on the vinyl diner seat and took a sip of his ice water. "I told the police—I saw the girl standing on the sidewalk, and then she was gone, and then the truck drove away, but I didn't actually see her get into the pickup." His tone was solemn, as if he were already on the witness stand. "Only other two things, probably don't mean anything, but they struck me wrong. The lights dimmed, right before the truck left, and there was a strange smell in the air that I ain't never picked up around here before."

The conversation paused as the waitress refilled their coffee, pouring the dark brew into hard-used white stoneware. The

Barkeyville truck stop was one of a chain of outposts along Interstate 80, the highway that cut across the top third of Pennsylvania. Good road, but treacherous in the winter with the altitude, and long stretches cut through remote, trackless forest, dotted by tiny, forgettable towns where the exits were few and far between.

"Tell me about the lights," Travis pressed, with the sense he was finally getting a break.

"Wasn't much, just that they all dimmed a bit, then came back," Chuck replied. "Didn't go out or nothin', but it was weird because there wasn't a storm."

"And the smell?"

"Sort of like rotten eggs," Chuck answered, and his lip curled as he remembered. "Figured someone was burning garbage, but it was strange because I hadn't smelled it earlier and it went away after the truck was gone. But for a moment, I thought I'd lose my lunch."

"Thank you," Travis said. He put down a twenty to cover their coffee and a generous tip for the server. They had kept the table tied up for almost an hour as he coaxed Chuck through his story, even though the police already had his account on record. Travis withdrew a business card and slid it across the table. "If you think of anything else, or see that truck again, please call me."

Chuck met his gaze, his light blue eyes unwavering. "If I see that truck again, imma run the other way and not stop 'til I get to the next county. It gave me the creeps."

Travis left the truck stop and drove across the intersection to the all-night convenience store. Angie, the clerk, looked up as he walked in. Her blond dreadlocks were caught back in a thick ponytail. The style made her face look fragile in comparison, although the pierced eyebrows and the snakebites on her lips suggested defiance, and her flinty gaze challenged anyone who might want to make an issue about her choices.

"Travis. What brings you here?"

"You're the pre-cog. You tell me."

Angie glanced around the store. Its aisles were laid out to make it easy to see anyone lurking or shoplifting, and the cameras and mirrors made sure there were no blind spots. She and Travis were alone.

"You want to know about the black truck." She made it a statement, not a question. "And you're the second person today to come asking."

Travis swore under his breath. "Let me guess. Tall, beefy guy, short blond hair, ex-military, looked like he'd been in a fight?"

"That's him." Her reply confirmed that Brent hadn't given up his dangerous game.

"Forget about that guy. Have you seen the truck?"

She gave him a look. "*Seen* or seen?"

He shrugged. "Either. I'm not the cops. Your word is worth a photo to me."

"Good to know." Angie pulled out her vape pen and took a long drag. "*Seen*," she clarified, tapping a finger to her temple. "First time, I didn't know what to make of it. I mean, lots of trucks come through here. Black's a popular color. But the truck I saw in the vision was scary...I don't know why. It just was."

"And after that?" Travis stayed where he could see out both side doors to the small store, so they wouldn't be surprised by newcomers.

"I heard people talking about a little girl who disappeared. Sherry. And a black truck." Angie inhaled the fruit-flavored mist and blew out a smoke ring. "So I started paying attention. I didn't get a bad vibe off any of the real trucks that came through here. Then I saw the creepy truck again in a vision. And, bam! Next day, everyone's talking about a woman who went missing down by Knox. Alicia something. Black truck again."

"Anything special about the truck, other than being freaky?" Travis asked. The fluorescent lights made Angie look dead pale, and leeched the color out of everything around her. The store was hard used, overdue for remodeling, and crammed full of merchandise to take advantage of every inch of space. The overcrowded shelves looked like they might collapse, burying Angie beneath them.

"I don't see windows tinted like that very often." Angie took another puff. "Didn't think it was legal up here. Didn't see a license plate on it either, and I know that's not legit." She shook her head. "Otherwise? No dents or scratches or damage that I could tell. Just... spooky as fuck." She hesitated, and Travis waited out the pause, knowing she had more to say.

"I saw it again, in a dream, night before last."

"A regular dream?"

"No. It was a vision. So if that truck's got something to do with people going missing, then someone's either gone, or they're gonna go soon."

"And you didn't get any sense of where or when?" Travis pressed.

"Uh-uh. People don't believe me when I tell them this psychic stuff doesn't work like in the movies," Angie replied. Outside, two cars pulled up to the gas pumps, and Angie watched the video cameras as the drivers slid their cards and started pumping. "If I'd had something solid, I'd tell you. It's not like I can call the cops. They won't believe me, or they'll think I had something to do with it."

Travis knew Angie was right. His own ability to talk to ghosts was inconsistent and never seemed to work when he wanted, or it fired up at the most awkward times. "Thanks," he said, sliding a twenty across the counter as one of the gas pumpers headed toward the store.

"If I get something you can use, I'll let you know," Angie said. "You didn't say if you'd heard anything."

Travis's smile was sad. "Your mom said to say hello," he replied. "She wishes you'd stop smoking." Angie's mom had been dead for five years.

Angie waved the vape pen. "Tell her I'm working on it." She turned her attention to the customer, who wanted cigarettes and lottery tickets, and Travis headed to his car.

It didn't take long to go from the bright lights of the Barkeyville service plaza to an endless ribbon of darkness on I-80. Travis headed east, away from Pittsburgh, deciding to drive the stretch to the next exit in case anything caught his attention.

He didn't mind passing along messages from Angie's late mother;

in fact, seeing what it meant to Angie helped to validate his gift. Growing up in a deeply religious family, he had been taught to feel shame and guilt about his mediumship, and anything else that didn't conform to their traditional views.

Travis had thrown himself into his studies, doing his damnedest to repress anything that might have made him suspect to the priests. But the dead never stopped talking, no matter how he tried to hide or send them away. Once he was ordained, he finally relented and held midnight confessional for the restless ghosts, giving them Last Rites and sending them on.

He'd served a small, elderly congregation on the North Side in a decrepit church that was a holdout from the neighborhood's post-war days. By the time he got to St. Eligius, named for the patron saint of metal workers, the surrounding streets belonged to the gangs and the dealers. Travis brokered a deal with the ghosts who weren't ready to move on, and they gladly "haunted" the area around the church. That at least meant Travis didn't have to sweep bloody needles, empty dime bags, and used condoms off the church steps each morning.

The ghosts couldn't stop the demon.

Travis had hosted four seminary students for a weekend retreat and neighborhood outreach. The demon caught them late at night, intent on destruction and defilement, as they were finishing setting up for the soup kitchen in the parish social hall. One of the students died before they even knew what stalked them. Travis had gotten the others to the safety of a small chapel, where the combination of holy ground and blessed relics, along with their desperately chanted prayers, kept the demon at bay until sunrise. Travis had fought the creature back with a silver candlestick and a monstrance, saving the lives—if not the sanity—of the other three young men.

Two of the students dropped out of seminary. One checked himself into a psychiatric hospital. And Travis had found himself recruited by the Sinistram, which didn't give a shit about him being a medium—as long as he fought the good fight, as they defined it.

He'd kept up his part of the bargain until his health, his faith, and his sanity were in shreds. When he walked away, his handler at the Sinistram told him that the priesthood, and demon hunting, were things you only quit when you were dead. Travis proved him half right.

That was four years ago, but it seemed like another lifetime.

Now, Travis drove his old Crown Victoria down a desolate stretch of dark highway, listening for the whisper of ghosts. He wasn't sure what he hoped to find, but he figured he'd know it when he heard it.

At first, the voices were so quiet he almost missed them. They grew louder, though still at the edge of his awareness. Travis pulled into the next rest area, which was deserted at this hour. He left the engine idling and made sure the doors were locked. Then he took a deep breath and opened himself to the ghosts.

Wisps of fog crept across the parking lot until each of the security lights overhead was encircled by a glowing nimbus. The rumble of voices sounded closer now, and as the fog grew thicker, Travis spied forms and faces that shifted with the wind. Restless spirits haunted the highway like spectral hitchhikers, unable to go home, and unwilling to move on. On more than one occasion, Travis thought he'd witnessed a horrific wreck, only to realize it was a repeater, a ghostly image replaying the last, tragic moments of someone's life in an infinite loop.

Repeaters weren't sentient. These ghosts still knew who they were, and how they died. The temperature in the car plummeted, and frost formed on the windows although the night was mild for October. Some of the spirits had died in accidents; others by violence along this lonely stretch, or at their own hand. But they flocked to Travis's power like moths to a flame, anxious to gain his help.

"I will hear all of you," he promised. "And help you pass over. But please, before I do, tell me what you know of evil in a black truck."

Travis felt a shudder and realized that his question had managed to frighten the dead. *Not mortal, then,* he thought, confirming his worst fears about the driver of the mysterious vehicle. He reached out with his gift, trying to bridge the gap between himself and the lost souls who milled about in the fog.

"He's kidnapping people, women and children. He'll kill them," Travis said, something he couldn't prove yet but felt certain of, bone-deep. "I want to stop him. But I need help."

Ghosts seldom spoke words, and even less often sentences. Images seemed to transcend the Veil more easily than language. Travis saw a barrage of fleeting images that flickered almost too quickly for him to process. The black truck, with dark tinted windows. A child with black hair done up with a pretty bow, crying. A blond woman, screaming and fighting, trying to open the door to escape. But of the driver, nothing but a dark, featureless form and an awful sense of wrongness.

"Where did he take them?" Travis asked the dead. But one by one, they shook their heads. Tragedy bound them to this stretch of road, and when the truck left their boundaries, they could not follow it. Yet if the entity behind the abductions killed his victims, their bodies hadn't been dumped near here, or their spirits would have heeded Travis's call.

"Can you tell me anything?" he begged.

Cooper City. The distant voice echoed as if it carried down a long corridor. The words were clearly spoken, but not repeated, and although Travis strained for more, the spirits fell silent.

"All right," he said. "Thank you. Come closer, and I will help you pass over."

Travis felt certain that not all of the ghosts had been Catholic in their lifetimes, but the core of Last Rites—confession, absolution, and blessing—was universal. He supposed that the trappings of faith mattered little to the dead, and that intent alone sufficed.

He withdrew the thin stole he kept in the glove compartment for emergencies and draped it over his shoulders. Guilt stabbed at him, that he had no business saying the words since he had renounced the priesthood when he renounced the Sinistram. But Travis knew clergy of many faiths, and each of them had a litany for the dead, so if he and the ghosts found comfort in familiar words, he refused to beg forgiveness because of a technicality. If this was sin, he had done far worse.

Travis didn't know who took more comfort in the rites—the ghosts or himself. His psychic gift communicated with the souls of the dead even as his physical voice lifted up the words of the benediction, and the ability to sense their passage felt equally as sacred as the mystery of the Eucharist.

When the ghosts were gone, and the litany complete, Travis opened his eyes. Both the fog and the frost had vanished. He paused for a few minutes to regain his composure, then pulled out of the rest area, drove to the next exit, and reversed course, heading back to Pittsburgh, deep in thought.

Something inhuman was behind the abductions, an entity able to frighten the dead. Travis didn't know why "Cooper City" was important enough to be shared from beyond the grave, but tomorrow, after he'd managed to catch a few hours of sleep, he had every intention of finding out.

———

THE NEXT DAY, one minor crisis after another kept Travis's mind on St. Dismas, instead of fretting about a troublesome hunter-wannabe, or the next moves of what he had mentally dubbed the "Silverado Killer" after the make and model of a very popular black truck.

"Okay, we got the shipment of ground beef, tomato soup, cabbage, and rice the soup kitchen needs to do stuffed cabbage tonight," Travis said to Jon, "and the overdue medical supplies Matthew ordered finally came in. Any news on the water heater?"

Travis and Jon had spent much of their time directing the halfway house's small staff through a day that seemed to go from bad to worse. The aforementioned water heater stopped working, the office printer was failing, and one of the ovens in the commercial kitchen was finicky enough that the cook not-so-jokingly asked if an exorcism was a possibility.

"Got a repair scheduled. Had to pay emergency rates because we can't do without," Jon reported, then took a big swallow of strong, black coffee. Travis had a cup of his own and felt certain the caffeine was the only thing keeping him on his feet after a late night.

"Good. And the van?" Travis asked. St. Dismas had a decrepit shuttle to take its temporary residents to any medical or social service appointments that couldn't happen on site.

"The repairs were more expensive than we expected, but at least we'll get a little longer out of the junker," Jon replied.

St. Dismas operated on the patched-together support of grants, donations, and nominal help from the Diocese. Travis, Jon, and Matthew, as three of the most visible faces of the organization, wrangled every connection and contact they had with local businesses to stretch their tight finances. Travis had spent half of the morning in an inter-agency meeting to coordinate resources, working closely with food banks, clothing drives, and volunteer organizations for medical, educational, and social services. Jon would cover for him at another event that night, while Travis went back to hunting.

"Can we cover the stipend for the Night Vigil?" Travis asked.

"As long as you don't add too many more people," Jon said, nodding. "That antique store owner in Charleston sent another large check earmarked for 'special purpose resource development.' It's almost as if he knows what the Night Vigil actually does."

For Travis, the Night Vigil was the intersection of St. Dismas's mission and his own obsession to fight supernatural evil. Jon had once called them "halfway house heroes," and he wasn't far wrong. Most, like Angie, had some level of psychic gift, or like Travis, they'd had their own run-in with the occult. All of them carried a heavy load of guilt over misusing their gifts or failing to protect someone they loved. Many worked the night shift because they didn't want to sleep when it was dark and because as sentries in the battle against evil, they needed to be alert in the hour of the wolf. They kept their eyes open for paranormal problems and fed that information to Travis. In return, they earned a small stipend, and Travis did his best to watch out for them. There was safety in numbers.

We're the misfits and fuck-ups, unwanted by Heaven or Hell, Travis thought, *looking for one last chance to atone for mistakes and missed chances, the pain we've caused others, the good things we were afraid to do, and the bad things we embraced with open arms. Might as well get the unfinished business dealt with before we cross over, so we don't become someone else's problem.*

"Given that particular shop, I'd bet on it, although I don't know how he gets his information," Travis said. "They handle any cursed or haunted items we come across and neutralize them."

"Nice," Jon replied. "You think you got a lead?"

"A slim one," Travis admitted. "Not sure what to make of it."

His phone buzzed, and Travis frowned as he saw the number, then put the call on speaker. "Father Ryan. It's been a while."

"It has indeed," the other man replied. "And I wish I were calling under better circumstances. Is there any chance you could meet me for dinner tonight? I've got a problem that I think is up your alley."

Travis checked his watch. "It's gonna take me about two and a half hours, assuming I don't hit construction." The fact that Father Ryan lived in Cooper City, the same place the highway ghosts had mentioned, had not escaped Travis's notice.

"It's important," Father Ryan replied. "I wouldn't ask you to drive out if it weren't...unusual. I've got a widow who is refusing to bury her husband's body—and she's the third family member this week who won't part with a corpse."

Jon and Travis exchanged a look. "You're sure it's not just extreme grief?" Travis asked.

"I've been in this business for a while," Father Ryan replied. He had been one of the younger priests when Travis was in seminary, maybe less than ten years older. Travis remembered the last time he'd seen Ryan. Being a small-town parish priest seemed to have aged him another decade, reminding Travis that if the big city didn't kill you, it kept you young. "I've buried a lot of people, seen a lot of bereavement. But this...it's like that Faulkner story."

Travis shuddered. *A Rose for Emily* was probably the only story he remembered from his college literature class, and it never failed to creep him out just thinking about it. "Okay. I get it. I'll be there."

"Plan to stay over. You can have the guest room at the rectory. I think you need to see what I'm dealing with."

He ended the call and turned to Jon. "Are you okay if—"

Jon waved him off. "Go. Sounds like the good father needs some help. I'll get one of the volunteers to help me pick up the coat donations from the radio station."

"I'm planning to be back tonight, but if that changes, you'll be the first to know," Travis assured him. He grabbed the duffel he kept packed for this kind of thing, and his laptop, just in case, and headed for his car, trying to remember where Cooper City was. The app on his phone gave him directions, and he saw that at least part of the route was on I-80, farther east than he had driven the night before. *Interesting. I wonder if there are any new ghosts who know something about the truck?*

October turned the forest bright red and orange, and the afternoon sun made the mountains ablaze with color. Travis tried to focus on the natural beauty to de-stress but found his thoughts cycling back to the disappearances, the black truck, and Father Ryan's problematic widow.

Could they be related? he wondered. Cooper City was almost in the middle of the state, while the missing people had vanished from farther west. Travis couldn't quite envision a common thread between the disappearances and the grief-fueled irrationality of Father Ryan's mourners. And yet the incident in the small town right on the heels of the message Travis had received from the I-80 ghosts about the same city seemed like too much of a coincidence.

Travis tried to remember who among his Night Vigil contacts were located mid-state. He couldn't recall off-hand but vowed to check his phone when he stopped. Even if the two situations were unrelated, it wouldn't hurt to have his network keep an ear to the ground, or use their abilities to uncover connections.

Just as Travis finally shook off his bleak mood, the phone buzzed. He recognized the number, seriously considered just letting it go to voicemail, then resigned himself to dealing with the caller.

"Travis. This is Father Liam."

"The answer is still 'no.'"

Liam's cold chuckle irritated Travis. "You can't run from your vows, my son."

"I'm no son of yours." Travis fought to keep his voice even, but his hands clutched the steering wheel white-knuckled.

"You are all my spiritual children," Liam said, with the cocksure confidence that had always set Travis's teeth on edge. His old Sinistram mentor was a man Travis knew could have easily done just fine for himself at the CIA—or the KGB—if he hadn't sworn his oath first to the Church.

"Get to the point."

"The point is, you need to return to the fold. There's work to be done." A hint of irritation added an edge beneath Liam's words.

"I'm out," Travis replied. "Out of the priesthood, and out of your little viper pit."

"Really, Travis. You're never really out. Or have you forgotten? 'Thou art a priest forever,'" Liam quoted, with the sanctimonious tone Travis had always resented.

"Tell me why you really called, or I'm hanging up."

Silence stretched long enough Travis thought the call might have dropped. "We've lost three more operatives," Liam said finally. "One to a vetala, another in a car accident, and the third to a gunshot wound."

"As usual, there's something you're not saying," Travis snapped. "Was the wreck a DUI and the bullet self-inflicted?"

The Sinistram was an ancient cadre of warrior-monks fighting dark magic and demonic forces, with a tradition of rigor and asceticism that drove men to an early grave. If the Knights Templar were the Marines of the Vatican, the Sinistram was its Black Ops. Between the horrors faced on the job, a pitiless culture that made a fetish of suffering, and the loneliness of the work, most Sinistram operatives never made it to their forties. Those who did were usually broken in mind and body. Alcohol blurred the memories, and when that failed, suicide ended the pain.

"I'll take that as a 'yes,'" Travis said when Liam didn't deign to reply. "You know, maybe you should ask yourself why so many of your men would rather commit a mortal sin than keep doing the work."

"The flesh is weak," Liam answered smoothly. "And in a moment of weakness, the Father of Lies prevails."

"Yeah, keep telling yourself that. Couldn't possibly be your 'real men don't show fear' bullshit."

"Language, Travis."

"You want language, Liam? How about this? Lose my fucking number. I'm done with you, and I'm sure as hell done with the Sinistram."

"Hell is closer than you think, Travis. Don't be too quick to burn bridges. You might need a fire escape." The call ended abruptly.

Travis swerved to take the ramp to the next rest area and pulled into a spot far removed from the other cars. He closed his eyes, taking deep breaths, trying to regain his composure and let his thudding heart return to normal.

Damn Liam, damn the Sinistram, and damn the rot that lets snakes like him make a mockery out of everything the Church says it believes. His faith had been as much a casualty as his mind and body, and while part of him longed for the comfort of certitude, he knew from bitter experience that not only was the devil in the details but within the shades of gray.

He leaned forward, resting his forehead on the steering wheel, wishing that just the sound of Liam's voice didn't trigger him. His stomach knotted hard enough that he thought he might throw up, and he knew if he lifted his hands from the wheel they would shake.

It's been four years. He doesn't control me. I'm out. He can't make me do anything, not anymore. But deep in his heart, Travis knew that wasn't completely true. Like the CIA and the Mob, the Sinistram knew how to work people like puppets, and neither extortion nor threats were off the table.

"Just when I thought I was out, they pull me back in," Travis quoted to himself, and the irony of the appropriateness of a line from a Mafia movie was not lost on him. "Not this time. Never again."

It took the rest of the drive to Cooper City for Travis to calm down after the phone call. He tried to keep from going over Father Liam's smug remarks, but just thinking about the Sinistram made his blood boil. He'd already paid too high a price in blood and nightmares and seen too many good men pushed to the breaking point. Now, Travis intended to wage the fight on his own terms.

He parked in the lot beside Our Lady of Sorrows church and walked up the steps to the rectory. Father Ryan swung the door open and greeted him with a hug and a smile. "Travis. It's been too long." The priest stood aside so that Travis could enter.

"Homey," Travis said, glancing around the snug living room. He set his backpack down inside the door. The old brick house was across the parking lot from the church and had housed innumerable priests in the century and a half that the parish had served Cooper City.

"It's more than I need," Ryan said with a shrug. "You know us priests. We travel light." The sturdy-but-comfortable furnishings were actually the property of the parish.

"Hey, if you've got a coffee maker and a TV that can stream movies, what more do you want?" Travis couldn't resist teasing his old friend.

"That, I have, as well as a couch to watch them on, and a cat for company," Ryan replied. On cue, a gray tabby appeared from beneath an armchair and wove in and out around his ankles. "Come into the kitchen. Dinner's in the oven. I figured this way we could speak privately."

Travis followed him into the dated but functional kitchen. It had obviously been remodeled over the years, but this incarnation appeared to be from the 1980s. No avocado and gold appliances, but the room's cabinets and tile looked well-worn. "Whatever you're cooking, it smells good."

Ryan smiled as he reached for an oven mitt. "You can thank Mrs. Kowalczyk, the housekeeper. Her motto should be 'feeding priests since 1976.'" He pulled out a tray of stuffed peppers, and a baking dish full of mashed potatoes, perfectly browned on the top. "Although I'll take credit for warming up the canned green beans, and I picked up the cherry pie from the grocery store myself."

Travis helped to get drinks and set the table. The rectory had the comfortable feel of a well-loved home, in stark contrast to his own apartment at St. Dismas. Although he was no longer a priest, he'd gotten out of the habit of needing a lot of stuff. Still, he thought, looking around, it might not hurt to make his place a bit more welcoming.

"So how goes the halfway house business?" Ryan asked as they sat down to eat.

Despite the call on the drive up, and the unsettling reason Ryan had requested his visit, Travis felt himself relax. He had only a handful of people whom he considered true friends, unencumbered by conflicting loyalties or by being his coworkers. Even fewer had known him as long as Ryan or remembered him before he had joined and then given up the priesthood.

"Well, we'll never be obsolete," Travis observed. "There's so much need, and nowhere near the resources to do what needs to be done."

"You're doing all that you can, and that makes a difference," Ryan replied. "Not to mention your extracurricular activities."

Travis rolled his eyes. "Yeah, good thing I don't need much sleep. How about you? Small town life looks like it agrees with you."

He and Ryan were a decade apart in age, with Travis in his early thirties. But where fighting monsters and unloading truckloads of donations kept Travis toned and fit, Ryan's routine of liturgies and committee meetings meant he'd gone a bit pudgy. His thinning hair and wire-rimmed glasses made him look comfortingly avuncular, but Travis knew that behind Ryan's mild veneer lay a sharp mind and a keen sense of humor.

"It's what I signed up for," Ryan replied. "As parishes go, it's as drama-free as you're ever going to get. No one's trying to stir up trouble, at least, not usually. This is a small town with an aging population. People just want to collect their pensions, play some bingo, watch a little football, and go about their business."

"Sounds like a nice gig," Travis replied.

"I imagine it seems boring to you."

Travis let out a long breath. "That depends on your definition of excitement. We help people fight their metaphorical demons all day long, and then after dark, I go after the real ones. Excitement is overrated."

They ate in silence for several minutes. "Has your Night Vigil had any news about what's going on out here?" Ryan asked after they had both done justice to their food, and helped themselves to seconds. He got up to clear their plates.

"I was just thinking that I need to see who's this far east," Travis replied, leaning back and enjoying a full stomach. "Most of what I've heard has all been about people going missing from truck stops on I-80. It feels hinky, like there's more to it than just human evil."

Ryan cut them both generous slices of pie, then returned with the pot of coffee and two mugs. "I've learned not to underestimate what people can do. Sometimes, I doubt we actually need the Devil, since people come up with horrors on their own."

"Don't let the folks in Rome hear you," Travis joked.

"Speaking of which," Ryan replied, "I gather that your...friends... there haven't persuaded you to pick up where you left off."

Travis sipped his coffee, suddenly wishing it had a slug of

whiskey in it. "No," he answered with a bitter edge to his voice that he knew Ryan would understand. "They keep trying. I keep saying no. Officially, they can't force me, but we all know that some arms of the Church follow the rules more closely than others."

Ryan was one of the only people aside from Jon and Matthew, and Father Pavel, Travis's confessor, who knew about his past with the Sinistram. Like many secret organizations, the group considered itself above both secular and Church law and employed tactics that officials disavowed in the light of day.

"Good for you," Ryan said, making short work of the pie. "Keep saying no."

Travis grimaced. "Easy for you to say. If I disappear someday, send someone to the catacombs to find me." He stared at the pie crumbs on his plate. "So tell me about what you've got going on here."

Ryan poured himself another cup of coffee. "Honestly, I debated whether to serve you dinner before or after we go visit Mrs. Laszlo," he replied. "Either way, it's bound to spoil your appetite."

"That bad?"

Ryan nodded. "I've dealt with a lot of pretty awful situations, Travis. I don't recall if I told you, but I spent a couple of years as an Army chaplain in Afghanistan, went on aid missions to Haiti and Puerto Rico after the hurricanes...I thought I'd seen everything grief could do to people. But this..." He shook his head.

"Since you called me, you must think there's more to what's happening that normal mourning."

"Come on. I'll show you. It's not really something I can explain." He handed Travis a bottle of anti-nausea pills. "Better take a few, just in case." Then he shared a small jar of menthol rub. "Put a little in each nostril. It's a trick I learned from a cop. Helps with the smell."

They walked outside the rectory, and Ryan sniggered when he saw Travis's Crown Vic. "I hope you got a good deal on that gunboat."

"It's a police interceptor model that didn't get neutered for civilian use. Bigger engine, higher speed. And room for more than one body in the trunk."

Ryan nodded. "All good points. I stand corrected."

They drove Ryan's small SUV, and Travis took in Cooper City. The town looked like most of the other central Pennsylvania communities Travis had seen, and much like those on the outskirts of Pittsburgh. Most of the houses dated from World War II or before, and while adequately maintained, showed wear and age. Few cars were new, fewer still were foreign or luxury models. Dollar stores and thrift shops outnumbered other merchants, although Travis had passed a Walmart on the way into town. He'd be willing to bet deaths outnumbered births, and that the average age was over fifty.

Decades ago, Cooper City and its neighbors relied on mines, timber, and small, local manufacturing jobs. When those dried up or shipped offshore, nothing took their place. Young people moved; old people stayed. The town's slow death was etched in its cracked sidewalks and potholed roads, in the shabby cars parked at the diner and in the peeling paint of its post office.

"This is the place." The trip had taken less than ten minutes. Ryan parked at the curb in front of a modest two-story frame house that had probably been built to welcome the troops home from Germany. The paint had grown chalky, and the picket fence was missing a few slats.

"No one's mowed for a while," Travis observed, taking in the overgrown yard.

"Mr. Laszlo has been indisposed," Ryan replied. "Let's pay a visit."

The smell hit Travis even before they rang the doorbell. Even on the porch, he caught the sickly sweet odor of advanced decomposition, despite the menthol and eucalyptus gel. "Jesus," Travis muttered as much a prayer as an oath.

A thin, hunched woman opened the door. Mrs. Laszlo looked to be in her late eighties, thin enough to blow away in a stiff wind. Her gray hair framed her face in a curly perm that went out of style in the

Carter administration. Travis noticed that her housedress and sweater looked clean, although the smell that assaulted them from behind her would certainly permeate everything she wore, no matter how freshly laundered.

"We just were in the neighborhood and thought we would pay a visit," Father Ryan said. Travis recognized the tone as his "conciliatory pastor" voice, used for coaxing good behavior from contrary parishioners. "I brought you cookies," he added, producing a bag he must have had stashed in the SUV.

"Why isn't that sweet of you!" Mrs. Laszlo said. "Please come in. I've just gotten Henry settled after dinner. He goes to sleep so early these days," she added.

They followed the woman through a tidy front hallway. If Travis had been expecting the clutter and piled junk of a hoarder, he would have been proven wrong. The house reminded him of his grandmother's, a neat, working-class haven filled with slipcovered chairs, dated draperies, and neatly hung decorative china plates on the walls.

Except for the corpse in the recliner.

Henry Laszlo's skin showed mottling where the blood had settled. He'd moved from pallid to greenish as rot set in, and his bloated belly strained at the tie of his bathrobe and elastic waistband of his pajama pants. His eyes were closed—a small mercy—but his mouth gaped open. Flies swarmed around the body, buzzing loudly enough to be noticeable even from a distance.

On a TV tray next to the recliner, sat an untouched plate of food. "Henry's appetite hasn't been so good lately," Mrs. Laszlo fussed.

Travis had to swallow, hard, not to puke. His eyes watered from the stench. He noticed that Mrs. Laszlo seemed inured to it.

"Have you noticed anything different with Henry lately?" Father Ryan asked.

Mrs. Laszlo sighed. "He doesn't get around so good anymore, with that bad knee of his," she tutted.

While Ryan kept Mrs. Laszlo talking, Travis closed his eyes and grounded himself, then opened his gift and called to Henry's ghost.

Travis had felt off-kilter ever since he'd been within fifty miles of Cooper City, an odd, jangly feeling that made his leg jiggle and his fingers drum, the sense that something wasn't right. Even without fully reaching out to his mediumship, he had felt a primal discomfort as they entered the Laszlo home. Now, just feet from a rotting corpse, his intuition was screaming for him to run.

Instead, Travis rooted his power and said a prayer of protection. The horrors of what he saw at the Sinistram might have left his faith in tatters, but he still took solace from the familiar words, and they proved valuable as he envisioned wrapping himself in a shield of white light against the horrors that sometimes prowled on the other side of the Veil.

Travis stifled a gasp as his inner sight flared. He saw Henry's spirit, but the ghost was covered with a quivering mass of what looked like black maggots that burrowed into the spirit's form and wriggled beneath its "skin." Thousands of the black worms bedeviled the revenant, and Henry's panicked gaze sought Travis with a silent plea for help.

The awful image made Travis recoil, but it did not break his connection to the Other Side. He felt the gaze of dozens of spirits, a cloud of witnesses, just at the edge of his perception. The emotions he picked up from the ghosts was a tangle of suspicion, terror, judgment, and guilt, so tangible that it made his stomach twist and his throat tighten. Before the specters could come closer, Travis strengthened his psychic shields, unwilling to be overwhelmed before he even had the chance to find out what tormented the dead and caused their unquiet rest.

He forced his attention back to Henry and knew what had to be done. With effort, Travis roused himself from his trance. Father Ryan was still chatting with Mrs. Laszlo as if sitting in a living room with a corpse was the most normal thing in the world.

Travis feigned a cough. "Can I trouble you, please, for a glass of water?" he asked Mrs. Laszlo, in a raspy voice.

"Oh, my dear! Certainly. I'll be right back, and I'll bring one for Father, too," Mrs. Laszlo said, bustling off toward the kitchen.

Ryan wasn't fooled for an instant. "What?"

"Not sure, but I think it's some kind of low-level demonic infestation. He's going to need an exorcism and Last Rites."

"I'm not cleared to do exorcism," Ryan replied.

"No, but I am." Travis gave a bitter smile. "And while I gave up the collar, the Sinistram says 'once a priest, always a priest,' so I consider it a loophole."

Ryan returned a conspiratorial grin. "You dissemble like a Jesuit."

"I learned from the best."

They heard Mrs. Laszlo shuffling back from the kitchen. "What's the next move?" Ryan asked.

"Restrain her," Travis replied. "Keep her from breaking my concentration, but stay close, and pray like your soul depends on it. It might. I don't think the things that are eating Henry Laszlo are going to give up easily."

Mrs. Laszlo came into the living room with a glass in each hand, trembling enough that the water sloshed and nearly overflowed. "Here you go," she said, setting them down on the coffee table.

"I was wondering, do you have a cat?" Father Ryan asked.

Mrs. Laszlo gave him a puzzled look. "A cat? Dear me, no. Why?"

"I thought I heard something coming from the closet," Ryan replied. "And I didn't want the poor thing to be locked inside."

Mrs. Laszlo frowned. "The closet? I can't imagine. Let me look." She headed for the coat closet, and Ryan followed her. The door opened, revealing a shallow cubby with a few winter coats and boots. "I don't see anything—"

"Sorry," Father Ryan murmured, giving her a nudge and closing the door, then leaning against it with his full weight. "Travis, go!" he cried, then began to chant the Hail Mary, resolutely ignoring Mrs. Laszlo pounding on the other side of the door.

Travis had already grounded himself, expecting Ryan to act. He rose and turned toward Henry's putrefying corpse, and experienced a kind of double vision, his inner and outer sight overlying one another so that he could clearly make out the writhing demonic maggots superimposed over the dead man's body.

"*Exorcizamos te, omnis immundus spiritus...*" Travis began, gathering both his authority as a medium and the spiritual power of the ancient litany. He might no longer have faith in the Church and its leaders, or in the doctrines he had been taught, but he clung to a ragged certitude that Light conquered Darkness, and it was that belief that empowered him to face the spiritual forces of evil.

"*Omnis Satanicas potestas...*" Travis continued. "*Omnis incursio infernalis adversarii...*"

Henry's body began to quiver, and Travis's double vision snapped into a single, unified view. Curls of black smoke, like hellish grubs, burrowed into the dead flesh, undulated beneath the skin, and massed in the chest and belly in numbers large enough to look as if the corpse breathed.

Father Ryan continued his prayers, and Travis hoped that his friend could make up for in faith what he lacked. The hell-maggots weren't the worst demonic threat Travis had faced, but the staggering number of entities required his full concentration.

They call us Legion, for we are many...

The idea of Henry's physical body becoming worm food didn't bother Travis; such was the way of all flesh. But the hell-maggots ate at his soul, feeding off its energy and the core essence of the dead man, and that was intolerable.

Mrs. Laszlo pounded on the closet door. "Let me out!"

Father Ryan leaned against it with his full weight, and chanted louder, offering Last Rites. Travis continued with the exorcism and hoped like fuck no one heard the old lady shouting and called the cops.

Travis's magic anchored Henry's spirit, as the sacred words exhorted the demonic parasites to depart and return to the Pit from whence they came. The dead man's body became a battleground, a war between eternal energies. But as demons went, the hell-maggots didn't have the juice that powered their more dangerous brethren.

Travis found that visualization helped to focus and amplify the currents that he channeled when he worked the sacred magic. Now he imagined himself surrounded by a field of glowing light, a sanctified bug zapper of sorts. As the litany pried the maggots loose, he saw the black smoke creatures vanish in glowing flares, first one at a time, and then handfuls of writhing curls. The flashes temporarily blinded him, turning his vision red with the afterimages.

A dark power fought him, pulling against the light that flowed through Travis, but gradually the resistance waned, and then stopped altogether. The abrupt end left him off balance as if his opponent had dropped the other end of the rope in a tug of war. Henry's ravaged soul glowed faintly, free of encumbrances, then faded out, moving on.

Travis finished the exorcism as Father Ryan completed the Last Rites, and Travis joined his friend in the familiar and comforting words of the benediction.

Henry's body was now a shriveled husk, a mummy in a stained bathrobe. The smell of sulfur and ash replaced the stench of decay. Travis nodded, and Father Ryan stepped away from the closet door. It swung open, and Mrs. Laszlo tumbled out, hair askew and eyes wild.

"Are you all right?" Father Ryan asked, managing to sound surprised and distressed.

"What happened?" She sounded genuinely confused, and Travis wondered if the hell-maggots created some kind of distortion that affected her mind.

"You went to get something from the closet, and the door slammed shut," Ryan replied. That wasn't exactly a lie. "It took a bit before I could get you out." Again, technically true.

"Oh my, what is that smell?" Mrs. Laszlo said, nose wrinkling. "And what's in Henry's chair? Oh dear god—" Her knees buckled and Father Ryan caught her before she fell. Travis hurried over to help, and with one man on each side, they half-carried the distraught woman to the kitchen.

"Henry's dead," Father Ryan said as gently as he could. "I think that you've been so overwhelmed with grief, it didn't really sink in until just now."

Sadness and horror warred in Mrs. Lazaro's expression. "He hadn't been well for a long time," she said, so quietly they could barely hear the words. "Felt like he was slipping away a bit more each day. I knew I was losing him. I just hope that he didn't suffer."

Travis looked away, remembering the parasites that ravaged the dead man's soul, unwilling to provide false comfort since he felt certain Henry's passing had been anything but easy.

"I'm sure he's at peace now," Father Ryan assured her. He frowned. "I'm sorry to ask this, but since I didn't have the opportunity to hear Henry's confession before he passed on...do you know if there were any sins that weighed heavy on his mind? Old failings, bad habits, those kinds of thing? I will ask for absolution on his behalf when I pray for his soul."

Travis knew that Ryan's promise was sincere—he would certainly remember both Mrs. Laszlo and Henry in his prayers—but he also was fishing for some clue as to why the infernal parasites had attached themselves to the failing spirit of an old man.

"Henry wasn't perfect, but he was a good man," Mrs. Laszlo said, wiping her eyes with a tissue she produced from the pocket of her housedress. "Never cheated on me or raised a hand in anger to the children or me. Paid every cent he owed in taxes. Didn't drink to excess. Gave to the church," she added. "He might have sneaked a smoke now and again, if he thought I wasn't looking, and taken the Lord's name in vain when he hit his thumb with a hammer, but if there wasn't anything worse than that, Father, I never saw it in sixty-five years of marriage."

Travis and Ryan stayed with Mrs. Laszlo until the mortician came to take the body, and a cop showed up to take their statements. The look the men exchanged with Ryan told Travis that it was not the first odd circumstances he had encountered. When the white van left with the corpse, Mrs. Laszlo laid a hand on Father Ryan's arm.

"Thank you for waiting with me," she said, including Travis with a glance in his direction. "But I'll be all right. I'll call my daughter, and she'll come stay with me a while. We already discussed it. Henry and I had a good long time together, and I imagine we won't be parted long," she added with a sad smile. "I'll see you at Mass in the morning."

Travis and Ryan drove back to the rectory in silence. By this time it was dark, and despite the streetlights and the warm glow from inside the houses they passed, Travis still felt chilled to the bone.

Ryan's cat, Lilith, met them at the door. They hung up their coats and headed into the kitchen. Ryan took down a bottle of scotch and poured them both a liberal draught. "Talk to me," he said, sitting across from Travis. "What happened back there?"

Travis was quiet for several moments, then gave Ryan as much of an account as he could bring himself to put into words. "I don't know why the rite still works for me," he admitted. "Because I stopped believing when I left the Sinistram."

Ryan shrugged. "The Eternal Power of Creation—call it by any name you choose—is not the same as the Church, and it's heresy to say otherwise. Although that's an unpopular opinion in some circles. You lost faith in a fallible human organization that often failed to live up to its ideals, and which, at its worst, hurt as much as healed. That's as it should be. Blind faith is a recipe for exploitation."

Travis took a swallow and let the liquor burn down his throat. "Better be careful who hears you say that."

"You know me, Travis. I won't say anything behind someone's back I wouldn't say to their face." Ryan took a slug of his own drink. "Lucky for me, there's a priest shortage."

"Still doesn't answer my question."

Ryan met his gaze. "It works for you because the energy you're calling forth in the rite belongs to itself, not to anyone else. You believe in *it*, so it doesn't matter if you don't believe in *them*. You don't have to completely understand. Just accept it as a gift, like your other abilities, and use it for the right reasons."

Travis wasn't completely convinced, but it was the best answer he was likely to receive, and so he nodded and raised his glass in salute before knocking back the rest of it. He was surprised when Ryan refilled both their glasses.

"I should probably drink less," Travis said with a sigh, regarding the amber liquid.

"Maybe," Ryan allowed. "Then again, life is short, and we should take comfort where we can."

"I don't remember them saying that in seminary either."

"Life taught me a lot of things they didn't cover," Ryan replied.

Travis sat back in his chair and toyed with his glass. "How did a low-level demonic infestation happen to pick a guy like Henry Laszlo? Do you believe his wife, that he didn't have some awful, hidden sordid secrets?"

Ryan considered his answer before speaking. "None he ever confided to me," he said. "And while no one ever really knows another person's heart, I don't think he was a serial killer or a secret rapist or a child molester. The worst I saw of him was his grief when the doctors diagnosed his wife's cancer."

Travis looked up, surprised. Ryan nodded. "They lost a son, last year, in a car accident. Henry took it hard. Then he found out Helen's cancer had come back—stage four, this time, so there was little anyone could do about it—and he was inconsolable."

"Was he desperate enough to do something like trying to bargain for her life?"

Ryan raised an eyebrow. "I really can't imagine Henry Laszlo striking a crossroads deal. He was honest to a fault."

"There's got to be a reason why the hell-maggots picked him," Travis mused.

"Not necessarily. Sometimes, random shit happens, and we wear ourselves out trying to make it make sense."

"You said there'd been other cases like this?" Travis sipped the whiskey, savoring the taste. Ryan didn't allow himself many luxuries, but the scotch was one of them.

"Yeah. But until I saw a pattern, I didn't think it was more than bereavement. In the other cases, there was family to help intervene. They got a doc to give a sedative to the person who wouldn't release the body, and then other relatives made sure the body went right for cremation." He wrinkled his nose. "There wasn't really any other option since the corpses weren't fresh. In a few cases, we didn't realize there'd been a death for quite some time."

"Cremation, huh?" Travis replied thoughtfully, absently tracing the rim of his glass with one finger. "Purifying fire."

Ryan nodded. "Which destroyed those particular infestations, but doesn't solve the bigger problem of why it's happening."

Travis rubbed his temples. "When I get back to Pittsburgh, I'll see what I can find at the Archives. Don't worry," he added. "I won't blab to the Keepers." The Archives was a secret repository of arcane knowledge deep in the underground warren beneath the Duquesne University seminary library. Travis retained access because of his history with the Sinistram. The Archive's librarians, the mysterious Keepers, were monks who dedicated their lives to preserving the old —and often dangerous—occult tomes. Many Keepers had taken a vow of silence.

"Creepy bastards," Ryan replied. "They're probably ninja assassins."

Travis grinned. "They're all older than Methuselah. Unless the rumors are true, and they're actually immortal." Seminary students gossiped like everyone else, although no one would dare have said a word within the hearing of the fearsome librarians.

"I'll keep my ears open," Ryan agreed. "Maybe I can figure out a pattern. Do you think that these...hell-maggots...caused Henry's death, or are they, I don't know, some kind of demonic soul-scavengers?"

Travis took another sip of his drink. The whole concept was

disquieting. "No idea. I've never even heard of that kind of infestation before. Sort of like satanic scabies."

"Let me do some digging," Ryan offered. "After all, I'm really only aware of what goes on in my congregation, unless something becomes newsworthy enough to get talked about down at the diner. Maybe there's been more happening than I know. I'm also overdue to have lunch with Pastor Jonas and Reverend Harmond," he added with a wink.

"That's very ecumenical of you," Travis replied with a wry smile.

Ryan shrugged. "Cooper City is a small town. Individuals may bicker, but behind the scenes, Jonas and Harmond and I—and some others—do a lot of collaborating on the food bank, the women's shelter, that sort of thing. Doesn't make sense to not work together. So I'll see what I can find out from them. And I'll ask Mrs. K," he added, referencing his housekeeper, "and find out what the ladies down at the beauty shop are saying. They know everything that's worth knowing in these parts."

"And if you would, keep an ear open for anything about a freaky black truck," Travis said. "Not that I think it's related, but I-80 comes right past here. So might that truck."

"You think there's something supernatural going on?"

Travis nodded. "I'm not sure what, but I don't think it's as simple as kidnapping. As if that isn't bad enough."

"I've heard about the disappearances. I think people are edgy about them," Ryan responded. "There's talk. Nothing but a rehash of what's been on the news, but I'll tell you if I hear anything really interesting."

Ryan made a pot of decaf, spiked with Jameson's, and they finished the last of the pie, then retired to the living room to stream a recent superhero movie. Travis's attention drifted in and out of the plot, but he enjoyed the rare camaraderie of being able to hang out with a friend without either of them feeling the burden of the collar.

He finally headed to the guest room around midnight, and the buzz of his phone surprised him. A glance at the ID puzzled him even more.

"Trece? Where are you?" Trece Baldwin was a long-haul trucker whose routes took him up and down the Eastern seaboard and back and forth across the heartland.

"Passing the exit for I-99 on I-80. I need to talk to you, man. I've been seeing shit, and you're the only one who'll believe me." Trece's far sight worked a little differently from Travis's own sporadic clairvoyance. Travis caught glimpses from the past, present, and future, and saw distant happenings as they unfolded in real time, but usually without context or any ability to intervene.

"Tell me."

"I saw a big black pickup stop beside a car pulled off on the side of the road."

"*Saw* with your eyes, or *saw* with your gift?"

"With my gift," Trece snapped, "else I wouldn't have cause to call you about it, now would I?" He was quiet for a moment. "Anyhow, there was a lady in the car, and she had the hood up, so I guess she'd had trouble. The black pickup stopped, and then it took off again, and the woman was gone. I never saw anyone get out..."

"But?" Travis prompted.

"But I got a glimpse through the front windshield." Trece's voice choked with fear. "Couldn't make out a face, but Travis, whatever was driving had glowing red eyes."

CHAPTER FOUR

"I JUST DON'T FIGURE Brian Mason to be the kind to kill himself." Doug Conroy led the way through the forest underbrush, and Brent followed a couple of paces behind.

"People do things for all kinds of reasons that only make sense to themselves," Brent replied.

"There's something weird about this, Brent. I wouldn't have dragged your ass out here if I thought this was just business as usual."

Doug left the Pittsburgh police force about the same time Brent left to start his PI business. He and his wife, Cheryl, used to be neighbors to Brent's family down in Columbia, SC, where Doug had been a cop before moving north for a promotion. He'd been on the scene the night Brent's family had been murdered and done his best in the aftermath to hunt the one responsible. It had been Doug's recommendation that got Brent the job in Pittsburgh, and they remained friends and fishing buddies, despite the difference in their ages. Now, he served as the Cooper City chief of police, which also covered the little hamlet of Merrick's Corners.

"I'm guessing all the easy stuff got ruled out? Debts, drugs, looming scandal?"

Doug snorted. "Brian wasn't an angel, but there was nothing shady about him."

"How about mental health issues?" Brent pressed. "Depression? Anxiety?"

"No more than anyone else. But the thing that gets me is, how come we've had five suicides from a town the size of Merrick's Corners, in the last four months, and all of them out in the same stretch of woods?"

Brent frowned. "Any link between the victims?"

Doug shouldered through the underbrush, which scratched against the sturdy tan canvas of his field jacket. "None anyone's turned up, other than just knowing each other from around town. Not related, didn't go to the same church, didn't even bowl in the same league. Not the same age. Hell, they weren't even poker buddies, and they didn't all drink at the same bars."

"Had any banks go belly-up lately? Bad investments?"

Doug shook his head. He still had a full head of hair, though it was steel gray now, instead of the silver-flecked brown that Brent remembered from his time on the force. "Nope. I do recall how to be a cop, you know."

"Yes, sir," Brent replied, respect hidden by a layer of sass.

"None of that. I need your help, Brent. I don't think that these deaths are *normal*." The emphasis he put on the last word left no doubt in Brent's mind as to what his old friend really meant.

He fought down a shiver. "What's so special about this stretch of woods?" Brent looked at the land around them. The trees were large, probably fifty to a hundred years old, he'd guess, although not much beyond that. As he studied the contours of the ground, he saw remnants of a road. Elsewhere, he spotted what remained of the foundation for a building, and an overgrown section of stone fence.

"That's what's left of Peale." Doug pointed to a clearing ahead. "Mining town, back about a hundred years ago. Built up out of nowhere when the mines around here opened, got bigger than Cooper City in just a year, and then dried up when the coal seams tapped out. Some folks stayed on into the early 1900s, but there weren't jobs, and so when they died, so did the town."

Curious, Brent followed Doug through the woods to see for himself. Time had taken a toll. If he had expected a ghost town like in the movies, full of rickety wooden buildings, he would have been disappointed. Depressions in the ground and the growth patterns of the grass and scrub bushes suggested where houses and stores once stood. Brent couldn't shake the feeling that something was watching him, and chalked it up to his imagination.

"Anything unusual about the bodies when you found them?" he asked.

"Three were gunshot wounds," Doug replied. "Two intentional overdoses of prescription medications plus alcohol. One man slit his wrists with his hunting knife." He walked a few paces farther down what had long ago been Peale's main street. "Found Peter Jessup over there," he said, pointing to the left. "Neil Ellison by those stones," he indicated. "And the other three were all between here and the old mine entrance."

"You think maybe someone's cooking meth in the mine?" Brent and Doug walked toward the old archway on the other side of town that had once been an entrance to the Lucky Pines coal mine. Rusted railway lines led away from the mine toward the tumble-down remains of the tipple and breakers, and then on to the horizon. No trains had run on those rails for a century, but pulling them up wasn't worth it, and so the trains and the miners moved on.

"Doubtful," Doug said. "We checked the entrances around Peale first thing, thinking drugs or vagrants. They were locked up tight, and when we did go in, we didn't see any evidence that people had been inside since they closed." He looked away, and Brent thought he saw a shudder run through the older man. "Although—"

"Yeah?"

Doug shrugged, clearly uncomfortable. "If there's anyone who'd understand, it would be you, I guess. Something about this whole area—and especially the mines—gives me the creeps. I'm not an imaginative man. I don't get the willies walking around in the dark. But lately…"

"I don't think that what's been going on lately is normal, in any sense of the word," Brent replied. "Do you happen to know if people are talking about seeing ghosts? What's the local gossip?"

Brent and Doug waded through thigh-high weeds as they walked along the old railroad tracks. "I'd have to ask Cheryl what she's heard. Most people watch their mouths a bit around me, except for down at Hanson's Pub. The boys down there haven't mentioned ghosts per se, but I did notice from what they've been saying that they don't seem to be wandering as far afield scoping out hunting spots or rambling in the woods. That's new."

Brent nodded. "I'd be interested to see what the ladies are saying. Are there any places around here that are supposed to be haunted?"

"Well, all of Peale," Doug said, taking in the abandoned town with a sweep of his arm. "In Cooper City, there are a couple of old houses that people tell tales about, and the old feed store, if you can believe it." At Brent's side eye, Doug chuckled. "There's a story about an unlucky guy named George who was standing in the wrong place when a pallet of bagged fertilizer fell. Helluva way to die."

"Seriously?"

Doug wheezed with laughter but held up a hand as if to solemnly swear. "I shit you not," he said, and then doubled over at his own joke.

"Funny," Brent replied, rolling his eyes. "How about the cemeteries? Or the railroad tracks closer to town? Maybe a crossroad that's had more than its share of bad accidents?"

Doug wiped his eyes, then grew serious. "I'll put Cheryl on the case. Get my granddaughter, Cici, to see what the teenagers say. Wouldn't do for me to go asking about ghosts, but they can do pretty much any damn thing they please."

"I'd be obliged," Brent replied. "Because I think you're right. There's something going on here, and I don't think it's just a run of bad luck. I hope with all my heart that we're wrong and that it's not really my kind of thing." Even as he spoke the words, Brent felt sure his intuition was on point.

"You'll have your own chance to ask Cheryl tonight at dinner," Doug said, jolting Brent out of his thoughts. "When she heard you were coming to town, she insisted on feeding you. And of course, you're welcome to stay at our house. It's not fancy, but we have a guest bedroom."

Brent grinned. "Dinner sounds fantastic, and I'll take you up on a hot shower. As for staying the night...I was thinking of coming back here with the truck and sitting up to see what I see."

Doug nodded. "You always were a ballsy bastard. Just make sure you have a charged and working phone with you, and extra flashlight batteries. I don't want any of this movie-of-the-week preventable danger stuff."

"I'm all about preventing danger," Brent replied. "And I might end up with nothing to show from it except a crick in my neck. But since I'm here..."

"Yeah. I get it. And I sort of figured you would. But if you change your mind in the wee hours, c'mon back."

"Deal."

They walked back to Doug's truck, but Brent couldn't shake the feeling that something was aware of their presence and watching as they left. When he came back tonight, he intended to bring all the tools of his trade, and see whether he could find out what really lay behind Peale's run of bad luck.

Doug and Cheryl lived in a comfortable split-level house that, despite dating from the 1960s, was one of the newer homes in Merrick's Corners. Most of the houses dated from before the Second World War, and the stretch of red brick shopfronts downtown boasted cornerstones or keystones from the turn of the past century.

A skeptical pug sniffed Brent's boots when they entered, then padded off toward the kitchen. Cheryl emerged as the men hung up their coats on hooks near the door.

"Brent Lawson! You're a sight for sore eyes. I can't believe how much you look like your daddy!" Cheryl threw her arms open, and Brent accepted an embrace that managed to be fierce and pillowy at the same time. If he blinked a few extra times at the mention of his late father, Cheryl couldn't see.

"Go get cleaned up," she ordered, after giving them both a once-over to assure neither had managed to get hurt on their outing. "I'm just taking dinner out of the oven. Be quick about it—you don't want the roast to get cold." Doug waved Brent toward the downstairs bathroom, while he went to wash in the laundry room.

When Brent returned, Cheryl was bringing out stoneware bowls of steaming mashed potatoes and corn to go with a delectable roast on a platter in the center. The furnishings were a combination of styles and periods, a mix of pieces acquired early in the Conroy's marriage and those that came via inheritance or estate sales. The result was homey and comfortable, and so much like the house Brent had grown up in that he had to clear his throat to get rid of a sudden lump.

"I put water out for the meal, but there's a fresh pot of coffee brewing to go with the pie I baked," Cheryl said. She left her apron in the kitchen, revealing a t-shirt that read *"too many books, too little time"* over blue jeans and fancifully colored wool socks.

They took their seats, and Brent bowed his head while Doug gave thanks, although he had stopped praying that night, long ago, when everything had gone to hell. Chit-chat waited until they had passed all of the serving dishes. Brent ladled the gravy over his roast and potatoes and drew in a deep breath, savoring the aroma of a real, home-cooked meal.

Conversation started out light, with the weather, sports, and movie blockbusters, as well as Cheryl providing Brent with a quick update on people he might remember from back in Columbia. Doug turned the topic to the deaths out in Peale, and Cheryl shook her head.

"Funny you ask about ghosts." She added another small piece of roast to her plate. "Sandy, down at the salon, was just saying that her friend who works over at the Happy Endings Tavern—the one in the old Moser Inn building? Anyhow, there've been stories for years about that place. Supposed to have been a duel there back in Revolutionary War times, then it was a stop on the Underground Railroad during the Civil War, and then back when it was a Prohibition speakeasy, there was a shoot-out between bootleggers and the Feds," Cheryl told them with a grin that said she enjoyed telling the tales.

"Well, Sandy's friend has had stories from time to time about weird things happening—cold spots, doors that open by themselves, bottles and things that move around by themselves or go missing and turn up somewhere strange. Apparently, that's been happening a lot lately. But when I was down there getting my hair cut, Sandy was saying that her friend Ginny actually *saw* a couple of the ghosts. One of them was a woman in an apron in the pantry, and the other was a young man in a uniform with a bandaged shoulder. Almost scared her badly enough to quit, but I guess she decided she needed the money, so she stayed on."

"About when did Ginny say things got more active?" Brent wiped his mouth on a napkin. He reached for a warm roll and butter, resolved to enjoy the feast.

Cheryl thought for a moment. "Sandy's had something new to tell me each time I've gone in for the last three months or so," she said. "And that got the other women talking. Now mind, some of this might just be people who don't want to get left out of the conversation, making up nonsense, but it seemed like everyone's had a story lately about seeing something strange at night on the road, or getting a glimpse of a weird creature out in the woods, or some such. I guess George down at the feed store scared a couple of truckers silly by popping up behind them and then disappearing."

"Are the ghosts just making themselves visible more often, or are they acting out?" Brent took a sip of his water. "Throwing or breaking things, pushing people, playing pranks?"

Cheryl nodded. "Seems I might have heard that, although I didn't pay a lot of attention. Sandy could tell you better, or Maryanne over at the diner. Not much gets by them."

Brent was so busy thinking about how to approach the two women for their stories, he wasn't prepared for Cheryl's next question. "You been down to Columbia lately?"

Brent caught his breath, then spoke when Doug frowned and looked like he might jump in. "No, not in a while. Maybe it's my imagination, but I still think people look at me funny when I go back, so I guess the old rumors haven't died yet."

Cheryl grimaced. "I'm sorry, honey. People can be ignorant. And I guess now that your aunt and uncle moved to Florida, you don't have any ties there."

"Not really," Brent admitted. "I was glad to get out of town after everything happened, so I left right after the funerals and stayed up at the hunting cabin the rest of that summer until I went to Basic Training. Aunt Mellie and Uncle Ted handled all the estate stuff since I was barely eighteen. By the time I came back from Basic, all that was left was a bank account."

Senior year, Brent and his twin brother, Danny, had been the stars of the high school football team, with college scouts taking notice. That summer, the brothers were supposed to go to training camp together before going to play for the Georgia Bulldogs in the fall on football scholarships.

Then Danny got mono and had to drop out of camp. Brent wanted to skip because it didn't feel right going without his brother, but Danny made Brent go anyhow. While Brent was at camp, someone brutally murdered his family, then set fire to the house. The news speculated about a serial killer, but local gossip turned darker, with rumors about some supernatural involvement, maybe even demons.

Doug had been on the Columbia police force back then and had done his best to shield Brent, but some of the other cops made it clear they wondered whether drugs, gambling, or some other criminal activity played a role. Even when Brent was cleared, and the tragedy declared the work of a possible serial killer, the gossip followed him, as did the odd glances from people around town. Even his aunt and uncle seemed to look at him differently.

That had been the first time demons had touched Brent's life, but it wouldn't be the last.

"I'm sorry," Cheryl said, her cheeks coloring with embarrassment. "I didn't mean to spoil the mood. I should stop to think before I talk sometimes."

"That's all right," Brent assured her. "It's been a long time." Thirteen years, a couple of tours of duty and a new city wasn't enough to rid him of the dreams or keep his chest from tightening every time he saw a fire engine streak past. And it certainly hadn't stopped Danny's ghost from visiting him over the years, waking or sleeping.

Doug steered the conversation back to Steeler and Nittany Lion football, and Cheryl went to redeem herself by serving the pie and ice cream. Brent hoped he faked recovering a good mood, and the excellent dessert meant the night ended on a pleasant note.

"I hope you don't mind if I drop by for a shower in the morning," Brent said as he got ready to leave. "With luck, it will be a very boring night, but I'd like to clean up before I get on the road."

"Doug and I are up at six-thirty," Cheryl assured him with a pat on his arm. "So any time after that is fine. Plan on breakfast. I'll make waffles and bacon." Her voice made it clear the invitation was really a summons, and Brent gave in gracefully. Cheryl also insisted on packing him a roast beef sandwich, a bag of chips, another piece of pie, and a Thermos of coffee for his vigil in case he got hungry during the night. Only after he assured her that he had several heavy blankets in the truck and he'd be warm enough on his stakeout did he manage to escape, much to Doug's amusement.

Cheryl's mothering made Brent feel cared for and sad at the same time. His own parents would have been about Doug and Cheryl's age. It had been so long since Brent had been mothered that he forgot how much he still craved it, even at thirty-three.

His whole life had changed in one night. Football wasn't the same without Danny to share it with, and the thought of going to college without him was unbearable. Brent had gone into the Army to get away, jumping from the frying pan into the proverbial fire. He'd eventually earned his degree online, in a program for veterans, and that and his combat and Special Ops experience got him the job at the FBI. But the demons kept showing up, first in Iraq, then on a job for the Bureau, and then with the Pittsburgh PD. That got the attention of other, less welcome organizations.

Which was how he ended up as an ex-cop private eye, staking out a ghost town with a shotgun full of rock salt and cold iron.

Brent drove his pickup carefully on the overgrown road that he and Doug had followed earlier that day. The sign *"closed to traffic"* seemed redundant, since no one would mistake the barely visible trail for a viable thoroughfare. That didn't stop him. He'd made some modifications to his vehicle and his arsenal over the years since he'd begun fighting monsters and demons, just for situations like this.

Branches slapped against the windows and rear-view mirrors. The truck powered through tall weeds and scrub that scratched against the undercarriage. It might have been quieter to just hike in, but if any of the range of creatures he had considered were behind the spike in suicides, Brent didn't want to face them without options.

By nine-thirty, Brent had his truck positioned so that the lights would catch both the mine entrance and much of the town ruins, if he turned them on. He got out and liberally scattered a mix made of salt and iron filings in a circle around the truck, and for good measure uncoiled a rope that had been soaked in holy water, aconite, and colloidal silver and laid it out at the edge of the salt circle. Then he climbed up into the bed of his truck with his weapons bag and waited.

An hour later, Brent heard rustling in the darkness. He adjusted his night vision goggles and readied his shotgun. He had a Glock with silver rounds tucked into his waistband at the small of his back, and a Beretta with steel hollow-point bullets in his shoulder holster. A variety of knives in sheaths all over his body gave him options. All he needed was a clear shot.

A man stumbled from the underbrush, with a whiskey bottle clutched in one hand and a revolver in the other.

Brent shifted to high alert. If the poor wretch with the empty bottle of hooch had been lured to this godforsaken spot, then whatever desired his death must also be nearby.

His left hand went out of habit to the silver medallion he wore with his dog tags, a St. Michael medal that he trusted more for the silver than the saint. The night goggles cast the ghost town in eerie shades of green. Brent didn't rely on thermal imaging to alert him to anything lurking in the forest; many of the creatures he hunted lacked a heartbeat or warm blood. Then he saw it; a slight movement in the tall grass that didn't match the wind, the signature of a predator closing in on its prey.

The man leaned back to take the last dregs from his bottle, then threw the empty container away with a curse. It shattered against a tree, breaking the silence. The drunk stopped and planted his feet, face upturned to the night sky. In the moonlight, Brent could just make out the man's features: average height, slim build, light hair, no beard, probably early thirties. Grief and despair etched the man's features, making him look haggard.

"After everything, you've got nothing to say to me?" he challenged the heavens. "Everything I did...followed the rules...tried to do it right...and for what?" he shouted. "What the fuck was all that for? Huh? Answer me, you goddamned cheat." His voice hitched, and he sobbed openly.

"Buncha lies, that's what it was. All of it. Sucker's bet—and I'm the sucker. Just one...damned...thing after another, and I'm done."

He turned in one direction and then another, as if unsure where the target of his ire might be. "You hear that? I'm fuckin' done!" He waved a pistol at the night as if to make his point.

The man's words tore at Brent, too similar to his own thoughts on many a night. He hadn't counted on having a would-be suicide show up, and it complicated his mission. But Brent couldn't let the man die.

"Shit," he muttered, knowing he was about to do something stupid. Brent triangulated the distance between the truck, the suicidal man, and the unseen predator. He still had no idea whether the creature in the tall grass meant to attack, or had come to enjoy the show. Even if the cryptid did not intend to do the killing itself, Brent knew there was no assurance it wasn't equipped to kill.

Brent eased down from the truck bed, weighing his options. He disliked all of his choices. He left the shotgun behind, pulled his Glock, and ripped off his night goggles, dropping them into the truck bed. Then he clicked his remote, and the truck's high beams flared to life, blindingly bright, behind him.

Brent leaped over the protective barrier of salt and iron, running full out. He closed the distance between himself and the newcomer, landing a right cross before the man saw him coming, then caught the stranger as he sagged toward the ground. Glad that the man was not hefty, Brent slung him over his shoulder and ran back, jumping into the unbroken circle again and depositing his unconscious companion in the bed of the truck. In another minute, he cuffed the man's wrists and ankles to keep him from getting away or getting *in* the way and wrapped a strip of cloth over his eyes to avoid future complications. Then Brent rested his hands on his hips and looked around the desolate area, wondering where the predator had gone.

There. He spotted movement in the high grass. Was the creature nocturnal? Brent hadn't thought to ask if the suicides shared a time of day. The bright lights had taken the stalker by surprise, perhaps even temporarily blinding it, but that advantage probably wouldn't last for long.

Only then did analysis catch up with adrenaline. For the seconds Brent ventured beyond the salt-and-iron circle, his mood had plummeted as dread and hopelessness washed over him, threatening to pull him into the undertow. Training and experience forced all other thoughts aside, keeping him focused on saving the stranger. Now, the dark thoughts and self-loathing made him gasp for air and nearly doubled him over.

And yet...the painful thoughts felt muted, almost second hand as if Brent were somehow replaying someone else's mental collapse. He forced his emotions down and retreated into the cold logic that so often had saved his life and the lives of his soldiers. Quick triage assured him he was not injured. Yet the assault on his thoughts and feelings had been sudden, overwhelming, and nearly incapacitating.

Maybe the men who killed themselves had help, he thought. *Maybe something lured them here, preying on their vulnerability, exploiting their loss and grief, cranking up the pain. But why? The dead men weren't ripped apart or gnawed on. It didn't use the psychic attack to trap them. Then what was the point?* He stilled as realization dawned.

It fed.

And with all his unresolved grief and the guilt and blame he could not shake loose, Brent had practically served himself up as a feast.

Brent walked the perimeter of his safe zone, Glock in one hand, silver-edged Ka-Bar in the other. "Come out, come out," he called softly. "I know you're there."

Standing in the silence of the night, Brent realized that the utter stillness was unnatural. No owls hooted, no forest creatures scrabbled through the dry leaves and branches. He knew from night maneuvers that the only time nature fell silent was when apex predators hunted.

Instinct told Brent that the creature would not approach from the front and brave the blinding lights. He moved through the high beams, averting and closing his eyes for a few seconds to avoid compromising his night vision, using the glare as a way to force his quarry to lose track of him. Brent dropped to the ground and belly crawled beneath the truck from front to back, emerging at the rear.

The stranger lay bound in the truck bed, quiet and motionless. As Brent started to crawl beneath the tailgate, he saw movement beyond the protective barrier and drew back. Instead, he rolled out from under the right side, hunched beside the wheel well and eased forward, peering into the darkness, where the headlights did not dispel the shadows.

The night had grown cold, and Brent wondered if the ghosts of Peale roused at the intrusion. Before he could think much about it, a pallid creature with a nightmare face hurled itself at the bed of the truck—and bounced back, repelled by the protective barrier.

Brent took the shot as the being stumbled, firing a silver round and striking the predator where its heart should have been. Black blood gushed from the wound, and the thing gave an ear-splitting howl that nearly deafened Brent even as it raised a primal dread deep within.

"Fuck that shit," Brent muttered, firing two more rounds. The force of the shots staggered the creature, but it stared at Brent with silver eyes set in a corpse-pale, elongated face, still standing after close-range hits that would have killed any mortal. Brent shot again, this time a kneecap, and the monster fell, screaming, then pushed off with its good leg and landed just short of the salt line, scrabbling with its clawed hands in the dirt.

Trying to break the warded circle.

This time, Brent fired down on the monster's skull, a shot that entered at the crown of the head and took off the back of the skull, spattering gobbets of black ichor and goo. The body shuddered, then went still. Brent didn't intend to take any chances. He emptied the rest of his clip into the creature, then dropped his gun and drew a machete from the sheath on his belt.

The monster lay just a step beyond the barrier. Gory exit wounds from skull to pelvis showed where Brent's shots had hit true. Still, he had no idea whether the thing could regenerate, or whether it could actually die, no matter how badly wounded. Only two ways to be certain: lop off the head and burn the son of a bitch to ash.

Swallowing fear, Brent took a two-handed grip on the machete and stepped across the protective line.

The creature lurched up, its eyes wide and maw open, pallid face streaked with black blood. One inhumanly strong hand locked around Brent's ankle so tight he expected to hear bones crunch. Gritting his teeth against the pain, he put all his strength into the downward swing of his blade. It bit into flesh and bone, parting the vertebrae, hesitating on the sinew and corded muscles before sliding through soft tissue and cartilage. The blade came free suddenly enough that Brent took a step forward to keep his balance, and the severed head dropped to one side. The rest of the monster's body went slack, and the hand released his ankle, though Brent felt certain he would have deep bruises in the morning.

While the fury of the fight still animated him, before he had time to think or feel, Brent grabbed a can of lighter fluid and a pack of matches from his gear bag in the bed of the truck, as well as more of the salt-iron mixture. He gingerly toed the head over to be face-up and snapped a photo with his phone to research later. Then he doused the body, covered it in a thick dusting of iron and salt, and lit it up.

Only then did the horror of the night fully hit him. Brent's hands shook as he replaced the equipment and supplies in his bag, and he leaned heavily against the tailgate, as his guts debated bringing back supper. He tasted bile but choked back the urge to puke.

A backward glance revealed bright flames and a plume of smoke.

Doug was on his side, but Brent didn't want to try to explain what was going on should other cops come to investigate the fire. Bitter experience had taught him that too many cops arrested first and asked questions later.

Brent coiled the perimeter rope and tossed it into the bed of the truck. He eyed the cuffed man in the back, who had just started to groan. With a muttered apology, Brent dragged the stranger out of the truck bed, chucked him into the back seat of the cab, and pushed the pickup to its off-road limits to reach the main road before first responders boxed him in.

If Doug hadn't brought him in on the situation, and he didn't have an unwilling passenger in the back, Brent would have hightailed it back to Pittsburgh. He might not be covered in blood spatter, but he was sure to have residue on his hands from firing his gun, and he didn't want to explain the reasons to the local cops. Still, he needed to offload his new "friend" and fill Doug in on what had happened. Instead of driving back to the house, Brent headed for the tumbledown barn of an abandoned farm he had passed on the way into town.

Doug answered on the first ring and promised to come meet him alone and unofficially. "Jesus, Brent. You don't do things by halves," he said.

"Yeah, well. Half measures get you fuckin' killed," Brent replied. "See you in ten."

Brent drummed his fingers on the steering wheel as his right leg jiggled nervously, waiting for Doug to arrive. By the time the police chief pulled in, Brent's prisoner was stirring. Brent ignored the cuffed man for the moment and stepped out of the truck.

"I think I've solved the Peale problem, at least until word gets around and another asshole drifts in to take over," he said, holding out the picture on his phone as Doug walked forward.

"What the hell is that?" Doug asked, recoiling.

"I'm not sure what it's called. Gonna send this to a buddy of mine to find out," Brent replied. "But I know what it does. It's a psi-vamp. Feeds off emotions and intensifies them—right up until the poor son of a bitch dies."

A thud from inside of the truck drew both men's attention. "Speaking of sons of bitches—I picked up a passenger," Brent added. "Kept him from offing himself. He's probably not going to be happy with me, and I'd rather not get arrested for saving his ass."

"Works for me," Doug said. "How about I stay quiet, and you dump him here in the barn, then head out of here. I'll wait a bit, then come 'save' him. Can he identify you?"

Brent gave Doug a look. "Do I look stupid? No. But I don't think the psi-vamp put the idea of suicide in the guy's head, so he needs help, or he'll probably try again on his own."

"I'll do what I can," Doug promised. "Thanks for helping."

Brent clapped a hand on his shoulder. "Any time. Let me know if other weirdness pops up—or you hear anything about that black truck. And thank you for dinner. I'll catch a shower elsewhere. I want to get going." He jerked his head to tell Doug to get out of sight, then went to open the back of the cab, expecting his prisoner to lash out.

His unwilling passenger's hangover made him clumsy, and while the kick he attempted might have worked under other circumstances, all it did was send him careening out of the truck and onto the barn's dirt floor.

Brent dropped his voice to a gravelly rasp. "Listen up, asshole. I saved your life. So you're gonna sit right here, nice and quiet, and wait for rescue. And if you try to kill yourself again, I'll know, and I'll come back and thrash you. Got that?"

"Who are you?" The blindfolded man's voice was thin, frightened.

"I'm Batman."

Brent walked away with a shit-eating grin, climbed into his truck, and drove away. He pulled into a truck stop once he was back on I-80, and sent the photo via an encrypted network to his friend and researcher, Simon Kincaide.

"Nice beauty shot. You clean up well," Simon responded.

"Very funny. Any idea what this is or where it came from?"

"Got a few ideas, but I'm not positive. Let me look into it and get back to you."

"Thanks. And I really want to know if they hunt solitary or in packs."

"I'm on it."

Brent grabbed a clean change of clothes from his go-bag, got a shower, and then ambled into the restaurant, finding a seat where he could eavesdrop on nearby conversations. He ordered a bacon and cheese omelet, then sat back in his chair, nursing his coffee and trying not to think about the fact that he'd been awake for more than twenty-four hours.

"...damn black truck again." The comment caught Brent's attention, but he made sure he did not look in the direction of the speaker.

"...heard she had car trouble. Called for a tow truck. But by the time they got there, she was gone."

"...ought to look at that guy who's been sniffing around, asking questions. You want my opinion? He's probably the one behind all this."

Sounds like Travis has been here. That's the last damn thing I need.

Brent's server delivered his breakfast just then, and the people at the other table rose to leave. As the waitress refilled his coffee, Brent glanced up. "I heard those guys talking. Did something happen?"

The dark-haired woman might have been old enough to be his mother. She looked as tired as he felt. "Another girl's gone missing, out by Dubois. Ya'd think the cops could do something about it, but..." her voice trailed off, and she shook her head.

"Real sorry to hear that," Brent replied. "I hope they find her."

The server fixed him with a look. "They ain't found none of them yet. Don't imagine they'll find her, neither." Beneath her anger, fear glinted in her eyes, and Brent could imagine how often the waitress had to drive home by herself on desolate stretches of road, wondering whether her own luck was about to run out.

He left cash to cover breakfast and a generous tip, grateful she had poured him a coffee to go. On the way out, he stopped by the bulletin board and looked at the hastily photocopied missing person fliers. Photos and descriptions were linked by a thread and a red push pin to the location on a map showing where they had disappeared. Brent snapped a photo, in case the display revealed something new on later examination.

The faces of the missing girls and women would haunt his nightmares. Sherri was the youngest, staring out from what looked to be an elementary school photo. The others were cropped from snapshots showing them laughing and happy, a moment frozen in time. Brent forced himself to look away and headed back to his truck.

He had barely gotten back on the highway when his phone rang. He saw the number and debated not answering, but he knew they would just keep calling. "Go away," he said before the caller had a chance to say anything.

"You know we can't do that." The ID said "unlisted," but Brent recognized the voice. "Shane" from CHARON, making sure Brent knew the secret organization did its best to keep an eye on him.

"Go fuck yourself. You'll feel better, and you'll forget about trying to fuck me over."

"It's a fool's game chasing the darkness all by yourself."

"And I'm a damn fool. That's not news."

Shane paused, and when he spoke again, his tone grew more serious. "You're not making much of a living, hunting down insurance fraud and cheating husbands. Bet it doesn't go far paying for your pain meds, or for the PT to ease up on those old injuries. It doesn't have to be this way."

Brent's jaw tightened. "We've had this discussion before. Nothing's changed. Go away."

"You're doing the work. Hunting monsters. How's the pay?" Shane goaded. "Come back inside, and we'll make sure you've got all the best tech, classified research, and intel, backup teams...regular paychecks and the best healthcare Uncle Sam has to offer."

Brent had tried changing his number. Shane always found him. "Or maybe throw some money to the VA so I can actually get an appointment, with the benefits I've already earned," Brent countered. "Nope. Not buying your shit."

"We'd prefer you come back on your own, but we don't have to ask nicely." Shane's voice grew cold.

"You try to conscript me, and I commit suicide-by-monster on the next hunt," Brent returned in an icy tone. "I'm no use to you dead or in Gitmo. So...go bother someone else. I don't have a soul to sell anymore."

"The demons aren't going to go away."

"I'll take them over you any day. Get lost." Stabbing the end call button wasn't nearly as satisfying as slamming down an old-style receiver. Despite his bravado, Brent's heart raced, and his palms sweated.

He pulled into a rest stop, grabbed a scanner from his gear bag, and ran it over the pickup, checking for tracking devices. He'd already turned off the GPS on his phone and only carried a burner cell with him out on jobs. A mechanic buddy up in Atlantic had disabled the truck's automatic reporting functions and handled his inspections and repairs to keep it that way.

When he found nothing, Brent swore under his breath and kicked a rock across the parking lot. Shane probably wiretapped all of Brent's known contacts and watched to see when an unknown caller popped up on the grid.

CHARON—he didn't remember what the acronym stood for, but the image of the ferryman of the damned from Greek myth was hard to forget—was a small, elite black ops team that reported directly to the vice president, and moved against supernatural threats deemed to be a danger to US interests anywhere in the world. CHARON operated without rules, off-the-books, accountable only for results, and without regard to collateral damage.

They hadn't bothered with the demons that killed Brent's parents and Danny, or Mavet, the creature that obliterated his unit in Iraq. And Brent would buy his own ticket straight to hell before he'd take orders from an amoral asshole like Shane. *Never forgive. Never forget.*

CHAPTER FIVE

"I THOUGHT you needed to hear what they had to say." Dr. Derek Peters, Jefferson County Coroner, ushered Travis into the autopsy room.

Travis steeled himself for what he was about to see. Four bodies lay on the steel tables, just released to the coroner's office by the cops. The victims had nothing physically apparent in common. One was a middle-aged woman, another a man in his twenties. The third was a teenage girl, and the fourth, an old man. Two were white, one African-American, and one Latina.

"What happened?" Travis asked. He'd long ago gotten over losing his lunch at the morgue except in the most extreme cases, but what twisted his gut now was sadness rather than revulsion.

"Guess which one was the shooter," Derek said. Travis frowned, not in the mood for games.

"The stereotype says it's the young guy."

Derek shook his head. "Nope. The old man. Pulled a gun out from under his newspaper in the food court and started shooting up the place. Thank heavens his aim was lousy, or we'd have bodies everywhere. One of the cops patrolling the mall shot him. The victims are all local. The families know each other. It's a goddamn mess."

Travis hung back, still in the doorway. "So what's the deal? You're a necromancer. What do you need a medium for?"

"Shh!" Derek looked around out of habit, but Travis had already assured they were alone.

"Validation," Derek replied with a glare. "I want to know what they say to you when you can't compel them to show up and talk."

"Did you summon them?"

Derek shook his head. "No. But spirits can tell I could if I wanted to. So having them talk to you is like confiding in a friend instead of getting called in to see the principal."

"It's easier with names," Travis said.

"Edward Hillard," Derek replied, pointing to the old man. "Sharon Dillinger," he added, gesturing toward the older woman. "Dequan Smith and Brandi Ramirez," he finished. Travis nodded in acknowledgment; knowing the names made their deaths more personal.

Talking to newly dead trauma victims was one of the scenarios Travis hated most. Since leaving the priesthood and the Sinistram, he had helped a few friends among the Pittsburgh cops on cold cases and when leads dried up. If the situation permitted, Travis called in a sympathetic priest like Father Pavel or Father Ryan to administer Last Rites, but if that wasn't possible, he had bent the rules more than once to offer rest and absolution to troubled spirits.

Unfortunately, no one offered true rest and absolution to Travis.

Travis centered his energy, closed his eyes, and reached out, opening himself to the dead. To his inner sight, the old morgue felt like a crowded ballroom, full of restless ghosts. Some had the faded resignation of long-dead revenants who either could not or did not want to move on. Others felt confused and jangled as if they had not yet accepted their deaths. That was to be expected here in a place few came to peaceably.

He gently sorted through the ghosts, looking for the four he sought. Some of the spirits clung to him, begging for his help. Those he blessed and sent onward. Others avoided him, and a few regarded him balefully as if he might force them to go elsewhere. He ignored them and pressed forward until he found the three victims huddled to one side, and the shooter's ghost pacing on the other.

Why? Travis confronted Edmund. He looked to be almost eighty and had a frame to suggest that in his day he had been large and powerful. Now he was a shrunken remnant, with too-big clothing hanging from his frame. His mouth twisted down and his eyes were alight with fury.

Thieves, all of them! Out to take what I've worked for. They follow me...taunt me...hide in the bushes around my house...trying to drive me out. And I said, "I'll show them!" He waved one hand as if he still held the gun he had used in the rampage.

Travis fell back a step. Edmund's ghost undulated with thin, black wisps of smoke that clung to him like leeches and burrowed beneath his skin. His spirit wasn't quite as covered with the hell-maggots as Henry Laszlo's had been, but it was only a matter of degree.

Taking a deep breath, Travis composed himself and turned to the huddled victims. Sharon wrapped her arms around Brandi, and Dequan planted his skinny frame in front of both women, presenting a barrier should Edmund attack again.

I'm sorry, Travis said in his mind. The three spirits startled, apparently surprised that he could see them. *Do you have any idea why, out of the crowd, he shot at you?*

One by one, they shook their heads. Up close, Travis could see worry and exhaustion in Dequan's features. Brandi fidgeted in Sharon's arms as if even in death she could not stand still. Sharon wore a defiant expression, but Travis saw pain and loss in her eyes.

I'll help you pass over, Travis promised. *But I have to take care of something first. You're safe here.*

"Travis!" Derek's voice echoed in the tiled room, and Travis spun in time to see Edmund's spirit launch himself in an attack, only to come up short as an iridescent green curtain of power cut him off, then encircled the belligerent ghost.

They want to take my things! They'll steal me blind. You don't understand! Edmund's eyes held the madness of a wounded animal.

"Hold him," Travis told Derek, who nodded. This time, with Derek's necromancy to restrain the wild-eyed ghost, Travis did not need to bother with holy water and a circle of salt. He began to chant the ritual of exorcism, and the words sent Edmund into a frenzy, careening against the foxfire glow that trapped him inside. Edmund's spirit howled and cursed, screaming threats and promising bloody vengeance, but as Travis persisted, the hell-maggots fell from Edmund's body and wriggled loose from beneath his spectral flesh, burning and turning to ash on the floor.

I have nothing left. Edmund cried, dropping to his knees. Travis didn't know whether the dead man meant that without his anger, he had no purpose, or whether a reversal of fortunes prompted his shooting spree. But quivering on the floor, he looked spent and empty.

"It's time to move on," Travis said out loud, mustering as much compassion as he could for the old man. He turned back to Sharon and the other two ghosts and gestured for them to come closer, while Derek maintained the green, glowing prison around their killer.

"I can help you pass over to the other side," Travis offered, his quiet, confident tone hiding how much confronting the hell-maggots had rattled him. "Listen to my words, and when you're ready, just let go."

The familiar litany of the Last Rites came from long experience, and Travis lost himself in their comforting cadence. His voice rose and fell with the old words, believing in the creative energy of the universe, even if he could no longer, after all he had seen, believe in a god.

His tattered faith sufficed. The warm glow of a summer twilight suffused the room, supplanting the harsh fluorescent glare, and the three victims' ghosts vanished between one breath and the next. The light shifted as if shadows covered a waning moon. The hair prickled on the back of Travis's neck and rose on his arms. He turned and stared into a fearsome darkness that drew Edmund's screaming ghost into its black heart and swallowed him whole before blinking out.

The phosphorescent protective light faded. Travis sagged against the wall, while Derek reached to steady himself against the foot of one of the steel tables.

"What the fuck?" Derek demanded. Derek was one of the Night Vigil, and as with most of Travis's loose alliance of psychic allies, Derek's power was only part of his story. His previous position as head coroner in Chicago placed him in the media cross-hairs as an expert witness on high-profile murder investigations.

Derek had reveled in the fame, working hours that left little time for his wife and children. When his testimony helped to put a notorious mobster in prison, the man's associates retaliated by burning down Derek's home with his family inside. Taking a nearly anonymous position in a rural county was both penance and self-imposed exile.

"I wish I knew," Travis admitted, staring at the spot where the ghosts had vanished as if he could still see the doorway. "Talk to me, Derek. I need the big picture. There's more going on here than just a mall shooting."

Derek sighed and nodded. "Come with me." He led Travis to a small break room. They poured coffee and took a seat at the table farthest from the door.

"Jefferson County isn't Chicago," Derek said when they settled in. "Yes, we have murders, but not on a big-city scale. Violence out here is personal, most of the time, and usually involves alcohol, old grudges, and jealousy. Bar fights. Someone cheats with the wrong person or decides they aren't going to take being beaten up anymore. A robbery or a meth deal gone wrong. But lately..."

"What?"

Derek shook his head. "It's like people have gone nuts. We're at two hundred percent of the number of murders from last year, and it's only fall. The mall shooting today isn't the only one of its kind. We've had shooters in offices, schools, parks, concerts. People are afraid to go out. I've had to bring in the coroners from neighboring areas on a part-time basis some weeks because it's more than one person can handle. If we keep this up, there won't be anyone left breathing."

"Has it been all year? When did it start?" Travis pressed, far more interested in Derek's story than his lukewarm, bitter coffee.

"I figured you'd ask, so when we aren't up to our asses in bodies, I've been running some numbers." Derek might have fled the big city, but his methods and perspective were still shaped by major metropolitan best practices.

He pulled out his tablet computer and brought up a set of slides. "See this line? It's the murder rate for the county for the past five years." Travis saw a mostly flat line with a few shallow bumps. "And then there's this year." The line veered up sharply, almost vertical.

"And it's not just Brookville or Jefferson County. Centre County's even worse," he added, showing another set of numbers. "This is just since summer, and it's getting progressively more fucked up each month."

Travis stared at the screen, trying to make sense of the data. "Aren't most of the people out here older? It's like some kind of Social Security rampage."

Derek nodded. "There's not much for young people to do for a living out here, and they can make more money in the bigger cities. So they leave, and the older people stay. Which is one reason we don't usually have a lot of murders. But the suicide rate looks even worse—this year."

"What's going on?" Travis asked. "Layoffs? Pension fund gone bust? Lots of people get bad diagnoses?"

"No more than usual on all of the above," Derek replied. "I've been researching whenever I'm not stuck in here pulling double shifts. Good thing I don't have a life," he added, and while he said it jokingly, that didn't hide the bitterness.

"Did the people involved have anything in common? Prior employment, family ties, old school friendships...anything?"

Derek nodded. "Plenty of small connections. After all, out here people cross paths because the population isn't that big. There aren't that many places to work or go to school. Lots of people are related, by blood or marriage, and they can tell you who's who, out to third cousins twice removed," he added. "But that didn't cover everyone. Only one thing did. They had all experienced a tragic loss prior to committing the violence."

Travis gave Derek a look. "Should I be worried about you going postal?"

Derek shook his head. "Whatever's going on is feeding on fresh grief, not old wounds."

Travis thought as he stared at the graphs and tapped his fingers. "Any evidence of supernatural activity? You work with enough cops, you hear things."

"If you mean, is there a coven of bloodthirsty witches cursing retirees into going on killing sprees, the answer is 'no.'"

"I sense a 'but.'"

Derek grimaced. "I caught up with Roger. Remember him? The homeless guy who sees death omens?"

Travis nodded. He had connected his Night Vigil people to one another within their area, to watch for signs of trouble and to help each other, since none of his crew came into their abilities or lived with their psychic talents without scars.

"He was almost one of our suicides. Thankfully, someone found him and pumped his stomach. I wouldn't have picked my gift if I had a choice, but his is worse. I understand why the guy's messed up." He shook his head. "So when I went to check on him, he said that for the last couple of months, he's seen so many omens that he's tried to hide from people and stays blind drunk most of the time."

"Shit. Does he have any insights other than that people are gonna die?" Travis knew that Roger's questionable "gift" had ruined the man's life, cost him his job and marriage, and sent him spiraling into drugs and alcohol. Roger had given up trying to warn people when the cops arrested him for making threats, and then he realized that the warnings, even if heeded, didn't change the outcome.

"I think that's what pushed him over the edge this time," Derek said. "He was raving about black maggots and creatures with red eyes and sharp teeth. Said they were being hunted."

"Fuck. I was afraid you were going to say something like that," Travis replied. "No idea where these creatures came from?"

"Roger just sees the omens. He gets the who and the how, but not the why or the when and where," Derek said.

"So we know there's a supernatural component, and the deaths have ramped up in the last four months," Travis said, running a hand across his arm in frustration.

"And one more thing," Derek said. "I got on a research streak and started looking for trends. It looks like something similar happened in this area fifty years ago. Lots of articles in the newspapers about it. Violent deaths and suicides spiked, the whole thing came to an ugly head, people thought it was the end of the world, and then...it stopped."

"Just like that?"

Derek nodded. "The death toll had been pretty horrific because it wasn't just the murders and suicides. There were train wrecks, farm accidents, mine collapses, bridge failures. Ministers were calling for wholesale repentance to avert the wrath of God."

Travis snorted. "Did they ever figure out what was behind it?"

"Nope. When it stopped, everyone seemed so relieved that they didn't want to tempt fate by looking into it. But those old articles made me go back farther—and look for new info on the current deaths."

"And you found out there's a cycle?"

"Bingo. The records were a lot sketchier going back a hundred years, but fortunately they've digitized a lot of old newspapers," Derek replied, showing an unsettling passion for his research. "And from what I could dig up from the headlines and obits, there was the same spate of unnatural deaths and an alarming number of floods, fires, mining, and industrial accidents, and a couple of epidemics, between here and the area around Cooper City."

"Cooper City, huh," Travis mused. "Anything special about that area?"

"Just a lot of bad luck, for a long time," Derek answered. "Not as bad as Peale, but then again, people still live in Cooper City."

Travis had never heard of Peale, Pennsylvania, but decided he would look it up when he got back to St. Dismas. "All right." Travis finished his coffee. "I've taken up enough of your time. Thanks for calling me in on this, and keep me posted on what your research turns up. I think you're on the right track—I just don't know where it will lead."

"Watch your back," Derek warned. "Whatever is behind this has been playing this game for a long time. It's not going to like being challenged."

Travis mulled over the information Derek shared as he headed farther east, toward State College. He smiled at all the Penn State signs and banners as he rolled into town, even though he'd gone to Duquesne. Nothing said "football" in Pennsylvania like the Steelers and the Nittany Lions, and he'd grown up watching both ride to victory more times than he could remember.

He found a parking space near the hospital and wound through the corridors to the nurse's station as close as he could get to the hospital pharmacy. "Paige McLachlan, please," he requested. "She's expecting me." He had messaged Paige from the truck, so dropping in wasn't a total surprise. If she'd talked to Derek, then she probably knew Travis would come by sooner or later.

"Hi, Travis. Come on back," Paige greeted him a few minutes later. She had a visitor's badge in hand, which Travis clipped to his shirt. He followed her through back corridors to the hospital pharmacy, an area that was usually off-limits to non-employees.

"Derek gave me a head's up to expect you." Paige got coffee for them from a Keurig in her office. She shut the door and settled behind her desk, gesturing for Travis to take the other chair.

"I'm trying to figure out what the hell is going on," Travis admitted. "And Derek said that for as bad as it is in his neck of the woods, it's worse here."

Paige nodded. She was a thin woman in her early forties, with bobbed brown hair and intelligent blue eyes, and a sense of self-awareness and purpose that made her attractive. "Not necessarily here in State College, but throughout the county, yeah. I think we actually have it a little better here in town, maybe because there are so many resources with the university to head off trouble early. But in the small towns and rural areas..." She shook her head. "It's bad."

"Especially around Cooper City," Travis finished for her.

Paige looked up. "I see Derek really did do his research."

"Yeah. So...what's Penny been hearing?"

Paige dropped her gaze and chewed on her bottom lip, a dramatic shift from the confident, professional pharmacist who had greeted Travis at the waiting room. She twined her fingers, looking like a nervous teen. The impression was valid. When her sister drowned at thirteen in a tragic boating accident, Paige spent years learning magic to find a way to be reunited with her. The black magic she found in an old grimoire enabled her to house Penny's soul inside her body with her own spirit. That gave Paige a simultaneous insight into the worlds of both the living and the dead.

"Something really scary is happening," Penny said, speaking through Paige. Penny never moved beyond her age at death, so the voice and mannerisms were those of a young tween. "The other people are worried."

Travis figured she meant the other ghosts. "What are they worried about?" Travis probed gently.

Penny's gaze flicked everywhere except to Travis. "Things," she said. She swallowed and gripped the arms of the chair. "Things in the dark. They like to scare you, hurt you, chase you. Bad things," she said and shivered. "Some people say they can eat ghosts."

Travis leaned forward, trying to be confidential and comforting. "Tell me what you've heard, Penny. I'll do my best to protect you and the other spirits."

Penny fiddled with her fingers, and Travis guessed that she struggled with how to voice concepts far beyond the normal reach of a teen. "They say the things are demons," Penny said in a voice almost too quiet to hear. "Something called them here, opened a door. But... they've come before. Some of the ghosts remember."

"Who called the demons, Penny?" Travis asked, sounding like he was talking to a spooked horse.

"They don't know. Maybe they've always been here. The demons go away, but they come back again. Always come back."

Penny's voice sent a chill down Travis's back. He knew that for Paige, cohabitating in her body with her sister's ghost was the best of a bad situation. From what little Paige said about the incident that claimed Penny's life, it was clear that his Night Vigil colleague blamed herself, although she would have only been a few years older than Penny at the time. Whatever hardships the situation posed was a penance Paige gladly served, unworried about the consequences when it came her time to die.

I'd rather have a lifetime with Penny here on earth than wait and see whether there's a heaven with her in it, Paige had told him once. *And if that would make God throw me out of heaven, then I don't want to be there anyhow. Not without Penny.* Not for the first time, the things Travis witnessed and experienced fighting the supernatural made him doubt everything he had learned in catechism.

"Is someone controlling the demons?"

Penny hesitated, chewing her lip hard enough to raise dark red teeth marks in the flesh, then shook her head. "Don't think so, but no one really knows. Maybe this is just a bad, bad place. If the demons were here first, we should leave."

Travis raised an eyebrow at that. He resolved to look up demonically tainted places when he went back to Duquesne's secret library. "Why do you think that?" he asked.

Penny still did not meet his gaze. "Because they're old. Really old. Like maybe they were here before people came, ya know? And they're hungry." She shivered, then clutched herself, gripping her forearms and running her hands up and down to warm herself. "And it's going to get worse."

"How?" Travis asked. He tried to be gentle, but so much was at stake. "How will it get worse?"

"I don't want to know!" Penny wailed, finally looking him in the eye. He saw the terror of a disoriented young girl, without the filters and sophistication of her sister. "The old ghosts say so. They try to hide each time it happens. Then, new ghosts come."

Shit, Travis thought. Penny confirmed exactly what Derek's research had turned up—a cycle of supernatural activity followed by a period where the dark powers went dormant. What was missing was any clue to what triggered the cycle, or how to stop it.

"Do the old ghosts say anything else?" Travis questioned. "How have they kept from being eaten?"

"You have to hide," Penny told him earnestly, fixing him with a wide-eyed stare. "I might be okay, in here with Paige. I'm not like the others."

Travis had always wondered whether Penny knew she was dead and hitching a ride with Peggy. Confirming that to be true made his heart ache for both of them.

"I think you'll be okay," he comforted. "What about the others?"

"The demons aren't in control," Penny said. "I think they just like the food." She leaned over like she was sharing a secret. "And I think that they're scared, too."

Travis didn't want to think about what might scare demons, although his training and experience gave him some ideas. He had learned the hard way that ghosts weren't always right and that their sources could be just as much driven by hearsay as the living. Just being dead didn't make a person infallible.

"Do you know who is running things?"

Penny shook her head, making her dark hair whip from side to side. "No. The other ghosts don't say much about that. Maybe they're afraid it might hear."

Perhaps, Travis thought. *Or maybe the ghosts truly didn't know.* "Can you do me a big favor? Can you keep your ears open in case the other ghosts talk about something bad happening that might hurt people? This 'it' you mention. I want to stop the demons from hurting anyone else—ghosts or otherwise."

Penny shook her head vigorously. "Yes. I can do that." She looked down, suddenly shy. "I'm scared. I don't want to get eaten."

Travis gave her a sad smile. "I don't want you to get eaten, either. And your sister, Paige, is fierce. She won't let anything happen to you."

Penny looked up. "I know. Paige is the best sister, ever. She found me when I was lost and brought me home, and she says we can be together forever."

Travis felt a lump in his throat and swallowed hard. "You're very lucky," he said, and if his voice broke, Penny didn't notice it, and Paige was too submerged in her sister's persona to hear. "She'll take good care of you." He paused. "Thank you for talking to me. Now, would it be all right to let Paige come back? I'll talk with you again."

Penny nodded. "I like you. You understand."

In the next moment, a subtle change came over the woman who sat across the desk from Travis. When she looked up, Paige was back in control, with a sadness in her eyes that went beyond her forty-something years.

"She told you everything she's told me," Paige said. The voice sounded so different with an adult's modulation, but Travis could hear shades of Penny's younger tones. "I hate to see her so frightened." She toyed with a pen, a nervous habit. "I didn't want her to be scared anymore, once we were together."

Travis shrugged. "The world is a scary place, no matter which side of the Veil you're on. I just need to figure out what started up the cycle again, and what—or who—has attracted the demons."

Paige met his gaze. "Do you think they'll come after her, with me?"

Travis frowned, then shook his head. "No. I really don't. The situations I've run into, people who seem to have the most problems are in turmoil. You and Penny, you're settled. The loss is old news, and you're happy together."

Paige flinched. "As happy as we can be, considering," she said, as a wistful expression stole across her features. Travis guessed she was thinking of all the life events that might have been, had Penny lived.

"You're together," he repeated. "That's something very rare. Enjoy it." He didn't add the rest of what he was thinking. *You paid for it.*

On the drive home, Travis fielded calls from Jon and Matthew, dealing with a late supplier, an employee who quit without notice, and an argument that broke out at one of the substance abuse support groups. The problems weren't earth-shattering or even unusual, but by the time Travis hung up, he felt utterly worn out.

At least for the return trip on Route 22, the scenery was different. After the day's events and the long drive, Travis thought he would fall asleep as soon as his head hit the pillow. He had battled fatigue on the dark, meandering highway, but when he finally stretched out on his bed, he tossed restlessly.

When sleep finally came, his dreams were jumbled, filled with images of vengeful spirits and creatures he had fought. Eventually, the dreamscape cleared to become a darkened plain with tendrils of mist. Even half-awake, Travis recognized that he had shifted from a brain dump of memories to something real, maybe even prophetic.

"Who's there?" Travis called into the darkness, knowing that he was not alone.

A figure approached through the mist. The young man appeared to be about eighteen years old, athletically built, and his expression radiated defiant purpose. Travis stared at the newcomer, wondering why he seemed familiar, although he felt certain they had never met.

"You and Brent need to work together, or you're both going to die."

Travis looked closer at the newcomer and realized the source of the resemblance. He'd bet his paltry paycheck this was what Brent Lawson looked like in high school. "Who are you?"

"Brent's twin brother, Danny. I watch out for him. Right now, he needs a wingman. So do you. I don't want him here with me before his time."

Danny's fierce determination and deep sadness touched Travis. "What kind of danger do you see?"

Danny gestured as if indicating everything around him. "The stuff he fights, because of me. Monsters. Magic. Bad stuff. It's gonna get worse."

Travis felt a chill at Danny's warning. He had roused from true sleep and experienced the conversation in a lucid trance, one he would remember when he was fully awake. He had no doubt that the spirit— and the conversation—was real. "Do you know what's causing the danger? Why are the monsters and the bad stuff happening now?"

Danny shook his head. "I don't know. Just—watch out for him, okay? I know he can be an asshole," he added with a lopsided smile, "but he's a good guy to have watching your back. Tell him I said so— make sure you mention the 'asshole' part."

"How did you—" Travis began, but the vision had already begun to fade. Danny's ghost raised a hand in farewell before vanishing in the mist.

Travis lurched awake with a gasp, alone in his darkened room. "Shit," he muttered. Travis felt certain that Danny's warning was right, but he was also sure that neither he nor Brent Lawson would find it easy to work with a partner. "I just can't wait to see how this turns out," he grumbled, falling back onto his mattress in resignation.

CHAPTER SIX

EVEN AFTER ALL THESE YEARS, the Keepers of the secret Archive in the Duquesne Seminary basement creeped Travis out.

They all looked weirdly similar. Travis knew that the men weren't identical, but the old-fashioned tonsures and cassocks blurred individuality. *Maybe that's the point,* he thought. *Stealth in numbers. No one expects the Spanish Inquisition...*a snarky voice in his mind added unhelpfully.

"What you're looking for is in the Restricted Reading section," Father Julian said as he led Travis deeper into the maze of tall shelves and endless corridors. Travis decided he would be only slightly surprised to see snarling, sentient tomes or grimoires bound with human skin that had a blinking eye in the center of the cover. *After all, Hollywood has to get its ideas from somewhere.*

Duquesne University sat atop a high cliff overlooking the Monongahela River, a sentinel keeping watch over the city of Pittsburgh. Most people held the university in high regard for its academics and sports, but few knew the role it played in preserving and safeguarding rare occult manuscripts or training the Sinistram.

Travis resolutely ignored the unmarked stairwell that led to the offices of the Sinistram contact, hoping that Father Julian hadn't ratted him out. Since Father Liam hadn't been waiting for them in the Archive, Travis felt reasonably safe.

"Just because we all serve the same God, don't assume we agree on the nature of that service," Julian said as if he could guess Travis's thoughts.

"I'm just here to look at the books," Travis replied.

"Father Pavel has missed you at Confession," Julian added, without a glance in Travis's direction. Apparently, the Seal of the Confessional applied only to what was said, not to whether or not one was overdue. Travis knew very well that priests indulged in gossip as much as the laity; some of them just felt guiltier about doing it.

"I've been busy," Travis replied, hating the discomfort that Julian's mild reproof created. His rational mind warred with the ingrained habits of a lifetime, and managed, at best, a truce.

Julian chortled. "The beauty of the sacrament is that you can confess being tardy along with everything else when you finally do show up. I suspect Father Pavel will be reasonably forbearant."

The university dated from the 1850s, but the Sinistram's presence predated the seminary by at least a century. Rumor had it that Duquesne was built in its fortified location because the tunnels and Archive already existed deep within the bedrock, and the college buildings merely provided a convenient way to hide in plain sight.

Out of the corner of his eye, Travis caught sight of the Archive's resident ghosts. He felt their icy touch as they passed by in the narrow corridors, or glimpsed the swish of a robe or the momentary glimmer of a spectral lantern. He stretched out his Gift but felt no uneasiness or discomfort from the spirits. Some were Keepers who chose to stay on, guarding the manuscripts indefinitely. Others were faculty or unlucky students who decided, for reasons of their own, to put off crossing the Veil and remain in a place where they had found meaning and community.

"I find the presence of our long-term residents very comforting,"

Julian said, and Travis wondered if the Keeper had hidden telepathic abilities. The Keepers were as mysterious a secret society as the Sinistram, and although Travis avoided politics as much as possible, he gathered that there were points of contention between the two clandestine organizations.

Travis had no intention of haunting his alma mater. As for his views on the afterlife…it was complicated. Being a medium brought with it a unique set of spiritual challenges. "I find it difficult to reconcile what I've seen of lost souls and the undead with the idea that 'to be absent from the body is to be present with the Lord.'"

"I've always thought that the route matters less than the destination."

Travis knew that a full-blown theological argument could take days, and he had more pressing matters. "That's insightful," he replied tactfully. "Let me think about that."

Julian might have sneezed, but Travis suspected the Keeper gave a quiet snort, fully recognizing Travis's deflection for what it was. "The Restricted Reading Room," Julian said, standing to one side of an unsettlingly solid oak door reinforced with an iron grill worked with protective runes. Travis was sure that a salt barrier reinforced with iron filings and refreshed with holy water made the room its own spiritual containment center. Nothing inhuman or infernal could get in—or out.

"Thank you," Travis said. "I'll be needing a couple of hours to research."

Julian nodded. "And I'll come back for you in three, as always. You know I can't leave you in there longer. And you know why."

Travis stifled a sigh of frustration. The Keepers regarded the items in the restricted room as being sullied at best, dangerous at worst, and carefully monitored access to protect the souls of those whose work necessitated contact. Since overriding protocol required intervention from Father Liam, Travis did his utmost to keep his usage of the special library to the bare minimum.

"I promise I won't end up with two heads or start breathing fire," Travis assured the Keeper.

Julian gave an eloquent shrug. "I've learned that we're rarely the best judge of the inroads the Darkness makes on our souls."

"You'll know where to find me when time's up," Travis replied, doing his best to keep his tone civil. Julian was one of the most approachable of the Keepers, and he tried to remind himself that staying locked away in a cellar on top of taking vows might not make for good social skills. Still, the priest's condescension rankled as Travis closed the door behind him.

"Brother Penrod? I know you're here," Travis called in a quiet voice. The large subterranean room offered no hiding places, not that Penrod would need one. Floor-to-ceiling shelves were filled with books, manuscripts, and scrolls, with two large study tables and four chairs. The electric lighting seemed to struggle against the shadows here, though it was adequate elsewhere in the building, and Travis attributed the perpetual chill to more than good air conditioning. He could almost picture what the room had been like back when the Archive was founded, lit only by lamps with fluttering candle flames. Despite himself, Travis's hand found the rosary in his pocket.

Without waiting for a reply, Travis moved around the familiar room, mindful that his time was limited. He had secreted his phone in his pocket—a sin of omission—despite the rules and knowing that deep beneath the rock he would not get any signal. Instead, the camera and recording features were what he valued since he suspected the resources he needed might exceed quick note-taking.

He plucked familiar tomes from shelves, stifling a shiver at the residual darkness he sensed when his flesh touched the bindings. Knowledge came at a price, and some of the priests who had diligently explored the Dark Side forfeited their sanity, their lives, and perhaps their souls. He wondered how many of those men had become obsessed out of a need for penance and revenge, or perhaps survivor guilt. Hunters, like himself. Travis could identify with the emotions, still unsure whether they counted as sins or merely scar tissue.

"I know you're here," Travis spoke to the empty air as he added to his pile on one of the tables. He clicked on a reading light and made a face at how little its glow helped to drive back the gloom. "Don't play games. I need to talk to you."

After he had pulled more than a dozen volumes from the shelves, Travis stood with his hands on his hips and regarded the rest of the collection. "Demonology" comprised a significant portion of the special library, but the types and manifestations were so varied that most of those books would be overly general for his purposes. Unfortunately, even the archaic card catalog was no help in narrowing his search for "hell-maggots."

Travis felt Brother Penrod's presence, but the ghost still hadn't shown himself, so he sorted the books on the table, setting out his pens and tablet, and finding the notes he had jotted of things to look up or ask about.

"I'm a medium, you know," Travis said with a sigh of exasperation. "I can see you, even if you don't make the effort to appear."

A puff of air gave Travis the impression Penrod had huffed in frustration. Gradually a form took shape from mist until the image of a short, stout man in his middle years looked nearly solid. Travis wasn't sure how long Penrod had been dead, but something about the monk made him suspect it was within the past century.

You shouldn't come here so often, Travis, Penrod warned with a somber, jowly face like a depressed bloodhound. *You'll end up like me.*

"You're here because you chose to be locked up in this room, Pen," Travis replied, familiar with the warning and their ongoing disagreement. "That's taking an abundance of caution too far."

Better safe than sorry, Penrod replied. *What awful happenings bring you here this time?*

Travis was well aware than Penrod disapproved of his demon hunting, even as the dead priest grudgingly acknowledged that someone had to do it, or the battle would be lost by default. The regret and self-loathing that clung to the spirit like a shroud made his judgment tolerable since Travis chalked it up as a misguided attempt to protect others from the man's own fate.

"People who won't bury their dead. Spontaneous outbursts of violence from people who aren't likely suspects, and tormented souls infested with hell-maggots, plus a mysterious black truck that might be snatching people, and all of it linked to the area around Cooper City," Travis recapped. "Anything sound familiar?"

Sternetur tinea et inferni, Penrod murmured in Latin, crossing himself. *You are playing with fire, my son.*

Travis gave a shrug, palms turned upward. "Just doing my job. I can tell by the flinch that you know something." Any subject that made the dead uncomfortable ought to send the living screaming in panic. Travis had spent a lifetime rushing in where angels—or their proxies—feared to tread.

Penrod looked as if he were fighting an internal debate. Finally, he relented. *The infernal worms you call "hell-maggots" are known. But they do not appear on their own.*

"Tell me," Travis begged. "People are dying and being driven insane. And I think this is only the beginning."

Penrod's pained expression worried Travis. *These hell-maggots are low-level demons—more correctly, imps. Perhaps not even that powerful. An infestation, like lice. They feed on dark desires and hidden weaknesses, and as they eat away at souls, they magnify the worst attributes.*

"Could they latch onto a person who was depressed and make them suicidal?"

Penrod nodded. *They feed on negative emotions like grief, despondency, anger, jealousy. And if they can push the host into committing a mortal sin, they would gorge themselves.*

Travis wasn't convinced that desperation great enough to end one's own life counted as "sin," but he didn't have time to argue. "You said they didn't appear on their own. What did you mean?"

If you had a battlefield covered with corpses, it would draw flies and vultures, Penrod replied. *Their presence didn't cause the deaths; they are an aftereffect. So the hell-maggots are a symptom, but not a cause. Something draws them to an area—something darker and more powerful.*

"Full demons? Nephilim? Warlocks?" Travis pressed. Penrod tended to talk around the point, but Travis had no way of knowing whether it was a side-effect of being dead or merely carried over from his living self.

Penrod shook his head. *Those will also be attracted to whatever calls the hell-maggots, but it requires a nexus to pull that much dark energy to it. A hell gate opening, perhaps. Or a reoccurring cycle of some sort—ritual magic, for example.*

"What about something like a genius loci?" Travis pressed. "A natural spirit of a place. Could one of those be corrupted?"

Penrod considered for a moment. *Perhaps. Or it might have always been twisted. Just because something is part of nature doesn't make it benign. Disease is natural, but it slays millions.*

Travis's heart sank. He had battled his share of demons and other supernatural creatures, but even with the Sinistram, he had not fought anything powerful enough to be a magnet for other dark entities. He had heard rumors—legends, really—that some of the Sinistram's more storied warriors had overcome threats like that, but now that he thought about it, details were sparse.

"How do I stop it?" Travis looked at the mound of books that he could barely skim in the time remaining.

Find the source, Penrod said. His shape had started to waver and grow less defined, and Travis felt the spirit's energy waning. *There is always a way to close a door—but the cost might be more than you wish to pay.* With that, Penrod's form dissipated, leaving Travis to stare at thin air.

"What is it about dead people that they like to speak in riddles?" Travis shouted to the empty room, gambling that Penrod could still hear him even if he had vanished from Travis's Sight. In response, one of the books suddenly moved several inches and dropped from the table, landing on its spine. It fell open, and pages riffled until it finally lay still.

"Thanks," Travis called out. "I'm still annoyed." He bent to pick up the old leather-bound tome and frowned as he read the section to which the ghost had opened.

"Hell gates and Liminal Spaces," he read aloud, translating from Latin, then settled down in his chair. He had already resigned himself to merely scratching the surface in the books he had selected, but if he could at least narrow the subject, he could note which manuscripts might be the most useful when he returned for another research session.

"Hell gates are formed when great tragedy, an excessive expenditure of dark energy or significant bloodshed occurs in a place where the boundary between our reality and the next is already thin. Some call these places 'liminal space,' since they are a line between the world we know and somewhere else. Often, but not always, these gateway places are found at crossroads, the edge of the forest, the shore of a body of water, the foot of a mountain, the mouth of a cave. These places are not inherently evil, but they are like lodestones for power, and if they do not attract dark forces, they often become revered as shrines or sacred spots. Some call them genius loci and consider them to be imbued with a sentient spirit.

Hell gates can also be formed from the sheer magnitude of evil concentrated in a single, massive act of destruction, such as a massacre, catastrophic accident, or brutal battle. In some cases, the supernatural energy of a place makes it inherently unhealthy. Such places gain a reputation for being 'unlucky' or 'haunted.' If the energy is strong enough, it may attract malicious people and entities who deepen the dark energy through additional and repeated acts of violence.

When a location with natural power is repeatedly violated with bloodshed and dark magic, it can become a nexus, a supernatural maelstrom that strengthens itself by pulling in similar energies. Such loci can become a constant hazard—as with places said to be evil—or may appear on a cyclical basis, such as the anniversary of a battle. A cyclical loci will manifest periodically to draw in new malevolent energies and eventually go dormant again after it has re-enacted the tragedy that formed it. Such loci are not necessarily hell gates, in that they do not open into the infernal planes, but they draw on the primordial energies of chaos and destruction, which are by their nature opposed to the will of the Creator."

"Well, fuck," Travis muttered, snapping photos of the pages with his phone, as well as one of the frontispiece and cover. More occult collections existed, at the Vatican and a few other secure locations, but Travis doubted he could easily gain access without alerting the Sinistram.

The remaining hour of his research passed all too quickly, and Father Julian's knock startled Travis. Reluctantly, he set aside another book that had proved helpful, glad he had taken photos of everything he could find that looked relevant from the indexes, to read later on his phone.

"I trust your effort was successful?" Julian asked as Travis reshelved the book he had been reading. He had replaced each tome as he finished with it, unwilling to let Julian retrace his steps. He did not need the Sinistram second-guessing him or getting in his way.

"Tolerably so," Travis replied with a shrug, hoping he gave the impression that he had not been especially productive.

"Searching the manuscripts can be a needle-in-the-haystack experience," Julian said, and Travis could not tell from the other man's tone whether he believed Travis's evasion.

"I'm ready to go," Travis said, walking over to slip his notes inside his bag. "The room does have an unsettling vibe." He wondered whether Julian knew about Penrod, curious about what had made the monk lock his spirit into the library in penance. He doubted the priest would tell him, even if he knew.

Travis stepped across the threshold, feeling a frisson of energy at the wardings. He closed the door behind him, waiting while Julian locked it, and then tried to remain patient while his guide insisted on saying a rite of purification and blessing over him, before permitting him to leave the area.

"I didn't get spiritual cooties in there, you know," Travis grumbled as they retraced their steps to the surface.

"It's entirely possible for dark energy—or even spirits—to attach themselves to someone who has been in proximity with tainted objects," Julian responded.

"Hello? Medium here. I think I'd know if I picked up a ghostly hitchhiker."

"Lucifer is the Father of Lies, the Deceiver," Julian answered smoothly, not bothering to turn to look at Travis. "We are most easily deceived when we believe ourselves to be in control."

Travis reminded himself that Julian was an ally, even if he was sometimes insufferable. *It's not only a mortal sin to murder him, but my soul is probably on iffy grounds already—and it would be damned inconvenient to hide the body.*

Travis breathed a quiet sigh of relief when he was aboveground once more. He thanked Father Julian and took his leave, then headed off-campus to a small neighborhood church where Father Pavel agreed to hear his Confession away from prying ears.

St. Thomas the Doubter Church anchored a working-class neighborhood that, like the church itself, had seen better days. The old brick building looked tired, and its sills and doors needed a fresh coat of paint. Inside it had barely changed, Travis wagered, since it was built back in the early 1900s. The declining, elderly population embraced the familiarity of the traditional interior, including the old-fashioned confessionals.

What did it say about him that he found comfort in the liturgy and rites, even when his faith was fragile at best? Travis was unwilling to examine that question too closely most days, and he knew from his short tenure as a priest that he was not alone in editing the sins he confessed. Maybe that was why he preferred this particular church, named for the disciple who needed proof, who had lost hope, and whose faith resisted resurrection.

"Father?" Travis said when he was near the dark wooden booths with their lattice screens.

The door peeked open, providing a glimpse of Father Pavel's familiar face. "Travis. Welcome, my son."

Travis opened the other door and knelt in the cramped, shadowed space that always made him feel like he had crawled inside an armoire. "Father, forgive me, for I have sinned. My last confession was—I don't remember. It's been a while."

Father Pavel chuckled. "That's all right, my son. God knows, even if we lose count."

"I may have committed six mortal sins, if the human hosts of the demons I killed weren't dead already." He paused. "I have committed more venial sins than I can count. I have lied and misled in the course of hunting infernal creatures. I have broken laws—especially trespassing, breaking and entering—in those hunts. I, um, have exceeded the speed limit and parked in fire lanes when circumstances required haste."

Travis did not confess regarding his psychic gifts or his sex life. He considered both to be an intrinsic, God-given part of his core being, and as such, part of Creation itself. That "difference of opinion" led, in part, to his decision to leave the priesthood, and resign from the Sinistram. Father Pavel might not agree, but he understood.

"Is there something else on your mind, Travis?" Pavel knew him well enough to interpret his silence as well as his words.

"I repent of my hubris," Travis said. "I came upon another man hunting the same supernatural creature, and I'm ashamed to say I briefly considered not helping because he had gotten in my way."

"Did you help?"

Travis nodded, then realized the priest couldn't see clearly through the screen. "Yes. He didn't have the right weapons for the type of monster. I killed the thing, and took the hunter back to the Center to be healed."

"Then, in the end, you did what was right. Thoughts come to our mind unbidden," Pavel replied. "Even Christ was tempted. It is what we do with those impulses that matter. You faced temptation and rose above it. There is no sin in that."

"I have been very rude to Father Liam."

On the other side of the screen, his confessor might have sneezed or perhaps coughed. Or, more likely, choked back a laugh. They had long ago wordlessly established a mutual dislike of the Sinistram priest. "Was he attempting to sway you to act against your conscience?"

"Doesn't he always?" Travis said, before catching himself. "Sorry. I meant, yes."

"It is no sin to tell the devil to get behind you."

"I might have used somewhat less Biblical phrasing."

"The Lord knows your thoughts—and your heart. Pretending to use mild language when you mean something else is a form of lying and indicates that you do not trust Our Heavenly Father to love you just as you are," Pavel replied.

"I think that's it, for now," Travis said. "I'm sure I'll rack up a few dozen more before supper."

"Come back, and we'll talk it over," Pavel offered. "And now I must ask, how is the depression? Are you taking care of yourself?"

Pavel was one of the few who knew the truth about Travis's background with the Sinistram, and that what he had seen and done in those years rocked his faith and darkened his dreams. Travis had wanted this particular priest because Pavel understood about the monsters. Pavel had bargained that part of hearing the hunter's confession included holding him accountable for his physical well-being along with his immortal soul.

"As well as I can, given everything," Travis hedged. "Jon and Matthew keep me fed and patched up. I rest when I'm able but between the monsters and the needs of St. Dismas—"

"It's like what they say on airplanes, with the oxygen masks. You can't care for others if you don't take care of yourself."

"I will try to do better," Travis promised. He meant it, too. Except that things tended to go awry.

"Then may God give you pardon, and I absolve you, in the name of the Father, the Son, and the Holy Ghost. Go in peace," Father Pavel said as both men made the sign of the cross. Perhaps it was merely his imagination, but Travis always felt lighter after Confession. Only with Father Pavel could he admit his fears and how often he second-guessed himself. Then again, Travis knew from experience that any peace he felt would be as short-lived as his absolution.

CHAPTER SEVEN

THE OLD CHURCH was as empty when Travis left as it was when he came. He headed back to St. Dismas on foot, although twilight had fallen. It was a distance of perhaps a mile, and while the neighborhood wasn't the best, Travis felt confident that he could protect himself from human threats. A few streets over, cars gridlocked in a sea of red tail lights for rush hour. Travis kept to the smaller streets that were still well lit, but didn't attract bumper-to-bumper cars or homicidal city buses.

His thoughts jumped between what he had learned at the Archive, to the mess in Cooper City, to wondering whether the donations for the food bank and shipments for the soup kitchen had arrived. Travis felt a stab of guilt at leaving so much of the day-to-day management of St. Dismas to Jon and Matthew, although he knew both men had the necessary skills and temperament to do the job. And neither had any desire or aptitude to hunt monsters. That was Travis's personal geas and atonement.

His skin prickled, and Travis had the sense he was being watched. A glance behind him showed no one in sight, and none of the cars slowed or gave any indication of following him. Wary, Travis picked up his pace, unwilling to discount his intuition. Something or someone knew where he was, and that couldn't be a good thing.

The smell of sulfur jarred him, and Travis instantly went on alert. He let the silver blade he carried in a wrist sheath fall into his hand, and took comfort in the weight of the Glock with its silver bullets nestled in the small of his back, tucked into his waistband.

He glanced around the empty side street, trying to figure out the most likely hiding place for a demon. Travis was familiar enough with the area to know the smell wasn't normal. He saw a boarded-up restaurant, a defunct bail bonds shop, and a convenience store with steel grates over its windows and doors, although a light burned inside and it appeared to be reluctantly open for business.

Travis decided that the convenience store was an unlikely shelter, and the bail bonds office window provided a poor hiding place. That left the shuttered restaurant on the corner. He approached it cautiously, reaching for his gun.

The front door faced a street with enough traffic that going in that way would be noticed. Travis slipped around to the back, eyeing the alley skeptically. The light from a dim security fixture barely dispelled the shadows, and a battered dumpster blocked visibility. The restaurant had filled the first floor of a wooden building that looked like it pre-dated both World Wars. Darkened, dirty windows of what might have been an apartment on the second floor convinced him that the building was uninhabited. That made some things easier.

Travis moved down the alley, holding his gun and a small Maglite in front of him to clear the space, sweeping the light from side to side. Unwilling to be ambushed, he checked all around and inside the dumpster before returning to the nondescript black door that led into the back of the restaurant. The lock was broken, and the door swung open at his touch.

"Shit," he murmured. Had squatters attracted the demon's attention? Or had the infernal creature come to this transient neighborhood to hunt for food, expecting easy prey? Travis hadn't been expecting a fight when he headed to see Father Pavel, but he had learned from bitter experience to always prepare for the worst.

He had his rosary in one pocket, a flick-top container of salt and iron filings in the other, as well as a small squirt bottle of holy water. His backpack carried a few more surprises. He weighed whether to go back to St. Dismas and get more weapons and decided it wasn't worth the risk that the demon might escape. Whatever brought the creature here, it boded ill for anyone nearby. Travis wasn't about to permit that kind of incursion, not on what he considered to be "his" territory.

The sulfur smell was so strong it nearly made him retch. Roaches scurried to flee from the piercing beam of his flashlight, and he tried to ignore the crunch of their shells beneath his feet. The back door brought him in by a storage closet and the bathrooms—all empty. The old restaurant looked to have been closed for a while; a thick layer of dust lay across the diner's counter and tables. The old, hard-used equipment must not have been worth selling off since the last owner apparently just closed the door and walked away.

The boards that covered the front windows made the room unnaturally dark, giving his quarry the advantage. Travis sent out a light psychic touch, checking for recent ghosts, but no spirits answered his call. He wondered if he would be able to smell fresh blood over the stench of sulfur.

Travis made a thorough sweep of the main restaurant and found no creatures. He heard scuffling in the back toward the kitchen and wondered if the demon was aware of his pursuit. Outside, car horns blared, and the pulsing bass of a car's subwoofer throbbed before he was alone once more in the silence.

Time to bring the fight to me. He reached into his backpack for a jimmied special-purpose IED. He pulled the pin and lobbed the device through the opening where cooks once passed plates up from the kitchen.

A deafening boom accompanied a burst of light that illuminated the kitchen like the sun, sending dust and debris raining down on him. Even braced for it, Travis winced from the noise, though he knew to look away from what little of the glare would penetrate the rest of the seating area. The flashbang also sprayed out salt and iron, guaranteed to piss off most troublesome supernatural creatures.

A dark, hunched form let out an ear-splitting wail and flew through the opening from the back kitchen, landing in a crouch on the counter. In the seconds before he fired, when the demon was caught in the beam of his flashlight, Travis got a good look at his opponent.

Its leathery skin looked almost as dark as the shadows around it, covering a compact body probably only four feet tall, but strongly muscled, with vicious claws on its hands and feet. The head was round, too large for the body, with gleaming yellow eyes and a wide maw full of teeth.

Drude, Travis thought. He squeezed the trigger twice in the instant before the creature sank its talons into the counter and pushed off, flying through the air right at him.

Travis shot one last time before throwing himself out of the way, pivoting to remain facing the creature when it landed. At least two of his shots had winged the demon, though he'd missed both head and center mass.

The *Drude* moved before Travis could get a bead on it, coming at him with its long fingers and sharp claws extended. He fired again, and this time his bullet at close range tore into the *Drude's* shoulder, and the creature crash-landed into one of the tables, breaking through the Formica-clad wood.

Travis leaped over the back of the nearest booth, gun ready to fire down on the wounded demon. Before he could take the shot, he heard a shriek, and another dark shape hurtled toward him from the kitchen, swiping for him with its talons.

"Fuck!" Travis threw himself out of the way, thudding against the glass window, which shattered between his heavy jacket and the plywood on the outside, clattering all around him. The second demon clawed its way up over the back of the booth, shredding the old vinyl and revealing the guts of the dated bench seats. Travis fired again, point blank, but the demon jerked to one side at the last second, so that the bullet lodged to the side rather than squarely where its heart should be. In the other booth, Travis heard the first demon scrabbling to regain its feet.

Travis squeezed the trigger once more, and this time he caught the second monster squarely between the eyes. Its skull shattered, spraying ichor and goo. The first creature hurled itself over the booth, underestimating the distance between itself and Travis. His point-blank shot tore through the demon's chest, and the body tumbled backward.

Before Travis could begin to speak the exorcism that would send the demons back to Hell, the back door burst open, and a man he had never seen before lunged toward him. A foxfire green light filled the stranger's eyes, telling Travis his opponent was possessed. The attacker started to close, but a shot from the back hallway split the man's head like a ripe melon. The body collapsed, and tendrils of eerie green smoke flowed from the corpse.

"Start the fucking exorcism already. I'll cover you." A familiar voice shouted from the hallway.

"*Exorcizamos te...*" Travis began the litany, as Brent Lawson sauntered out, taking up a shooter stance with his back to the wall where he could cover the entrance and the entire restaurant.

The green mist swirled angrily, held by the power of the rite but clearly fighting the words that constrained it. Travis glanced at the black-skinned bodies of the two *Drude*. They were demonic in origin, but not possessed like the stranger. While the liturgy tore at the glowing fog, thinning and draining its power until it was sent back from whence it came, the corpses withered like mummies, shriveling to bone until they went up in flames like dry timber. He waited until the bodies crumbled to ash, and used the holy water he carried to extinguish the embers.

Brent remained covering the darkened diner, still on high alert. "Is it done?"

Travis nodded and reminded himself of his confession. Brent was clearly working on the same case from a different angle. Resisting his help was pointless and prideful.

"Thanks," Travis said. Brent grinned as if he knew what that word cost him. "How did you find me?"

"I was following the possessed guy. He was following you. What were those other things you roasted?" Brent lowered his gun but did not holster it.

"*Drude*. Minor imps. They feed on nightmares and dark impulses," Travis replied, checking to make sure the embers had gone out. He did not need to set a city block on fire. "I've seen them before. They like neighborhoods like this. Plenty of anger and frustration."

"We need to talk."

Travis glanced around the diner, picking up spent shells to leave nothing behind to show they had been present. "Okay, but I'm splattered with monster guts. I can't exactly go to a coffee shop looking like this."

Brent gave a snort. "I've seen worse."

"We're only a couple of blocks from St. Dismas. You get coffee, I get a shower, and no one will disturb us or overhear." Travis did not give him time to argue, striding past him for the door. Brent brought up the rear, moving with predatory agility that confirmed his military background.

"Do you have to be a priest to do an exorcism?" Brent asked as they walked. They holstered their guns to avoid trouble with passersby or the cops, but neither man relaxed.

Travis opened his mouth and shut it again. Once, he would have said that yes, ordination was required, or at least faith. But he had renounced his vows, and his faith was fragile.

"Depends on who you ask," he said finally, figuring this counted toward humility, in penance for his earlier arrogance. "The Vatican says yes, but they have a job security issue. I'd say that you have to believe in...a higher power, but I'm not sure. Maybe you just have to believe in the litany itself."

"Huh," Brent replied. Travis waited for a smart remark, and when it didn't come, he looked over at his companion. Brent's alert posture and the way his gaze scanned for danger betrayed nothing of his thoughts. "Does it have to be in Latin?"

Travis laughed. "I don't think so. Or at least, not since Vatican II." When Brent gave him a blank look, Travis grinned. "That's when priests got the okay to say the Mass in the language of their people."

"Did the Devil get the memo?" Brent crooked an eyebrow.

"Whatever works," Travis replied.

To his surprise, the tension that had bristled between them in their first run-in had lessened. Maybe in the time since, they had rethought the benefit of back-up. Travis still wasn't sure how he felt about working with anyone, let alone forming a partnership, but if the danger was really as big as he feared, it was suicidal to go it alone.

Travis let them in the back door to St. Dismas. The street in front and the parking lot were full, reminding him it was the night for all of the "Anonymous" groups that met at the center.

"Busy place," Brent remarked as Travis locked up behind them.

"That's a good thing, and a bad thing," he replied, motioning for Brent to follow him back to the staff kitchen. "Bad, because a lot of people need our services. Good, because we're here to provide them. The goal is to work our way out of our jobs." He dumped the old coffee grounds and washed out what remained in the pot, then made fresh as Brent took a seat at the second-hand, scarred table.

He looked up to find the other man watching him quizzically. "What?" Travis asked with a touch of defensiveness.

"Just thinking that you can take away the collar, but—"

"No. I'm not a priest," Travis said, more sharply than he intended. "Doesn't mean that I don't want to make the world a better place."

"By running a halfway house—and killing monsters."

He shrugged. "You're a private investigator, chasing down wrongs the cops won't handle. So you traded in the badge—"

"Okay, I get it." Brent sounded testy. He took a deep breath and released the tension in his shoulders. "We've both got issues."

"No one gets into this business unless they do." Travis pulled out a mug and gestured toward the powdered creamer and packs of sweetener. "Make yourself at home. I'll wash off the goop, and be right back."

True to his word, Travis returned in under fifteen minutes, to find Brent seated at the table. From the level in the coffee pot, Travis figured the other man was already on his second cup. "Better," Travis said with a sigh as he settled at the table, happy for clean clothes and a hot cup of java.

"You're chasing the black truck disappearances, too," Brent said.

Travis nodded. "I heard you were in Barkeyville."

"Yeah. I heard you were sniffing around Cooper City."

"There's more going on than just people being abducted by a psycho in a truck," Travis replied and paused to take a sip of his coffee. It was warm and rich on his tongue.

"No shit, Sherlock. I fought off a couple of psi-vamps near Peale. They'd been suckering in hard luck cases, feeding off their misery until they killed themselves."

Travis winced. "You took care of them?"

Brent nodded. "I got called in because people are living with their dead relatives, or going postal on their neighbors. That's why I think we would do better working together instead of marking territory," Brent replied, with a sheepish grin. "We could both do with having someone to watch our back."

"Agreed. I'll share my research if you'll tell me what you know. I think we've got some kind of supernatural 'blast zone' out around Cooper City, but why it exists and what caused it? I've still got no clue," Travis admitted.

"I think you're right about the zone, and we'd better figure it out fast because I have the feeling whatever's causing it is just getting started."

"Thanks again for saving my ass back at the diner," Travis said after an awkward pause.

"That makes us square." Brent shrugged uncomfortably. "Pretty sure we'll have a chance to trade the favor back and forth. That green fog reminded me of a story I heard when I was on the force. Couple a years ago, there was a cop who had a hostage situation on his hands. Shot the would-be shooter, and then the cop swore a 'green mist' came out of the guy and possessed the hostage, who drew down on him. He claimed self-defense when he shot her, and Internal Affairs cleared him, but..."

"I can't imagine that went over well."

Brent shook his head. "It didn't. The guy resigned, went somewhere down South, I heard. But the hell of it is, the cops here still talk about it, because he wasn't the only one to see something weird. Our kind of weird. He was just the only one to say so out loud."

Travis nodded. "Doesn't surprise me. What makes you different?"

Brent looked away. "Demons killed my family when I was in high school. Then I had a run-in with a big-time demon named Mavet when I was in Iraq. Lost some good men. Got out of the army and went FBI. Kept running into demons, even when I left the Feds and went to the police. So...I figured if you can't ditch them, kill the sons of bitches," he added with a bitter smile.

Travis frowned, remembering his ghostly visitor. "Your family... did you lose a brother? Danny?"

Brent jerked upright, fists tightening, eyes narrowed. "What do you know?"

Travis held up his open hands in appeasement. "I'm a clairvoyant medium. You know, ghost whisperer? And a kid named Danny showed up a couple of nights ago, begging me to warn you about danger and maybe look out for you."

"You saw Danny? He was worried about me?" Brent's tension seemed to war with an almost desperate need to know.

Travis slowly lowered his hands. "He said his name was Danny, and he looked like you, only younger. A teenager."

"He was eighteen. We're twins."

That explains the strength of the bond, Travis thought. "He watches over you. And he worried that you might not accept help, even when it was needed."

Brent looked away again, sadness and regret replacing his earlier anger. "That's Danny," he said, and his voice tightened. "I was the one who went charging in. He liked to hang back and strategize. We were a hell of a team."

"I don't mind bearing messages," Travis said, offering an olive branch. "He's not always close by, but I have the feeling he's played an active role in your life, even if you didn't know. And he said it was important that we team up, even if you are an 'asshole'—his word, not mine," he added.

Brent sighed. "I...suspected that he's been around. There've been times when I had close calls, and something would happen to save my ass. I'd get a feeling things weren't right, and so I paid attention to my surroundings and didn't get ambushed. A couple of times there was a weird distraction—like glass breaking or something falling—right when I needed it." He looked up. "Thanks, Danny."

"You know he's not on the ceiling, right?"

Brent flushed, embarrassed. "It's just, I always figured he went up instead of..."

"And I'm sure he will, when he decides it's time to rest," Travis replied, falling into the comforting tone he used so often in his former profession. He let it remain unsaid that given all he had seen of restless ghosts, undead and resurrected creatures and the like, his own views of heaven and hell were complicated. "But he's decided to stick with you, for now."

Brent looked down at his coffee cup. "We were both supposed to go to football camp. We had scholarships to college that fall. But Danny got sick and wasn't up to it. I wanted to stay home with him—

no fun by myself, after all. He insisted that I go. The demons came..."
He blinked and swallowed. "I never saw Danny or my parents again."

Travis regarded him silently for a moment. "Random demon attacks are pretty rare. Do you have any idea—"

Brent shook his head. "Don't you think I've asked myself that a million times? My parents weren't the kind of people to sell their souls. I haven't found any hidden scandal or financial problems. They didn't even believe in the devil, for Chrissake!"

"Maybe when we clean up this mess, I can help you figure it out —if you want," Travis offered.

Brent looked surprised. "Yeah. Thanks. I would."

Travis let it remain unsaid that he was intrigued—and a little worried—about the way the demonic had dogged Brent's steps throughout his life. They had that in common, and Travis didn't think it was a particularly good thing.

"I need to go do some administrative stuff," Travis said, draining his coffee. "We're good, right?" He made a vague motion to indicate the two of them. Brent nodded. "So how about we road trip northeast tomorrow? I've finagled an interview with the family of one of the black truck abductees, and a few of my Night Vigil people alerted me to some problems out toward the State College area."

"Night Vigil?"

"I'll fill you in on the way tomorrow, if that works for you."

Brent finished his coffee and set aside the cup. "Sure. And maybe we can swing by Cooper City and see my cop buddy."

"I've got a priest friend out that same way," Travis said. "Two birds, one stone."

"My truck or your—"

"Crown Vic," Travis supplied, trying not to wince at Brent's smirk. "Gas mileage stinks, but it's got a police engine and room for more than one body in the trunk."

"Fine. You can drive," Brent said. "See you at eight."

CHAPTER EIGHT

THE ALARM JOLTED Brent from his restless sleep. He slapped the button to shut off the annoying klaxon, and dropped back onto his mattress with a groan. *What idiot suggested leaving at eight? Oh yeah. Me.*

A shower, two donuts, and half a pot of coffee later, Brent felt barely sentient. He couldn't even blame his fuzzy head and lousy sleep on booze or pain pills. No, his dreams had been troubled by memories and images of what might have been. He relived the day he went to football camp, and the way Danny's expression mingled real excitement with disappointment. Not for the first time, Brent wished he had stayed home and died with them.

Is there something tainted about me that drew the demon to them? That keeps attracting demons wherever I go? Maybe I can get Travis to tell me, but I doubt I can talk him into a mercy killing. God, I'm tired of this shit.

Brent grabbed the rest of the box of donuts, poured most of the remaining coffee into a travel mug, and headed out. He had stayed up late, handling as much on his investigation cases as he could, reminding himself that demon-hunting soothed the conscience but

"

didn't pay the rent. Still, he managed to make enough progress on his cases—and respond to several inquiries for new projects—that he could take the day out of the office with minimal guilt.

When he pulled into the St. Dismas parking lot, Brent took a moment to get a good look at the place, since his prior visits had not afforded the opportunity. He managed a wry smile at the idea that even the halfway house appeared to be resurrected, and guessed it had been an apartment building or hotel in its previous life. The structure looked tired and worn, but clean and adequately maintained. Nothing fancy, a hand-me-down haven for folks who desperately needed a second chance. It did not escape Brent that had a few twists of fate gone differently, he might have been among its residents.

Brent took in the sketchy surroundings, wondering whether his truck would still be there when he returned. He was glad for his alarm system and wondered if any of Travis's friends-with-psychic-benefits had bothered to put a safety spell on the lot.

Pushing his doubts aside, Brent grabbed his coffee and the box of donuts and headed over to where Travis waited, leaning on the Crown Vic.

"That's a gunboat," Brent observed. He held out the donuts like a peace offering.

"I prefer 'land cruiser,' and it's fast," Travis replied, but he took the box, surveyed the remaining contents, and picked a chocolate iced donut. "Thanks."

Brent shrugged. "Figured it's a long drive."

The three-hour drive to Snowshoe, a small town just off Interstate 80, passed less awkwardly than Brent had feared. The Crown Vic rode smoothly, with a suspension that had obviously been tightened up for better handling. The purr of the big engine reminded Brent of his grandfather's car, and a 'classic vinyl' playlist boomed through the car's speakers.

"Cake or yeast?" Brent asked, after a period of silence.

"Huh?"

"Donuts. This is important. Keep up. Cake or yeast."

Travis couldn't help smiling. "Yeast. With icing. And sprinkles."

"Filled or unfilled?"

"Hmm. That's a hard one. Both—and I won't turn down lemon filled if I have a chance."

"Coffee. Flavored or unflavored?"

Travis made a face. "I'll drink pretty much anything that hasn't been on the burner all night."

"Yeah, me too. But now and again, vanilla is a nice splurge," Brent confided.

"Hamburger or hot dog?" Travis lobbed back.

"It depends on the toppings," Brent replied, pretending to think about it. "I want bacon and cheddar with onions and pickle on the burger, or blue cheese and onion straws. Otherwise, a footlong with chili and onions."

"Now I'm hungry," Travis said. "But at least you've established we can stand to eat in the same places."

Brent grinned. "Hey, I was a cop. We think with our stomachs."

Brent had plenty of questions he wanted to ask about demons and the priesthood, but since he didn't feel like reciprocating the scrutiny just now, he kept them to himself. Instead, they chatted about the music and the weather, quibbled over pizza toppings and brands of beer and agreed that the only real football teams were the Steelers and the Nittany Lions. Brent had gotten off to worse starts with partners back in his police days, so he counted the unlikely camaraderie as a win.

The conversation gave him a chance to take Travis's measure when they weren't fighting for their lives. Growing up in the South, Brent had known plenty of clergy—although, admittedly not priests— but Travis didn't remind him of any of them. Despite the Latin and the liturgies, Travis seemed more like a soldier than he did the Army chaplains or small town pastors Brent remembered. Travis had dropped some of the defensiveness Brent had picked up on in their first encounter and seemed genuinely interested in partnering to bring down whatever big bad was causing the problem. For as much as Brent really hadn't been looking for someone to ride shotgun, he couldn't argue that this union made sense, and he'd already seen proof that Travis could watch his back.

I'm sure we'll find ways to irritate the fuck out of each other eventually, Brent thought, sipping his now-cold coffee from the travel mug. His own record with partners in the military and with the police hadn't been sterling. Then again from their encounters so far, Travis already had seen enough to know that Brent was quick-tempered, impulsive, and unpredictable—and suggested teaming up anyhow. *And he can talk to Danny.* If Brent needed any additional reason to agree to work together, that was it.

"Let's hit that place after we do the interview," Travis said, jostling Brent out of his thoughts. He looked up in time to spot a small mom-and-pop dairy isle. "I bet they serve killer pizza burgers and onion rings—and soft serve."

Brent grinned. "You're on."

———

TRAVIS PULLED up in front of an unassuming yellow house along a quiet side street in Snowshoe. The small flower garden, neat picket fence, and trimmed lawn were the epitome of Americana.

"This is it," he said, double checking the GPS on his phone. "Aisha Anderson vanished from a convenience store at the highway exit two weeks ago. She was eighteen. People saw her step out for a smoke break, but she never came back in. The security camera showed her getting into a black truck, but didn't get the plates."

"So what do you think the family can tell us that we don't already know?" Brent asked as he got out of the car.

"We won't know until we hear it," Travis replied. "But there's got to be a connection to everything else that's going on."

Brent let Travis take the lead heading up the walk. They stood on the porch, waiting for someone to answer the doorbell. "Mrs. Anderson?" Travis asked in what Brent had come to think of as his "priest voice."

The woman in the doorway was probably in her late thirties, but worry and loss made her look at least a decade older. Her brown hair was pulled back in a ponytail, and the rumpled sweats and lack of makeup told Brent the woman was too consumed by grief to care about anything as trivial as appearance.

"You're the one who called. I recognize your voice." She eyed Brent as if wondering how he factored into whatever story Travis had given to win them access. "You're not a reporter, are you?" she asked.

Brent shook his head. "No ma'am," he replied, with a little more drawl than usual. "I'm a private investigator."

"Come on in." Shelby Anderson led the way into a cluttered living room. The couch and end tables were covered with newspaper clippings and printed-out screenshots from TV news, all of them about the black truck disappearances. She cleared room for them to sit and took the recliner opposite the couch.

"I don't know what I can tell you that I haven't already told the police," she said, tucking a strand of stray hair behind one ear. "Aisha liked working at the QuickMart. Her co-workers were nice, and she said there wasn't as much drama as there had been at the last place she worked."

"Which was?" Brent prompted.

"Aisha wanted to go to college when she graduated," Shelby said. "She'd been working since she was fifteen to save money. And none of that money has been touched, so I know she didn't run off with some boy like the police suggested." She took a deep breath. "She waited tables, flipped burgers, cleaned houses, and babysat. My Aisha's a good worker," she added, slipping into using the present tense.

"So she hadn't fought with anyone recently? A boyfriend, a girl-friend, someone from a former job?" Travis asked.

Shelby shook her head. "People like Aisha. She's the one who brings everyone together. The whole town's been upset." Shelby sniffed back tears and pulled a tissue from a pocket to dab her eyes. "It's got everyone up in arms," she went on. "There've been search parties and roadblocks looking for that truck, and people chipped in on a reward. Aisha was everyone's friend. It's been hard."

Travis frowned like he picked up something Brent hadn't. "I'm sure it's been awful for everyone," he murmured. "I know you've had your mind on other things, but have you noticed anything else unusual going on lately? People reacting strangely?"

Shelby blew her nose, then wiped away tears. "It just seems like the whole world's gone crazy, if you want to know the truth," she confessed. "Mr. Van Patten hanged himself last Tuesday, and no one had a clue things weren't good with him. Then my neighbor's uncle fell inside a silo on his farm, and the methane gas killed him before they could get him out. Ted O'Connell got mad at his boss and shot up the hardware store, and the church youth group got into a bad bus accident." She looked overwhelmed. "And my Aisha is gone. I don't know what this world is coming to."

From the glint in Travis's eyes, Brent figured his new partner had a theory to tie all the horrible events together. That much bad luck couldn't possibly be a coincidence. *More like a big city-sized package of awful crammed into a teeny-tiny town. Something's wrong,* Brent thought.

"Would you mind if we took a look at her room?" he asked.

Shelby sniffled, then nodded. "Go ahead. The police already went through her things. It was...intrusive. But if it brings her back—"

"I promise we'll be respectful." Brent led the way, with Travis a few steps behind. He opened drawers, looked through her closet, checked under the bed, the way he had been trained by the cops. Nothing looked even slightly suspicious. He glanced at Travis and shook his head.

"We've taken enough of your time," Travis said, in the well-rehearsed tone Brent associated with pastors. It didn't mean the clergy were insincere, it just meant they had a lot of practice soothing people on the verge of freaking out. *Yet another reason to work together. I suck at those kinds of conversations.*

Shelby walked them to the door, and Travis assured her that they would continue to explore every lead on the black truck abductions. Brent held his tongue until they were back in the Crown Vic.

"Spill. You've figured something out."

Before Travis could answer, his phone rang. He raised his eyebrows when he saw the name "Derek" on the screen and thumbed the call to put it on speakerphone. "I've got you on speaker so my partner, Brent, can hear you. What's up?"

"Zombies," a man's voice replied. "I heard from Erin, over in Milesburg. She's been getting calls about people who should be dead showing up along Route 150. Several sightings called in, but when the cops show up, the zombies are gone."

"Shit," Travis muttered. "Is Erin picking up anything on her own?" he asked, and Brent wondered what necessitated the code.

"Yeah, but you know how it is with her," Derek replied, "she gets the message, but not the address. She's sure this isn't a hoax."

"No, I'm sure it's not. Okay," Travis said, pinning the phone between his chin and shoulder as he started the car. "I'm about forty minutes away from Milesburg. Any idea of where on Route 150 I should be looking?"

"Cemeteries, for starters," Derek replied. "Churchyards, family plots. Where else would zombies come from?"

"Morgues?"

"Not mine, and I think it would be on the news already if people were popping up at the County Hospital morgue."

"You've got a point." Travis put the phone down as he pulled away from the curb and headed for I-80. "Any idea why those particular zombies are on the move?"

"Nope. But Benjamin might."

"Fuck. I hadn't thought about that," Travis said. "We'll swing by on the way and see if he knows something. Thanks for the tip."

"I've asked off for the rest of the day," Derek replied. "I'm leaving now, so I'll meet you at the abandoned convenience store on 150. I figure maybe I can help. And I need to know what's going on, in case any of my corpses decide to go walkabout."

Travis ended the call, and they rode in silence for a few minutes until they merged into highway traffic. "You want to decode any of that?" Brent asked. It was clear that Travis had a relationship with the caller, one that included knowing exactly what sort of "side gig" kept Travis busy. "Was that part of your Night Vigil?"

Travis blew out a breath. "Yeah. Derek is the Jefferson County head coroner. He's also got some extra abilities that come in handy, like being able to talk to the dead."

"Not sure that's a good thing, in his line of work." Brent frowned. "How is that different from what you can do?"

Travis shrugged. "I'm a medium. I can hear and speak to ghosts, but I can't compel them. Derek is a necromancer. So if someone's raising the dead, he's going to take that personally. As for the rest, if he can get tips that help the cops catch the killer, he passes them along. It doesn't always succeed, but he tries to make the best of what he's got to work with."

"And the Night Vigil?"

"They're people like you and me...and others with a variety of psychic and magical abilities...who have made mistakes and want to do better," he answered quietly, keeping his eyes on the highway as if glancing at Brent would reveal too much. "Sometimes, pretty spectacular mistakes, since they've got power but no training, and human beings can make very bad choices."

"Pretty sure I have a gold medal in fuck-ups," Brent replied. "And other than being a demon magnet, I don't even know if I *have* any abilities."

"So the Night Vigil are the people I've gotten to know, all across the area, who have talents they can't admit, but they want to do some good with them, maybe make amends. One way or another, they found me, and I introduced them to each other, and they're sort of a first-responder network for the supernatural," Travis said.

"A lot of them work nights because they'd rather sleep when it's light out."

"I totally understand," Brent answered, having his own dread of the dark. He felt an odd pang of jealousy. All the years he had struggled with what he learned the hard way about fighting off demons and talking to ghosts in his dreams, and there had been no one to confide in who wouldn't think he was crazy. Maybe Danny was onto something when he pushed him together with Travis.

"I figured you would," Travis said with a rueful smile. "Anyhow, when they see or sense something weird, they let me know. Erin is a 911 operator, but she's also a clairaudio—she can hear cries for help from a distance."

"That must come in handy."

"Not when she has no idea where the person is or why they are calling," Travis responded.

"Ouch."

"That's the problem with a lot of 'gifts.' They don't come with instruction manuals, most people can't get anyone to believe them or don't dare ask until they're an adult and have lived with these abilities they can't control for years. If it doesn't destroy them—or they don't fuck up fantastically—they try to figure out how to make the best of it."

Brent had the very clear impression Travis included himself in that description.

"And Benjamin?"

Travis was silent as he maneuvered around a slow car, shifted into the passing lane, and accelerated. "Benjamin's brother, Tom, was dying. Rare disease. He researched every doctor, every treatment, no matter how unproven. When science didn't help, he turned to magic. Then Tom died, and Benjamin couldn't deal with that, so he found a way to raise Tom from the dead—as a zombie. Kept him alive for years on the brains of two-bit pimps and low-level drug dealers, until Tom finally put a bullet through his own brain to end it all."

Brent's throat tightened, and he turned to look out the window.

He could understand and identify with Benjamin's obsession all too well.

"Back at the house, with Shelby Anderson, you looked like you figured something out," Brent said after a long silence.

"I'm not sure," Travis admitted. "But when she said that everyone in town took Aisha's disappearance hard, it made me think about the people you and I have already run across who've been affected. They've all been grieving."

Brent thought about the suicides in the ruins of the mining town, and the stories he and Travis had shared about the spike in demonic activity. "Yeah. Maybe that has something to do with it," he mused. "Grief makes people vulnerable. Willing to do anything to fix what went wrong or stop the pain."

Travis nodded. "I don't think that's all of it. But I think the grief is involved with what's happening. And the shootings and suicides and accidents create more people who have lost someone, generating more grief."

Brent felt a spike of anger that went right to his gut at the idea of someone—human or demonic—using grief as a weapon. Despite the years that had passed, his own losses burned brightly in his dreams, wounds that might scar but would never completely heal. He remembered just how raw he had been in the days after his family's deaths, and in the weeks after his squad's encounter with Mavet. If he hadn't already vowed to hunt down whatever was causing the violence near Cooper City, Brent was fully on board now.

"Can Derek stop the zombies?" Brent asked. "I've run into demons and vengeful ghosts and shifters, plus a few ghouls, but I haven't fought zombies."

"We can stop the zombies, even without Derek," Travis replied. "Regular bullet to the head, or decapitation. Burn the bodies. I can send their souls on with Last Rites. But," he said, weaving through traffic to avoid a slow semi, "Derek can figure out what magic raised them. And if he can withdraw that magic, we might not have to fight at all."

Brent cleared his throat. "So...are they like on TV?"

Travis took his eyes off the road long enough to meet his gaze. "No. They're worse."

———

THEY DROVE INTO MILESBURG, a tiny town kept alive by Social Security and the visitors to the nearby state game lands. A budget hotel sat near the highway exit, along with a gas station and a couple of fast food chain restaurants. Not far away, the State Store occupied one storefront in a seventies' era plaza. Travis angled the Crown Vic into a parking space.

"Come on," he said. "Let's talk to Benjamin."

Brent looked around the state-run liquor store when they entered, and figured it told him a lot about the area. Unlike the Pittsburgh stores, this one had no wall of flavored vodkas and high-end scotch. The small store carried the basics—rum, vodka, and whiskey—without the trendy specialty items or expensive upscale brands. All someone would need to numb the pain, no frills required.

"Can I help you?" A man called from behind the counter. Brent guessed that the clerk was in his late forties, but he had the look about him of someone who'd had a rough life, and the reddened flush and sallow skin of a hard drinker. His face fell as he recognized Travis. "Oh. It's you. What's going on?"

Travis looked around as if to assure they were alone in the store with the clerk Brent guessed was Benjamin. Brent took up a spot near the door where he could hear their conversation while watching for incoming customers.

"I was hoping you could tell me." Travis picked up a bottle of Jack Daniels and walked to the register. "I got a call about zombies out on route 150."

Benjamin's eyes widened. "Oh, shit!" He reddened. "Sorry." Travis shrugged to excuse the language. "I don't know anything about it. I didn't do anything, I swear."

Travis took out a credit card to pay for the whiskey. "I didn't think you did. But I wondered if you've heard anything...sensed anything...that might be connected."

Benjamin paused, staring off into space as he thought. "Been busier this month than I ever remember, and I've worked here for close to ten years," he said. Brent had the feeling that Benjamin might be one of the store's best customers, a radar that came from shared abuse. "People just seem down on their luck, you know? Like they can't catch a break. Couple of house fires, some hikers got killed out in the state park, and from what people say at the diner, a slew of unfortunate diagnoses. People have a bad turn, they stop by here to get comfortably numb," he said with a shrug. "And there's been some crazy talk, about seeing dead people who've come back, but so far, no one's hauled one into town to show everybody."

"The zombies have been showing up on Route 150, going toward Mount Eagle."

"Fuck. You mean those stories are real?"

Travis nodded. "Afraid so. Can you think of anything out that way that might be where the zombies are coming from?"

Benjamin pondered the question while he rang up Travis's purchase. "There are a few churches that have graveyards," he said. "Used to be a funeral home on that road, too, but it closed down a while ago."

"Any local legends? Scary stories about that stretch of road that kids tell around the campfire?" Travis fished.

"About zombies?" Benjamin shook his head. "No. That's one of the things I liked about this town."

"Keep an ear open, okay?" Travis asked as he took his bottle and stuck his credit card back in his wallet. "I have the feeling we're going to see a lot more weirdness before everything's said and done."

The sour look on Benjamin's face suggested that he really didn't want to know, but he nodded. Travis headed out the door, with Brent a few steps behind him, and put the bottle in the trunk.

"You think he was telling the truth?" Brent asked as he slid into the front seat.

"Yeah. Benjamin was a one-shot problem," Travis replied. "He did what he did because he couldn't stand losing his brother. And that went so horrifically wrong that I don't think he's going to be tempted to go into business raising other people's dead relatives."

Brent repressed a shudder. "Good to know." As much as he missed Danny—and sometimes his absence felt like an amputated limb—he'd been content with memories and dreams. Raising him from the dead had never crossed Brent's mind, and it made him nauseous that he now apparently knew two people who could have made that happen.

"Derek should be waiting for us," Travis said, and if he noted Brent's reaction, he was tactful enough not to mention it. "Let's see if we can stop this party."

DEREK SAT in his gray Audi sedan in the gravel parking lot of a tumbledown empty convenience store. Travis pulled up beside him, and Derek got out, locked up, and slid into the back seat of the Crown Vic. "I figure the car'll be safer here than anywhere we're going," he said.

"You bring any weapons?" Brent asked, aware of the gun in his shoulder rig, and the weapons bag in the trunk.

"Don't need them." Derek tapped his temple. "It's all up here."

"Benjamin doesn't know anything about the incidents," Travis reported.

"Don't you think that's a little suspicious?" Derek questioned.

Travis shrugged, then eased the Crown Vic out of the gravel lot. "Not really. I get the feeling he keeps to himself. I doubt he goes looking for that kind of news." He glanced into the rearview mirror to make eye contact with Derek. "Can you sense anything?"

Brent caught a glimpse of Derek in the side mirror. The coroner took a deep breath, then closed his eyes. He remained still, eyes shut, for so long that Brent thought the man might have fallen asleep. As Travis neared a side road, Derek's eyes flew open.

"I feel the power," he said. "It's...all wrong. Not like it usually is. The power feels twisted, tainted."

"Is it natural?" Travis asked, splitting his attention between the GPS on his phone and the road ahead as he turned the car down a side road that led between forest and empty fields. A small white clapboard church sat on the left, and Brent saw a brick fence around a graveyard beside it. Travis pulled into the parking lot and turned the car, so it was ready for a quick escape.

They got out, and Brent drew his gun. Travis tossed him a sheathed Ka-Bar, which Brent caught one-handed and strapped to his belt. Travis withdrew a shotgun and a machete. Derek shook his head when Travis offered another shotgun and turned his hands palms up.

"I've got what I need right here," Derek replied. "How about I wander around in the graveyard, and you guys have my back? I get a little distracted when I go with the flow."

Brent and Travis fanned out, one on each side, trailing behind Derek as he strode toward the cemetery. Up close, Brent could see that both the church and its surroundings looked untended. The wooden siding was chalky, long past the need for fresh paint, and rot claimed some of the moldings around the doorway. In several places loose bricks tumbled down from the graveyard wall, leaving gaps and crumbling mortar. Tall grass around the headstones hadn't been cut in a while, and some of the markers were broken or vandalized.

"Off-hand, I'd say the congregation hasn't been paying much attention," Brent murmured.

"Probably down to a handful of retirees, mostly women," Travis replied. "Happens a lot."

The wind rattled through the branches of the woods just beyond and sent a chill down Brent's back. Derek walked forward slowly, eyes open but glassy as if he had tuned into a different reality.

"Picking up any chatter on the Dead Channel?" Brent asked.

Travis grimaced at the nickname. "Chatter? No. But uneasiness? Yeah. I'm sure all these folks had lovely funerals, but that doesn't mean people go gently to wherever they're headed next."

Derek climbed through a broken place in the low brick wall rather than fumbling with the wrought iron gate. Brent and Derek followed at a cautious distance, weapons ready.

"Either they've got grave robbers, or some of their dead parishioners woke up from their dirt nap," Brent remarked, noting the messy excavations in front of several markers.

"But not everyone," Travis mused. Both Brent and Travis had their guns raised, scanning for trouble, either living or undead. "So what made some of them special?"

Brent stared out across the small churchyard. Unlike the big Pittsburgh cemeteries filled with obelisks and angel statues, the headstones were modest and unremarkable. Brent had visited famous graveyards elsewhere that boasted gardens and beautiful landscaping, but this small plot felt desolate and forlorn, without even shade trees to soften the rows of tombstones.

Some of the markers were limestone, badly weathered with the years, nearly illegible. Most of the others were gray granite, probably the least expensive available. Several looked newer than the rest, and it was in front of those that fresh dirt formed mounds where the zombies had clawed themselves free.

"It's the recent dead," Brent said quietly.

"Yeah. I noticed that. Maybe because they still have people to mourn them?" Travis suggested.

Derek stopped abruptly and shook himself out of his trance.

"Well?" Brent asked, hearing an edge in his voice from the tension. He didn't care for role-playing *The Walking Dead*, waiting to be surprised either by the local cops or hungry shamblers.

"The energy that raised them isn't anything like my magic," Derek replied. "I think the bodies were reanimated against their will. The power feels sullied. No, I'll go farther than that. Not just dirty...

evil." He met Travis's gaze. "At the risk of sounding Biblical, I'd even say infernal."

"Demons again," Brent groaned.

Travis didn't look surprised. "The ghosts are afraid," he said. "Especially those outside the wall."

"What the fuck?" Brent felt his temper rise. "I thought that kind of thing only happened in movies." Burying non-believers, criminals, and stigmatized others outside the churchyard walls, beyond "sanctified ground," used to be common. Some thought it doomed the souls to wander, denying them eternal rest. Brent had always thought it sounded like petty bullshit.

"I don't think that's been done for quite some time, generations maybe, but Milesburg is an old town, and ghosts have long memories," Travis said. "They don't know what raised the dead, but they saw them rise, and they were afraid whatever power commanded the corpses could take them as well."

"They were right to be afraid," Derek replied. "I don't think anything human channeled that energy. So the question becomes— why them, and why here?"

"Benjamin said there were other churches on this stretch. Let's see whether they have the same problem," Travis suggested.

Two other small churches stood in lonely isolation along the highway between Milesburg and the state game lands. One appeared to be abandoned. None of its dead rose. The other, a small brick building that seemed slightly better cared for than the first church, had even more missing bodies. They made the same sweep, and Derek reported feeling similar dark power in the cemetery with the risen dead, but not in the undisturbed burying ground.

"No one might have noticed the dead rising during the week," Derek said, "but come Sunday, I'm betting it will be a topic of conversation."

"No one rose in the third churchyard," Brent pointed out. "Why?"

"And in the first cemetery, all of the newly buried people rose, while the ones who had been dead longer didn't," Derek mused. "But here, there are a couple of new headstones with recent deaths who didn't rise."

Brent bent down to examine one of those undisturbed graves. "The man who was buried here was ninety-six." He walked a few paces over to another new marker whose "resident" remained below. "And a lady who was ninety-two."

Trent seemed to catch his drift. "So maybe there was no one left to grieve them."

Brent nodded. "It would make sense if you're right about the Silverado abductions. Whatever's behind this is picking its targets to make the biggest emotional impact. A child goes missing. A teenager everyone liked. A young woman who didn't seem to have an enemy in the world." He swept one hand in a gesture to indicate the cemeteries. "And now, zombies where the loss is recent and the grief is fresh for families who are going to be out of their minds about the graves being desecrated."

"If they think the graves are bad, wait until they meet up with their loved ones looking a little worse for the wear," Derek muttered.

"So there were five from the first cemetery, none from the second, and six here," Brent said. "And from the dates on the headstones, seven of those were older adults, and four were between sixteen and thirty."

"Which holds with the theory about wanting to upset the surviving family members," Derek added.

"Do you think we've found all of them?" Brent asked.

Travis frowned. "Benjamin said something about a mortuary that went out of business."

"Oh, shit," Derek said, looking pale. "I totally forgot about that. Randall Funeral Home was in the news a month ago when it shut down without warning. Turns out that their crematory stopped working, and they didn't tell anyone. Some bodies only got partially cremated, others just got stored in freezers, and the families got a box of sand instead of ashes. Then the power went out."

"Fuck. What happened?" Brent asked.

"Families had started to get suspicious. The cops got a warrant, and found bodies in shallow graves, or stacked in a walk-in freezer. The owner committed suicide, the employees went to jail, and every forensic lab in six counties got called in to match dental records to badly decomposed remains." Derek grimaced as he recalled the horror.

"Let's go have a look at the funeral home," Travis said. Derek got into the car first. Travis stowed his gun under the front seat, and Brent covered them until Travis was settled and the car was running before he got in, too.

Randall's still showed up on the GPS, a short drive from the last church. The sprawling old home had been grand once before it was converted to a mortuary and fell into disgrace. The police tape was gone, but orange temporary construction fencing had been staked out along the perimeter of the grounds.

Travis got out of the car, and stumbled, catching himself against the chassis.

"You okay?" Brent asked.

Travis nodded. "Yeah. It's just, the impressions are pretty strong." A sudden gust of wind whipped by them, bending the tall grass and rustling the dry leaves in the trees. Brent felt gooseflesh prickle along his arms and at the back of his neck.

"I'm not sensing any of the undead," Derek said. "Just some restless, angry ghosts."

"Dangerous?" Brent had his gun in hand, but he knew an iron rod would do him more good if they were going to deal with vengeful spirits.

Travis and Derek shook their heads. "Angry for being mistreated, and for the heartache it caused their families," Travis relayed.

"Grief again," Brent noted. "Finding out that the funeral director stole your money and botched your loved one's send-off would be like losing them all over again."

Derek nodded. "I think you're onto something there. If the police confiscated the remains, there wouldn't be any bodies left here to turn into zombies, but I can feel the same energy imprint as I did at the graveyards. This isn't a dark witch, messing around. It's something old and powerful—and evil."

Brent could see where backhoes and excavating equipment had torn up the lawn behind the building. The air felt heavy, like a storm was brewing. Pressure behind his eyes gave him a pounding headache, and it felt difficult to breathe. The nearby woods were too silent, as if even the birds and forest animals had fled. Every primal instinct told him to run.

"I want to say Last Rites, and send the spirits here on to their rest," Travis said. "That leaves less unsettled energy for anything bad to draw on, and it's the decent thing to do."

Travis moved up to the fence and began the litany, while Brent and Derek remained at a respectful distance, watching for danger. Gradually, the air around them felt less oppressive, and Brent's headache eased, as did the sense of disquiet. Perhaps it was his imagination, but the sky seemed to brighten, and by the time Travis finished his prayers, Brent heard birdsong and the rustle of small animals in the brush.

"Whatever raised the zombies didn't exactly conjure up an army," Derek noted. "So what's the point?"

Travis led the way back to the Crown Vic. "Terror and grief. They aren't supposed to attack the town. They're supposed to get spotted and vanish, keeping everyone keyed up, not letting their loved ones let go and move on." He started the car as they got in. "Let's go back to where the drivers thought they saw the zombies. Maybe we'll find something there."

They drove in silence, each man lost in thought. Brent couldn't help reliving the awful memories of the viewing and funerals for his parents and Danny. None of them had been open casket, not with what the demon left behind. He'd identified the bodies, to spare his grandfather who had a weak heart. No amount of alcohol would ever wash the images from Brent's memories. The cops claimed it was a serial killer, but years later, after he'd encountered Mavet, Brent had figured out the truth.

Don't make it personal, Brent warned himself. He knew it was already too late. While he'd managed to keep his objectivity on regular cases as a cop or a Fed, demon hunting bordered on being a vigilante obsession. Every monster he killed was a hollow victory, and while it protected someone else's family, it would never return his own.

A glance at Derek yielded no insights; his expression was shuttered and unreadable, though the tense way he sat, leaning forward, suggested he was ready for a fight. Travis radiated anger in the white-knuckled clench of his fingers around the steering wheel and the set of his shoulders. Perhaps he felt the sacrilege even more strongly since he did not seem to have left as much of the priesthood behind as he claimed.

Travis pulled off on the shoulder. "There've been five sightings, all in this half-mile stretch. Seems like a good place to start."

Brent got out first, with a gun in one hand and his Ka-Bar in the other. Travis came around to stand on the same side of the car, holding his shotgun. Derek stood between them, unarmed except for his magic.

Travis turned to take in their surroundings, making a slow circle with his shotgun held at the ready. "They're out there," he said quietly. "In the forest."

Derek nodded. "I sense them, too. It's almost like they've been... deactivated. I'm not sure they can move on their own. I think they're being controlled."

Travis racked his shells, ready for a fight. "Can you locate them? If they aren't going to come to us, maybe we can take the battle to them and put a stop to this."

Derek's eyes widened, just as the sound rose of something crashing through the underbrush. "Shit. They're awake, and they're headed this way."

Seconds later, the smell of rotting flesh filled the air. Shadowy forms careened toward them, moving quickly but with the coordination of a drunkard.

"Great. Fast zombies," Brent muttered.

"Can you stop them with magic?" Travis glanced at Derek, gripping his machete as tightly as his gun.

"Gonna try," Derek assured them. "Cover me." He stretched out one arm, hand open and palm out, then closed his eyes, and while his lips moved, he did not speak aloud.

The two zombies in the lead were close enough for Brent to see their bloated, discolored faces. Two old men, still wearing their Sunday best suits, stumbling forward like they were running downhill, unable to stop. Brent had no idea what the zombies intended to do when they reached the road, but he did not want to find out. He raised his Glock, but Travis put a hand on his arm.

"Give Derek a moment."

Brent held his fire but did not lower his arm.

Derek gave a shout and clenched his fist. The front two zombies fell to their knees, and the closest of their companions fell over them. It might have been funny, if the zombies hadn't gotten back up again, fixed on their objective.

"The power that raised them isn't magic," Derek cried out, eyes wide with panic. "I can't stop them."

"Then blowing them to bits won't stop them, either, but it might slow them down," Travis said, handing off his shotgun to Derek. "Start shooting, and I'll try the exorcism."

Brent and Derek opened fire. The zombies might be moving at a medium jog instead of a slow shamble, but not so fast that it made targeting a problem. There were more of the undead than they had figured from the cemeteries, but not by many. Brent kept count as he shot, and his aim was true, striking in the head or center mass. Travis was right—the bullets sent the zombies reeling and forced them back a few steps, but within seconds they reoriented and started moving forward again with shattered skulls and gaping chest wounds.

"*Exorcizamos te....*" Travis began.

Almost with the first words of the litany, the wind shifted, and a clinging cold descended. The feeling that they were in the presence of evil, like back at the mortuary, grew stronger, reminding Brent of that night his squadron survived Mavet. Something wicked and powerful made its presence known. He fought the triggering memories to keep focused on the moment, aiming and firing to buy Travis time.

In the next instant, the zombies collapsed like puppets with cut strings. The oppressive tension in the air vanished, and with it the dark entity that animated the wretched corpses.

"Someone had to have heard that," Derek said, his voice unsteady.

"Get in the car," Brent ordered. "Start it up. I'll be there in a minute or less." He ran toward the stinking heaps of rotting bodies, drizzling each with a bottle of lighter fluid he pulled from his jacket pocket, then tossing a match to light them like a pyre.

"Are you crazy? You could set the forest on fire!" Derek yelped as Brent threw himself into the front seat and Travis peeled rubber to put distance between themselves and the flames.

"We've had plenty of rain, and the cops are going to be here soon," Brent replied, breathing hard. "But if whatever raised those bodies could drop them by leaving, it could start them up again if it came back. Gonna be harder now that they're fried to a crackly crunch."

They dropped Derek off at his car, getting back on the road seconds before police cars and fire engines zoomed past them, lights flashing and sirens blaring. Brent did not let out the breath he was holding until they and Derek were on I-80.

"That was—" Brent began.

"Horrific," Travis finished. He visibly loosened his grip on the wheel and rolled his shoulders to release tension. A glance to the rear view mirror told Brent that the other man expected to see squad cars in pursuit.

"Now what?"

"I'm going to talk to more of my Night Vigil, and then we head back to Cooper City and see if we can figure out how to pull the plug," Travis said with grim determination. "Because if this is a cycle of some kind, then it's building to a climax and I really don't want to see what happens next."

CHAPTER NINE

THEY DIDN'T MAKE it to Cooper City that day, although they did stop the zombie mini-apocalypse of Milesburg. Brent and Travis agreed to take two days off to handle their other responsibilities—barring a new looming catastrophe—and head east again mid-week.

Twenty-four hours later, Brent's cold, acrid coffee settled in the pit of his stomach as he sat on a stake-out, waiting for the suspect to make the drop. His client, Preston Energy, Inc., believed one of its engineers was selling confidential information about its natural gas exploration to a competitor. Fracking had turned the previously worthless land into energy goldmines, and the potential profit involved was more than enough to push desperate men to make dangerous choices.

The stake-out left him time on his hands with nothing to do but think, and his thoughts rehashed the trip to Milesburg, and the fight in the diner. *Travis and his Night Vigil are the real deal. Danny was right—I can't handle whatever this is on my own,* he thought. After flying solo for so long, working with a partner again was going to take some getting used to. *Still, he's not too bad—for a priest. Ex-priest.*

Yeah, right. He might not still actually be wearing the collar, but it's not really gone.

And what did that make him? Brent knew in his heart he'd never really left behind the Army, the FBI, or the Pittsburgh Police Department. He might have turned in his badge and his ID, but he still did the dirty work, even if his former employers would have struggled to believe that the supernatural foes were real.

Brent blinked and gagged down more coffee. Last night's dreams had been bad, triggered by the zombie fight and the memories of his butchered family. The only solace had been in that haze between waking and sleeping when he found himself alone on a gray plain with Danny. His brother had hugged him tight, and when he drew back, Brent could see that Danny looked more worried than he ever remembered seeing him in life.

It's going to get worse, Danny warned. *If you don't stick together, you won't be able to stop it, and neither one of you will survive.*

What do you know? Brent had begged. He'd always wondered whether the dead had access to the secrets of the universe. But Danny just shook his head.

I don't know how to stop it, Danny told him. *I just know you can't do this alone. And I'm in no hurry for you to join me. So don't be stupid.* Dream-Danny sounded so much like Brent's memories of his brother that he had to swallow hard to keep back tears.

Can't promise I won't be an asshole. It's what I'm good at, Brent replied with a lopsided smile. *But I'll work with Travis. And we'll figure out how to stop this thing. I'll be as careful as I can.*

He had expected a smart remark, but Danny was gone, and the alarm ripped away the last vestiges of sleep. Which left Brent tired and out of sorts, reminding himself that the paycheck for nabbing the white-collar thief would cover his expenses for a couple of months as he returned his attention to the stakeout.

Showtime! Brent thought as the suspect came into view. He triggered the video camera he had already set up, as well as a sequence of still shots with a telephoto lens that would leave no doubt about the man's identity or that of the person he was meeting.

A loud thump made Brent swing toward the noise, gun drawn. A large man in a dark suit with a grim expression leaned over the passenger side of the truck like he meant to tear off the doors.

Brent wasn't getting paid enough to get into a shoot-out, and being worked over by hired muscle wasn't in the contract. He floored it, practically running over the man's toes, but not before he had snapped a picture of the guy for good measure. Brent hoped that the shots he got of the meet-up would be sufficient because any future stakeout was going to require a different car to remain anonymous.

His phone went off as Brent navigated a tangle of narrow side streets and alleys. He checked his mirrors for a tail but didn't relax until he had gotten across the city without incident. Still, he thought, the bruiser had gotten a good look at him and probably took down his plates, so that cushy paycheck now carried the risk that the embezzler or his patron might decide to shut Brent up before he could supply damning evidence.

"Fuck. If the demons don't get me, Frankie Numbnuts might," Brent muttered. He took the long way back to his side of town, still alert for anyone following him. Then he pulled into a hotel parking garage, backed into a spot to obscure his plate, grabbed the cameras and his gear bag, then sauntered to the hotel's front doors to call a rideshare so he wouldn't have to park at the curb in front of his house.

Only when he pulled out his phone did he remember his missed call. He tapped the number and heard one ring before the person picked up.

"Hey, have you seen the news?" Travis asked without preamble.

"I've been kinda busy trying not to get my teeth knocked in," Brent replied, eyeing the surrounding area warily. "On-the-job hazard."

"Nice. There's been a bus crash—freak accident—that killed a high school sports team out near Sylvan Grove," Travis went on.

"And I think I've found evidence to prove that more than a few folks out that way sold their souls to turn their luck around."

"Seriously? You mean, like that old blues guitar guy?" Despite his recent brush with danger, Brent couldn't help being intrigued.

"Yeah. And it's all happening in a fifty-mile radius around Peale and Cooper City," Travis said. "I want to head out there in the morning. Are you up for it?"

Brent scrubbed a hand down over his face tiredly. "Yeah, yeah. Count me in. I've gotta get some work done today anyway. I can meet you at your place."

"Great. See you at seven," Travis said and ended the call before Brent had a chance to argue. That left him swearing at the phone in his hand before he remembered he still needed to call a ride.

He worked at a furious pace, uploading the photos and evidence that should give his client enough to prosecute the corporate spy. "Poor dumb bastard probably didn't get enough money out of it to buy himself a spiffy car, and he's likely to go to jail." Brent remembered what Travis had said about people in the "blast zone" around Cooper City selling their souls. He wondered for a moment whether the incidents could be related, then he finished the email to his client and hit the send button. Not every bad decision could be blamed on demons. Brent had made plenty of them himself, no infernal assistance required.

Before he sat down to work, Brent checked the locks and the security system to make sure his perimeter cameras were recording and tried to assure himself that he hadn't been followed. The old break in his leg—the one patched together with a metal plate and some screws—ached more than usual. He eyed his pain pills—harder to get these days, best to save them for when he *really* needed them—and poured himself a couple of fingers of Jim Beam instead.

The Pennsylvania cold settled in his bones when the weather turned, and up here, that was from early October through late April. It was a cold, dark place for a southern boy, Brett thought as he sipped his bourbon. He flipped channels, hoping for a good football

replay, and switched it off when he saw the Georgia Bulldogs playing. If the demons hadn't come for his family, if Danny hadn't died,
they'd have been on that team, probably earned matching bowl
game rings.

He wondered again what drew the demon to his family, and why
he attracted the demonic. Maybe when the solved the Cooper City
problem, he'd gain some insight, or at least work up the nerve to ask
Travis if he could exorcize whatever fault in him had led to so many
deaths. *Maybe if there are grief demons, there are guilt demons. If so,
I'm somebody's all-you-can-eat buffet.*

———

SYLVAN GROVE, PA, was more of an idea than a place, without
much to mark its existence besides an old white church and its cemetery. Farm fields, barns, and far-flung houses were the only settle-
ments Brent had seen for miles as he and Travis went looking for the
aftermath of the fatal crash.

A small converted school bus lay in a twisted pile on its side next
to the railroad tracks. Like many rural crossings, there were no barri-
cade arms, just a flashing light, and a crossing marker. Accidents
weren't unusual when a vehicle's driver decided to gamble that he
could beat an oncoming train, but what Brent remembered from the
fatalities that made the news back home, a dark night and a malfunc-
tioning signal could be a recipe for disaster. The train that hit the bus
had derailed, so there were injured train personnel, as well as
concern over the spilled contents of some of the freight cars.

Brent wasn't about to push his luck impersonating a federal
agent, but his PI license got him past the small town cops.

Travis didn't need a clerical collar. He showed up in a black t-
shirt with a blazer over jeans, and something about his somber
manner earned him grudging respect from the police, enough to keep
them from being run off as trespassers.

"Over here," Travis said with a jerk of his head, honing in on the hastily erected tent with a hand-lettered sign offering water and food for first-responders.

"We heard what happened, and wondered if you needed some help," he said to the harried middle-aged man who was simultaneously trying to tell several teenagers where to unload cases of bottled water and give orders to a handful of flustered volunteers on when to bring the sandwiches.

"Oh, thank the Lord," the man said. "I can use all the extra hands I can get. I'm Pastor Pete, Pete Sheldon, from the Snowshoe Baptist Church."

"I'm Travis, and he's Brent. What do you need us to do?"

Moments later, Travis headed off to set up folding tables and carry coolers for the cadre of volunteers that had shown up to feed the officers and responders who worked at the taped-off crash site. Brent helped relay cases of water and sports drinks, as well as manage huge thermal urns of coffee.

Brent kept his ears open as the other helpers chattered.

"...don't know why they even took this road."

"...seems like they went out of their way. Did they get lost?"

"...I heard one of the cops say, they couldn't figure out why there even was a train through here last night."

The longer he listened, the more Brent became convinced that the accident that claimed fifteen lives wasn't truly accidental. Everyone in the volunteer tent was either related to one of the dead teens or knew them personally. Every few minutes, someone would have to step away to collect themselves, as two or three of their co-workers enfolded them in a supportive hug, or embraced them as they sobbed.

His old leg injury ached, but Brent dry-swallowed a couple of Advil and kept going. He and Travis had come for information, but now that he saw the grief that consumed Pastor Pete's volunteers, he felt a duty to help, a holdover from his own small-town roots. A glance across the tent told him that Travis had gotten his fellow helpers talking. The sorrow was palpable, and even the officers and firefighters had to excuse themselves at times to deal with the gory accident scene.

All these people, swallowed up with loss. And something out there, feeding on their grief.

"It's not like we haven't had more than our share," Wanda, a woman with a long gray ponytail, said as Brent helped to set up the coffee station. She had a slender, raw-boned look to her that made Brent think of ranch girls in Texas.

"What do you mean?" he asked. When Wanda gave him a look, he managed a self-conscious smile. "I'm not from here. We just came to lend a hand."

"The dog food factory over near the highway burned down two weeks ago, and that put forty people out of work—not much else to do around here. Then Mrs. Slater fell and drowned in her tub, and old Mr. Hendricks shot himself out hunting." She shook her head. "Kelly Abrams's husband got diagnosed with a brain tumor, and she's got that sick baby at home. Cory Edwards overdosed. Now, this. It's just a lot for a little town to bear up under."

"There've been some good turns, too." A portly woman with bright red hair in a messy bun bustled up with a tray of cookies. "Jim Sanders's cancer up and disappeared from one scan to another, praise the Lord," she added, though Brent suspected a less heavenly power was responsible. "Vera Mason thought she was going to have to close her bakery, and then she got that life insurance payment from an uncle she hadn't seen in years. And Ned Thompson's wife came out of surgery just fine, when everyone said they thought she wouldn't make it home from the hospital. Good things still happen."

Brent's heart ached when he remembered what Travis had said about people selling their souls. As much as Wanda and the cookie lady needed a win, he felt certain that their "good news" was just another tragedy.

Brent finished up with the coffee urns and stepped away. Doug Conroy answered on the first ring. "Brent. Wondered when I'd hear from you."

"Hey, I'm over in Sylvan Grove. You know anyone over that way?"

Doug paused for a moment as if trying to figure out the connection. "The bus crash?"

"Yeah. I think it might be related."

"Shit. Yeah, I know the police chief, but he's going to be up to his ass in alligators for a while. His wife, Olivia, is friends with my Cheryl. Might be neighborly for her to check in and see if our church group can help in any way."

"I'd appreciate anything you find out," Brent said. When he ended the call and glanced up, he saw Travis slipping his phone back in a pocket. Brent wondered if Travis had placed a call to his priest friend, Father Ryan.

He rejoined the volunteers in the food tent and spent the next half hour putting out trays of sandwiches, bowls of salad, big buckets of potato chips, and platters of cookies. Hungry cops, firefighters, and others involved in the clean-up came by, hurriedly eating and mumbling their thanks as helpers pressed hot cups of coffee and fresh cookies into their hands.

The responders came in waves, and the volunteers scrambled to replenish, doing their best to greet the tired, harried workers with smiles and thanks. Brent could see the worry and sadness in the lined faces of the cops and knew from bitter experience that they were barely holding their own emotions together. Tonight, they'd drink their sorrows into a stupor, then get up in the morning and do the job all over again.

"It was nice of you and your friend to come help." A short woman who reminded Brent of his mother touched his elbow. She was in her early fifties, dressed in a booster shirt for the local high school over a pair of yoga pants, and she looked like someone who actually knew her ass from an asana.

"It just seemed like we had to do something," Brent replied, and while it wasn't the whole truth, it was close enough.

"I know the feeling." She smiled. "I'm Sadie."

"Brent."

She looked out over the accident scene, past the crime scene tape and the orange-and-white sawhorses. "It's bad, but we'll get through this," she said with quiet conviction. "We've been through worse."

"The way you say it, I might be able to believe you," Brent replied.

She nodded. "I know it's true. These are good people. When Phil, my husband, had a heart attack and left me with two small children, they took care of us. Found me a job, helped watch the kids, brought us food. We know how to take care of our own."

Her deep-seated certainty made Brent pause. "I'm glad they were there for you. But this—so many people affected, and Wanda says there's been a run of bad luck besides—everyone has a breaking point." Brent knew that for a fact. He'd had many of his own.

Old pain flickered in Sadie's eyes, then was replaced by a glint of determination. "Oh, yes. We do. That's when you find out who you are. And some folks will have a harder time than others. But we'll pull together. Do the best we can. Muddle through."

Brent saw a calm acceptance in Sadie's expression that made him wonder about the grief demons' hold on the area. "How long ago did you lose your husband?"

Her smile grew sad. "Ten years. Miss him every day. But we had a good run of it, and I wouldn't trade those years for anything. Now, I have friends and my children. Plenty of reasons to get up in the morning."

Someone called out to her, and Sadie patted Brent on the arm and took her leave. Brent pitched in, ferrying more trays of sandwiches and refilling the coffee. He saw Travis talking with several of the local men as he helped to direct traffic and carry supplies. Brent wasn't surprised to see a priest who looked a bit older than Travis drive up and park, then work his way through the small crowd to offer his help with the responders. From the way the local police accepted his presence, Brent figured he was a known quantity, and probably Travis's friend, Father Ryan.

After his conversation with Sadie, Brent started watching the volunteers more closely. Some moved as if in a fog, weighed down by shock and sadness. Others almost seemed energized by the opportunity to act, compulsive in their need to help, finding solace in organizing the relief efforts. And a few, like Sadie, kept busy but found the opportunity to speak to those who were having the hardest time, offering encouragement.

So the grief demons don't get their claws into everyone, Brent mused. *What makes the difference?*

A commotion outside the food tent caught Brent's attention. "Let me through!" a man yelled, pushing his way through the caution tape. Several of the officers converged, telling him to remain behind the barricades, but he pressed on.

"I want to see with my own eyes," he shouted. "I want to see the van. I won't believe it until I see for myself."

"Mr. Winters, please move back—" one of the officers ordered.

Winters pulled a handgun from beneath his jacket. "I'm going to see what happened with my own eyes."

One of the cops Tased Winters from behind. He squeezed off a shot as he fell, and the bullet caught one of the officers in the shoulder. After that, two burly officers pinned and cuffed the man, who kept ranting and shouting threats as they dragged him to a cruiser.

"That's Don Winters," Sadie said, slipping up beside Brent as if she guessed his thoughts. "Lost his only daughter, Natalie, on that bus. His wife hasn't been well, and I'm afraid this might push her into a relapse."

Whatever problems Winters had before he'd shown up at the crash scene, he'd just bought himself a whole heap more trouble after that stunt with the gun. "Why did he say he didn't believe the crash happened?"

Sadie shook her head. "Stages of grief, you know? Denial, anger, bargaining, depression, acceptance. Basic Kubler-Ross. Don always was an angry guy, and he never met a conspiracy theory he didn't like. So I imagine he'd want to see for himself what happened to his baby girl, and probably wanted to fight with someone, while he was at it."

"Stages of grief," Brent repeated, barely hearing the rest of Sadie's sentence. He gave her a one-arm hug. "You're a genius. I need to go talk to my friend," he said, rushing away before Sadie could ask questions.

Travis saw him coming and met him at the edge of the clearing. "I think I've got something," Brent said, breathless with his discovery. "The grief demons, they're twisting the stages of grief. But they can't hurt the people who have accepted their loss."

Travis frowned, absorbing Brent's revelation, then nodded. "That makes sense. Anger—the shootings and the fights. Denial—"

"The people who won't bury their dead," Brent supplied.

"Bargaining—explains the crossroads deals," Travis said.

"And depression...all those suicides."

"Shit," Travis said, running a hand through his hair. "We need to figure out how to fight this. Let's go back to Ryan's, get pizza, and see what we can come up with." He seemed to interpret Brent's wary look. "It's okay. He knows what we do. Well, what I do."

"Doug Conroy should come, too. He's an ex-cop, and he knows about...things."

It took another hour to extricate themselves from their tasks at the crash site, but Brent managed to text Doug, who promised to meet them at the church. Father Ryan finished offering support to the responders and headed back to make preparations.

They met up at Our Lady of Sorrows. Travis and Brent were ready to make introductions, but Doug and Father Ryan grinned at the sight of each other and shook hands like old friends, and the priest exchanged a nod with Cheryl.

"Son of a gun, I wondered if you were in on this kind of thing," Doug said.

Father Ryan shrugged. "I've known Travis since his seminary days, but this kind of...specialized information...doesn't come up all the time, thank heavens."

From the number of cars in the parking lot, Brent wondered if they could find the privacy to speak frankly, but Father Ryan waved them toward the rectory.

"No one needs me at the church tonight, and they won't bother me here," he assured them. "I've already called ahead for pizza delivery. Beer's in the fridge, and you're both welcome to stay over if there's more you want to investigate here tomorrow."

Brent followed Travis into the rectory. Father Ryan's cat wound around his ankles.

"Don't mind Lilith. She just hopes you'll drop food," Ryan called as he walked into the kitchen to set out glasses and plates. "The cookies are fresh—Mrs. Simko brought them to the parish committee meeting this morning," he added with a nod toward a large container of homemade treats. "They're good, but I've got to give them away. That's how priests get fat," he added and patted his belly.

Brent met the delivery man at the door and found that Father Ryan had paid in advance.

"I think this qualifies as a community meeting," the priest said at Brent's surprised reaction. "I have a budget for that."

They found seats around the scarred farm-style table that took up most of the kitchen. Lilith wended her way around all of the chairs, then found a spot on the windowsill where she could keep an eye on the neighborhood and settled in.

The conversation remained light as they ate, and everyone dug into the food like they were starving. It became clear to Brent that Doug and Cheryl were well-acquainted with Father Ryan, even if they didn't attend his church. Then again, Brent figured that as a small-town police chief Doug probably knew just about everyone.

Travis seemed more at ease than Brent had ever seen him, and he remembered what Father Ryan had said about how far they went back together. Ryan had known Travis before his ordination, before the Sinistram, before whatever it was that scarred him so deeply.

He felt a pang of sadness; when he'd left his home in South Carolina after the murders, no one he'd grown up with or played on the high school football team with had been interested in remaining in touch. They knew he wasn't responsible for the deaths, but Brent suspected they didn't want to risk having any of his bad luck rub off. Seeing how easy Travis and Ryan were with each other made him think of Danny, and how effortless their connection had been. He hadn't really needed a best friend before his brother died, and he hadn't let himself tempt fate by making one since then.

"—after the frozen yogurt place closed down," Cheryl was saying when Brent zoned back into the conversation.

"I'm a soft-serve fan, personally," Father Ryan replied. "Although the parish ladies do make an exceptional homemade butterscotch brickle ripple for our summer family carnival."

"Best I've ever had," Doug affirmed. "I might not be one of your parishioners, padre, but I believe all God's children deserve good ice cream."

"That's true, and you're always welcome," Ryan added with a wink.

"What do you know about Pastor Pete?" Brent asked. He winced as the jovial conversation ground to a halt. "Sorry, didn't mean to be a buzzkill. He organized the volunteer tent at the crash scene, and I didn't know whether he'd be an ally in...this..."

Father Ryan sighed. "Pete's a good man, but I'm afraid he's rather literal when it comes to anything supernatural. I'm as willing to accept that whatever is troubling this area came from another realm, another planet, or another dimension as I am to blame it on the Devil —which opens up a lot of different avenues to fight it—but I fear Pete's take on it will be more orthodox."

"Gotcha," Brent said with a nod. "We already know that exorcism won't work on everything."

Doug cleared away the pizza boxes and loaded the dishwasher. Ryan put on a fresh pot of coffee, set out mugs, and pulled several bottles of beer from the fridge. Travis grabbed his laptop, and Brent fetched the files he had brought in his backpack. When he returned to the table, he saw that Ryan had a worn spiral notebook, and Doug had unfolded a marked map of the area and put it in the center of their workspace.

"So the 'blast zone' seems to be an area fifty miles across, with Cooper City and Peale smack in the middle," Doug said. "There are too many 'events' to mark, but I put dots for the bigger ones, and I brought a list of everything I've found or that you've sent me that might be connected." He peered at them over his reading glasses. "It's a mighty long list, and it began about four months ago."

Doug pulled out a multi-page printout from a manila folder in Cheryl's big purse and set it down next to the map. Travis reached for it and thumbed through the names, dates, and notes. "Shit, there's a lot of stuff," he muttered, not even bothering to make an apologetic glance in Father Ryan's direction. "For a small area, that's a lot of dead people and bad luck."

Ryan nodded. "Within the circle on the map, I'd say pretty much everyone's been touched by those tragedies in some way. Friends, relatives, co-workers, neighbors, classmates—people in these parts know each other. Most of them grew up together, and sometimes so did their parents and grandparents. So bad news travels fast, and bad luck feels like it affects everyone when it strikes."

"Everything that's going on, it's part of a fifty-year cycle," Travis said. "We've found plenty of evidence to document that every fifty years this area gets hit with a string of catastrophes, some man-made, and others seemingly natural. When you know what to look for, that includes suspicious deaths, possible suicides, missing persons, bankruptcies, and a crime spike." He sat back and crossed his arms.

"I've had two ghosts—whom I'd call first-hand witnesses," Travis added with a glance toward Brent and Doug, daring them to disagree, "and they confirmed the involvement of demons, but said that the demons were a symptom, not a cause. One of them told me that whatever's going on attracts the demonic and the dark supernatural like flies on a battlefield. So the monsters and demons—and most likely, the Silverado killer—are part of the problem and we need to deal with them. But getting rid of them won't stop the half-century apocalypse."

"Which explains the psi-vamp I fought off at Peale," Brent said, "the zombies over by Milesburg, and the reports the local police have been getting about red-eyed wolves in the woods that are eating pets and farm animals. Plus the hell-maggots—low-level demons. They're the vultures, but they didn't start the war."

"There've been other strange creatures people didn't report to the police, but they told their friends," Doug said. "No one wants to be out in the woods after dark."

"You're talking about a hell gate," Father Ryan said quietly. "I'm surprised your 'friends' aren't all over this."

Travis cleared his throat uncomfortably as Doug and the others looked at him. "I used to work for a secret organization of demon-hunting priests. We didn't part on the best of terms." That tracked with what Brent's friend, Mark, had suspected. Oddly enough, it was nice to know he wasn't alone in his tug-of-war with CHARON.

"They obviously either don't know or don't care," Travis continued. "And since no one's bothered to break the cycle before this, and we're not swarming with ninja priests, my bet is that by their standards this is too small to bother with."

Cheryl huffed, rightfully offended.

Travis raised his hands in appeasement. "Clearly, I don't agree. Just saying."

"What's a hell gate, and how do we shut it down?" Doug asked. "And does it really go to, you know, hell?"

"Not always," Brent replied, glad for the information Mark had given him and what he had gotten from his lore expert, Simon Kincaide. "Some people call them a nexus or a vortex. It's a door between here and somewhere else—and what's on the other side is pretty nasty."

"There are several ways hell gates get created," Travis picked up. "Someone could work really strong, dark magic, bad enough to permanently stain the land. In other cases, there's a disaster—a huge catastrophe with a lot of deaths—and all of that pain and blood twist a place's energy somehow."

"And sometimes there are just places that are born evil," Brent finished. "Or at least, whatever made them bad happened so long ago there aren't even legends. People just avoid them and make up stories about why."

"That last one is what I think we're dealing with because the story of the area being cursed goes back so far," Travis said. "A genius loci is a primal spirit that is rooted in a place, an immortal entity tied to the land. Usually, when people consider a mountain or a grove or a cave to be sacred, it's because they sense a genius loci's presence and want to honor it."

"But it's possible for the spirit to become warped, turned to chaos," Brent jumped in. "And we think that maybe what we have is kind of a combination hell gate and genius loci, a doorway that opens every fifty years to let out the primal spirit, and then seals it away again until the next cycle. The spirit has to feed while the portal—the hell gate—is open. If it feeds really well, the bloodshed is even worse the next time the hell gate opens, because the spirit has gotten stronger."

"What you're saying makes sense," Cheryl said. "Because I can't say that the local historical society has any record of ancient satanic cults around Cooper City."

"I suspect that there was always something off about the area, but the lure of mines and timber—and now natural gas—was enough that people settled here anyhow," Doug said. "People will go against all their self-preservation instincts if they need money bad enough—or are so greedy that they don't care who gets hurt."

"If people hadn't settled around here, the genius loci would still have lured in sacrifices every so often, but it wouldn't have gotten so strong," Father Ryan mused. "It might have been a valley where unwary hunters disappeared, out in the middle of nowhere."

"But people built railroads and mines and highways—and permanent towns," Brent said. "And there was more for the spirit to feed on in each cycle."

"As far as the hell gate, it could be natural, the way cicadas live underground for seventeen years and come back again," Travis picked up the story. "Or maybe some forgotten witch back in the day tried to lock up the genius loci and failed. We don't want to destroy the hell gate, because I don't think we'll be able to destroy the genius loci, and we need to contain it. We want to limit the damage, and shut it away early if we can."

"So how do we make that happen?" Cheryl asked. "And are you sure we can't stop the cycle from happening again?"

Travis and Father Ryan exchanged a glance. "We don't know whether we can stop the hell gate from opening again," Travis said. "But if we can keep the genius loci from feeding well this cycle, maybe it won't be as strong the next time, and then we try to leave what we learn about fighting it so that the next poor bastards don't have to start all over again."

"Then we'd better get busy," Doug said. "Because we don't want to be here for the grand finale."

They talked late into the night until Travis had filled pages of his notebook with the ideas they came up with, and all of the cookies were gone. When Cheryl and Doug finally said goodnight and left, Brent knew they had generated a lot of possible tactics, but none of them knew for certain what would work.

"Do you think anything we just talked about will make a difference?" Brent asked Father Ryan, as the priest shut and locked the door and led them back into the living room.

"Won't know until we try," the priest answered. "But we've got more than we started with, including some good allies. Tomorrow we can sort through things again and make a plan. Right now, I've had about all the strategizing I can take for one day." He bent down to scoop up the big cat in his arms. "And a good night's sleep is worth a hundred Hail Marys when you're facing down the Devil."

"I don't remember that from seminary," Travis teased.

"There's a lot they forgot to mention," Ryan replied. "Now you're welcome to stay up and talk, but Lilith and I are ready to crash."

They were both too tired to keep working, so they followed him down the hallway to their rooms. But as Brent lay awake, waiting for sleep, he wondered what Danny made of their plans, and wished with all his heart that he could ask.

CHAPTER TEN

"HOW CAN IT BE MEGHAN? She died three years ago." The bewildered man buried his face in his hands, shoulders shaking. "Oh, God. What have I done?"

Brent and Travis exchanged a glance. Doug had called them before they left Father Ryan's rectory in the morning, with news that Cooper City had a new problem.

"You didn't do anything wrong, Clint," Doug said, placing a hand on the sobbing man's shoulder. "Far as you knew, there was an intruder trying to get into your home. You saw someone break down your door, with your wife and child inside your home. There's not a jury in the state that would fault you if it ever came to that."

"I swear, I didn't know it was Meghan," Clint said brokenly. "I buried her. She'd been so sick—"

"We'll take care of it," Doug assured the broken man. He'd had one of the officers escort Clint's wife and young daughter out the back door, with orders to drive them to a friend's house.

"Am I going to jail?" Clint looked up, eyes red, tears streaking his face.

"Can't kill someone who was already dead," Doug replied. "And it's not abuse of a corpse if the body was attacking you at the time. So...no. You're not in trouble. But I would appreciate it if you kept this quiet. We don't want a panic."

Clint nodded, but his eyes looked glazed. "Sure."

"I'll get Doc Brenner to stop by," Doug said. "Maybe he can give you something to help you sleep."

While Doug finished up with Clint, Travis and Brent walked the long way around the house to stay off the front porch. The door hung askew from its hinges, split down the middle and then blasted through with the shotgun shell that hit the unwanted visitor.

The corpse that had been Meghan Zimmerman lay sprawled on the steps, chest blown open. Travis and Brent waited by the cars while two young cops who looked like they were about to lose their lunch scraped up the rotted flesh and what remained of the decomposing body and shoveled it into a body bag.

"So this time, the zombies remember how to come home," Travis said, trying to rein in his anger and not having much success. Beside him, Brent looked unnerved and pissed off.

"Hell of a surprise," Brent replied. He looked a little green around the gills. "Do you think there's any chance she knew who she was? The other zombies, they were just shamblers. But this..." His voice trailed off, and Travis could hear the uncertainty in his tone.

"Did she really remember where she used to live, or did whatever pulled her body out of the ground give her a push and send her on her way for maximum shock value?" Travis kept his voice low, to keep the two police officers from overhearing. They looked like they were barely holding it together, as it was.

"I want to believe that she was a puppet," Brent said. "That's still horrible, but better than coming back to find out your husband had moved on without you."

Travis shrugged. "Isn't that what we tell people to do, after a death or a divorce? It's not like he ran out and got hitched the day of her wake." If Brent thought he had questions, Travis knew that his religious education created an existential chasm. *Can you have memory without a soul? Are our memories what makes our "self?"* The questions were huge, enough for a team of philosophers to debate for ages, and the implications might gnaw at Travis in the hour of the wolf, but they made little difference with the calamity facing Cooper City.

"How the hell can they keep this off the news?" Brent wondered aloud.

"Very carefully." Doug came up behind them. "The only people who know what happened are right here. My men aren't going to tell anyone, because I've told them they'll lose their jobs, their pension, and any recommendation I might have given them. Doc won't say anything. And frankly, no one's going to believe Clint."

"His wife—"

"Didn't actually see anything," Doug replied. "She and the kid were in the bedroom. As for what Clint saw—people have been seeing strange things around here for weeks now. Without a body, it'll just be one more ghost sighting."

Travis rubbed his eyes, trying to fend off a headache. "You said there'd been another situation."

Doug let out a long breath. "Yeah. I had meant to call about it, actually, and then Clint phoned 911, and everything went off the rails." He watched the cops transfer the body bag to the trunk of Doug's squad car.

"Not sure that's exactly by the book," Brent remarked.

Doug glared at him. "Did your police manual say anything about zombies? Neither did mine. Sure doesn't need an ambulance or a hospital, and that would just make the rumors fly."

"How about if I go say Last Rites," Travis offered. "And then you know we're going to have to finish her off, or she might be back."

Doug paled and nodded. "Yeah. I know. Go do your thing. I'll make sure Doc's on his way and that Chip and Jay," he added with a nod toward the officers, "head back to the station. I never thought I'd say this, but I know a place where we can burn the body without anyone noticing."

Travis usually felt peace settle over him when he said Last Rites, a calm that transcended even his hardwired guilt over speaking a prayer that, as a defrocked priest, he wasn't supposed to have the authority to offer. But now, remembering Clint's grief and Meghan's ruined body, Travis raged inside at the tainted energy bedeviling the citizens of Cooper City and wresting the dead from their graves. He hoped that for all his turmoil, the litany gave Meghan's violated spirit a final rest.

By the time he finished, the officers were gone, and a man in a late model gray sedan had pulled into the drive. From the way Doug greeted the newcomer, Travis guessed he was Doc.

"Didn't know they made house calls anymore," Brent remarked when Travis came back to the Crown Vic where he was waiting.

"Extraordinary circumstances," Travis replied.

"This whole place is like Schrodinger on steroids," Brent said as he got into the passenger side of the car. Travis knew him well enough by now to guess that the black humor was his way of coping.

"What worries me is, if we keep running around playing whack-a-mole with zombies and monsters and low-level demons, when do we have time to concentrate on shutting down the hell gate?"

Travis eased the car down the country driveway, following Doug's cruiser. Much as he lamented what the gravel would do to his undercarriage, he didn't want to think about how much worse it would have been if Clint had lived on a city street.

Doug led them toward the state game lands, then back a lonely drive to an abandoned farmhouse. Travis helped him lift the body bag from the trunk, then Brent covered them with his Glock as Doug opened the bag enough to sever the head from the spine. Gasoline from an emergency container fueled a pyre.

"You said there was another incident," Travis prompted as they walked back to the cars.

Doug looked like he had aged just since the previous night. "Yeah. Someone else got a surprise visitor. I might as well just show you."

They followed the cruiser down another country road, but thankfully not back to Cooper City. "I don't think we're very far from those cemeteries," Brent pointed out. "In fact, we're just on the other side of the woods."

"Yeah, I realized the same thing," Travis agreed. "Maybe whatever's creating the zombies can't control them long enough to have them hike all the way into town. Be grateful for small favors, I guess."

———

TRAVIS AND BRENT followed Doug after they left the burned-out pyre that used to be Meghan Zimmerman. "I'm afraid the next one isn't going to be any easier," Doug said when they parked outside a cabin near the state game lands.

"What's that godawful noise?" Brent asked.

"Follow me." Doug led them around to the back of the cabin, where a large, enclosed dog run took up a chunk of the backyard. The big cage was made from chain link, sized to comfortably hold several large hunting dogs. But the creature inside was not canine. A mournful wail sent a chill down Travis's back. He couldn't tell whether a creature was in pain or calling its pack, but it sounded feral and unnatural.

"What the fuck?" Travis recoiled as he realized what he was looking at. A boy who might have been about ten years old, hollow-cheeked and dressed in the rags of a nice shirt and slacks, crouched on his haunches, dead—and howling.

"Back away from there!" a man's voice commanded, and Travis heard a shotgun load. He and Brent raised their hands, but Doug turned slowly, hands still down at his side.

"It's just me, Ben. I brought people who might be able to help, like I promised."

Ben had the build of a linebacker who let muscle run to fat. His dark hair fell shoulder-length, and his thick beard looked more unkempt than intentional. He had frozen in place and paled as if he had seen a ghost.

"Captain Lawson?" he asked.

Travis glanced at the man beside him. Brent looked equally poleaxed. "Ben Thompson?" Brent finally managed, eyes wide as his gaze flicked between the wild man with the gun and the creature in the cage.

"I won't let you take him," Ben said, bringing the shotgun's muzzle up again from where it had dipped.

"It's me, Benny," Brent said, keeping his hands up but he chanced a step toward the man. "I got your back. Like always."

Travis glanced at Doug, who looked equally mystified.

"He wants to take my boy," Ben said, glaring at Doug, who had kept his hands in plain view.

"Put the gun down, Benny, and we'll talk. Like in Mosul. Old times. Okay?" Brent had eased a few steps closer, but not enough to make a grab for the gun without getting someone shot. The shotgun wavered, and Travis held his breath, hoping that neither Doug nor Brent did something stupid.

The dead child howled again, and Ben's expression went from defiant to despairing. He lowered the shotgun, and Brent moved in quickly to disarm him, passing the gun off to Doug as Ben collapsed to sit on the steps. Brent sat down beside him, while Travis and Doug kept their distance, not wanting to spook the man.

"Tell me what happened," Brent said. This was a different side to the ex-soldier than Travis had seen.

Ben's gaze fixed on the howling zombie inside the cage. "Jamie got hit by a car when he was riding his bike," he said. His tone was thick with grief, and he had a hopeless look in his eyes. "We buried him two weeks ago. His mama and I split up a while back, and she took off, so it was just the two of us." He paused and tried to compose himself.

"I shouldn't have let him go ride that day. But he wanted to go to his friend's house, and it was nice out, and he was almost eleven, and

I used to ride my bike places when I was his age, so I thought he'd be okay." He sounded frantic, as if he needed to justify himself to them. Or maybe, Travis thought, because Benny lived with his own relentless accusations every day.

"The driver was going too fast. Ran a stop sign. Jamie never made it to the hospital." Ben closed his eyes, straining for composure, and Brent laid a hand on his shoulder in support. "I watched them put his casket in the ground, and it was the worst day of my life," Ben said in a ragged tone. "And then, two nights ago, I heard a noise out back, and there he was, in the clothes we buried him in, wild-like."

Ben opened his eyes and glared at them in challenge. "But he's my boy, and he's back. I don't know how, or why. But I can't—I won't —lose him again."

Travis's heart ached for the man, and his anger spiked at the cruelty of whatever lay behind the zombies. The dark force that returned Jamie from his grave—and Zimmerman's dead wife from hers—was drawing its energy from their pain, toward an end goal that could only be even more horrific.

"Do you remember what we saw, that night in Mosul?" Brent asked quietly, leaning in as if only he and Ben were present. "That night we saw…her."

Ben's gaze darted like a frightened animal. "I try not to, but I see it in my dreams."

"So do I," Brent said, his voice low and reassuring. "It wasn't natural, wasn't something from this world."

Ben nodded in agreement.

"We think there's something like Mavet loose near Cooper City and Peale, and it's causing all the weird shit that's been happening," Brent said.

"But Jamie—"

"He's not the only one whose body's been animated," Brent said, and Travis knew his partner was choosing his words carefully. "We just came from a place where a man's dead wife attacked him."

"Jamie's gone feral," Ben confided. "Like his brain must not have gotten enough oxygen—"

"Jamie's dead, Benny," Brent said with quiet conviction.

"No! He's just messed up from what happened," Ben protested. "I wish God would just strike me dead because I let them bury my boy alive—"

"No." Brent's voice this time was a command, and Ben reacted reflexively, straightening his back and squaring his shoulders. "That creature in the cage over there is not Jamie, back from the dead. It's a hoax, by a spirit like Mavet, like we saw in Mosul, and it's just his corpse, brought here to torture both of you so the demon-thing can feed on your pain."

"Jamie—"

"His body—his corpse—is deteriorating," Brent said matter-of-factly. "We don't know that there's anything of Jamie left inside—his memories, or his soul. They're gone, the stuff that made him, him."

"But he found his way back," Ben said, utterly bereft.

"Or he was sent," Brent pressed. "Sent to torture you and maybe keep Jamie from his final rest. He can't heal. His body is decaying. Listen to him," Brent ordered. "If he can feel anything, it's pain. My friend was a chaplain," he added with a nod toward Travis. "He can help Jamie pass over. But we have to send him on."

"You got us out, in Mosul," Ben looked away. "When the others died, you knew what to do. I trust you, Cap. You know I do. But...he's my boy."

"You held it together that night, with Mavet," Brent said, dropping his voice in shared confidence. "You're a strong man, Benny. A brave man. And now you've got to do the right thing, for both of you."

"I can't put him down," Ben sobbed. "I can't do it."

"You don't have to," Brent assured him. "Just go inside."

"Can I say goodbye?" Ben looked up, eyes wet with tears. Travis guessed that Brent had put into words what Ben had known all along, even if he hadn't wanted to admit it.

"Of course," Brent said.

Travis saw Brent's gaze flicker between him and Doug, giving the okay for Ben to approach the cage.

The feral dead creature inside paused its howling to glare at Ben, recognizing him as prey if nothing else. It shuffled closer to the fence, sniffing and mumbling. Ben stopped a foot away from the chain link, out of reach, as if he recognized at least on some level that the Jamie-thing might be a danger.

"I'm so sorry," Ben said, tears streaming down his face. "I let you down. It's all my fault. I'm so very sorry, Jamie. And no matter what, I love you."

The Jamie-thing canted its head, looking at Ben through rheumy eyes, before it let out the thin, high howl of an injured wolf summoning its pack. Travis felt ice slither down his spine. He had no way to know whether some spark of Jamie retained enough memory to grieve—God, he hoped not—or whether he meant to call more zombies and kill them all.

"Go inside, Ben," Brent ordered. He gave Doug a look and a jerk of his head, asking him to accompany the man. When they were in the house, Brent met Travis's gaze.

"Say your prayer," he told Travis. "Then I'll take care of it."

Travis nodded and began Last Rites. The Jamie-thing shuffled closer, eyeing Travis and Brent curiously, more like a wary stray dog than anything remotely human. Halfway through the litany, Jamie began to howl, a soft, keening sound this time, and he fell to his knees, rocking back and forth. Whether a splinter of his soul remained intact enough to react to the prayer or the infernal power that animated his corpse knew its time was short, he didn't know. Travis stood behind him, hiding the gun in his hand, a silver round already chambered.

"Amen."

"Move."

Travis stepped out of the way. Brent raised his hand and shot. The high-caliber round hit the Jamie-thing between the eyes, shattering his skull. Seconds later, Travis broke the lock and brought his silver-edged machete down, severing the head from the body.

From inside the house came the muted sound of a gun firing.

"Shit," Brent muttered.

Travis knew Brent wanted to run inside to see what happened, and even without Travis's clairvoyance, he felt certain that Brent already guessed. Instead, Brent pulled out lighter fluid and set the pathetic corpse aflame, as Travis chanted a Psalm. Together, Travis and Brent headed toward the house. Doug met them on the porch.

"He went to the bathroom, and he either had the pistol on him or had it hidden there. It was done before I could stop him."

Brent sighed. "Had a feeling it was going to happen, now or later. Damn."

"It's finished?" Doug asked, looking past them to the smoking heap of zombie.

"Yeah," Brent replied. "It's over."

"For Ben," Doug said. "But there's more out there. Shit, I hate this part of the job." He ran a hand across his chin. "You two better get out of here before I call this in. You get the shell casing?" he asked.

"And the slug," Brent said.

There would be nothing to tie Brent's gun or their presence to the situation.

"Good," Doug said. "I'll say that we found the thing in the kennel like that, and Ben inside, who panicked when I came to the door. No one's going to look further, not with the shit that's going on these days."

"Call us," Brent said as he and Travis turned toward the car, then paused. "We'll be in the area for a while before we head back."

"Let me know what you hear," Doug said, looking worn. "I don't think it's over—not by a long shot."

CHAPTER ELEVEN

"I'M SORRY ABOUT BEN." Travis didn't glance at Brent when he spoke, but he didn't need to see his partner to know how the day's events had worn on him. Brent was hardly chatty, but since they had called a truce and decided to work together, he had gradually thawed a little, willing to make small talk on long car trips, and showing a dry sense of humor that meshed well with Travis's. Since the shooting, Brent had been quiet.

"That thing wearing Jamie's body—his spirit wasn't present," Travis said. He couldn't read minds, but he felt certain he knew some of what was bothering Brent. "Pretty sure Ben had been thinking of killing himself a long time before the zombie showed up. He's at peace now—yet another church dogma blown to smithereens," he added with a bitter edge to his voice.

Being a medium had given him enough of a glimpse into the afterlife to skewer most of what he had been taught in catechism and seminary. And while he was relieved to discover that suicide did not lead to eternal damnation, he still bristled at the damage done by such callous, ongoing teaching.

"Benny always expected the worst—and usually got what he

expected," Brent replied, head turned so that he remained staring out the passenger window. "That night in Mosul, when we survived Mavet, he had more trouble with it than a lot of the guys." He snorted. "I mean, don't get me wrong—having a major demon clean out a town like the fucking Angel of Death did a number on all of us, including me," he admitted.

"You seem to have figured out how to cope."

Brent gave a harsh laugh. "Is this coping? I kept running into demons or demonic activity when I was with the police, and before that, the Bureau, and of course, no one believed me except CHARON."

"CHARON?" Travis asked. He'd heard the name whispered more than spoken and figured it was a government version of the Sinistram, one of many that had come and gone throughout the years. Bureaucrats worried about psychics and came up with things like the Men Who Stare at Goats. The Church did marginally better since at least they were steeped in the world unseen. To Travis's mind, neither institution was to be trusted.

"Think of every movie you've seen with a black ops organization to stop occult threats," Brent replied. "And then make it worse. There's a reason those groups are never the good guys. CHARON lives down to the stereotype."

"And they want you?"

Brent nodded. "Demon magnet, remember? I keep saying no. They keep telling me that someday they'll make me say yes."

"Fuck them," Travis said, with enough heat behind his words to make Brent actually look at him. "I got recruited into something like that back in seminary until I got tired of doing their dirty work. Never again."

"The Sinistram?"

Travis startled. "How—?"

Brent nodded. "Maybe it's not as secret as they want to think it is," he replied. "I told a buddy about you, and he said that ninja priests were all Sinistram."

"Ninja priests, huh?" Travis managed a tired smile. "Yeah, maybe. But that kind of badassery comes with a price, and I got tired of paying it."

"So they let you walk?"

"Hell, no. They're biding their time, figuring they'll get me back sooner or later." He gave Brent a conspiratorial look. "Looks like we can be on the run together."

"Just like Butch and Sundance," Brent replied.

"Maybe we can skip the blaze of glory part." They fell quiet for a few minutes. "I figured we'd meet with the lead on the Silverado killings first, and then check in with Derek. He's heard chatter to suggest we've got a ghoul problem, on top of everything else. I've got a message from my friend, Jason, and I'm afraid that's what it's probably about."

"Works for me," Brent replied. He thumbed through screens on his phone. "I need some real Wi-Fi to send a report to one of my clients. Then I can focus on what we're doing, knowing the rent is paid."

"I got us a hotel in Bellefonte. Free Wi-Fi. I need to check in with Jon and Matthew, and plow through some emails." Travis turned his attention back to the road, but memories of what had happened in Cooper City were never far from mind. "Did you look at those news sites?"

Brent nodded, turning again toward the window, so his expression wasn't easily readable. "Yeah. Kind of a 'be careful what you wish for' thing, isn't it? Dead husband shows up and kills hubby number two. Dead kid shows up and pushes mommy off the balcony." He paused. "I thought you said that the zombies, like Jamie, didn't have sentience and couldn't remember who they were?"

Travis bit his lip, trying to figure out how to put his impressions into words. "I know that Jamie didn't have individual sentience. Could there be something like muscle memory, or like the 'stone tape' impressions of a repeater ghost? Maybe, but that isn't the same as awareness. I said Last Rites just to be careful, but I didn't sense a soul or a ghost, just like I didn't sense one at the earlier killing. But borrowed sentience...I think that's possible, and that it's malicious."

"You mean, whatever power is raising the dead knows enough to send a kid back home to his father or a wife back to her husband?"

Travis nodded. "Because it's maximum emotional damage, and like those psi-vamps you fought, and the hell-maggots, these grief demons feed on pain."

"So why ghouls?"

Travis shrugged. "Anything that desecrates the dead touches on very deep, primal reactions, even for people who didn't know the deceased. It's even considered an act of war. And I think that's exactly what this entity wants—to make as many people into bundles of raw emotion as possible so it can feast."

"There's your exit," Brent pointed out. Travis had to swerve to make the ramp, although he knew this stretch of highway better than he wanted to admit.

"Thanks," he grated.

Brent studied him. "Are you okay? You've been off since we left Cooper City. Is there something besides the obvious bugging you?"

"I grew up around here," Travis admitted. "So having the genius loci fucking with people in this area feels personal."

Thankfully, Brent left the topic alone. Travis hadn't pressed him for details about the FBI or the PD, figuring Brent would say more when—or if—he felt like it. They'd loosened up around each other enough to share a few more details, but Travis wasn't ready to talk about that part of his past, not yet, and maybe never.

TRAVIS HADN'T BEEN BACK to Bellefonte in years, but not much had changed. On one hand, that meant the town's good points were probably as he remembered them. On the other, so were the simmering tensions and small-town myopia. Change came slowly to second-tier cities like Pittsburgh, compared to major metropolises like

New York or L.A., but out here, the shifts in thinking moved at glacial speed. Those who stayed liked it that way.

"First up, another Silverado family," Travis said, trying to get himself out of his thoughts. He pulled the Crown Vic up to the curb next to a small neighborhood greenway with a sign proclaiming: "*Masulo Park.*"

"We're meeting someone here?" Brent glanced around. The grassy area held a few picnic tables, a basketball court, and benches overlooking Spring Creek. A pickup game was in progress on the court. Several people fished from chairs near the creek bank, and some of the benches were taken by walkers content to stop for a moment and enjoy the view.

"Ellie Durbin." Travis nodded toward where a woman sat alone at one of the picnic tables. He headed toward her with Brent a step behind, and Ellie looked up as they approached.

"Travis?" she asked, and he reached out to shake her hand.

"Hello, Ellie. I'm Travis, and this is my research partner, Brent." They took seats opposite the woman. "Thanks for meeting us."

Ellie looked flustered and smoothed her dark red hair back behind her ear. Travis figured her to be in her early thirties. "I wanted to come here because this is one of Rachael's favorite places. I thought you might pick up more of her energy here than in the house." Left unspoken was whether that connection would be with a vision or with Rachael's ghost.

"Tell us about what happened," Brent urged, leaning forward with his best "good cop" manner. Travis let him take the lead and sat back, observing Ellie and reaching out with his Sight.

"Rachael was coming back from an appointment in Milesburg," Ellie said. "Normally she wouldn't have driven I-80, but there's a bridge out and some detours on the back route, so she took the highway instead. That's what she texted before she left Milesburg. She never made it home." Ellie looked down, nervously twisting the stack of metal bracelets on her wrist.

"When did you call the police?" Brent nudged.

"I got worried when she was an hour late and didn't call," Ellie replied. "I texted her and didn't get an answer. Then I called. Nothing. After two hours, I got in the car and drove the route, thinking maybe she'd had car trouble and her phone died. So I drove to the truck stop, and that's where I found her car, but Rachael was gone." Her voice tightened, but she squared her shoulders and lifted her head defiantly.

"Did you ask around at the truck stop?"

Ellie looked at Brent as if he were stupid. "Of course. I talked to every clerk, every trucker, every person in the restaurant. They remembered seeing her talking to someone in a black pickup, but no one saw her after that."

"What about the driver of the truck? Any luck getting a description?"

Ellie shook her head. "The truck had dark windows, and apparently the driver was on the side facing away from the building. People remembered Rachael because her hair is so red. Reminds them of that actress from *Dr. Who*." She slid her phone across the table with a photo of a woman in her early twenties with long red hair and bright green eyes. The combination was definitely memorable, and Travis felt certain that anyone who saw Rachael would have remembered her.

"I don't know if you can read anything from objects," Ellie said, "but her phone was still in her car." She pulled a cell phone out of her purse and handed it to Travis.

Travis let the conversation fade as he opened up his Gift. Later, he and Brent would go to the truck stop and see what psychic residue he could lift from the scene. Now, he stretched out his awareness, trying to pick up any kind of vibe about Rachael, holding his breath and hoping that he didn't find her ghost.

He focused on Rachael's picture, then extended his focus to her phone. His gift wasn't psychometry—the ability to read an object's history or magic via touch—but he could usually pick up impressions about the energy of the person who owned a frequently-used item.

The energy he sensed seemed normal. A little tension, but if Rachael had been running late, that would make sense. Nothing about the vibe made Travis think that Rachael was afraid for her life, or was fleeing a pursuer. He pushed his Gift further, to include this park she loved so much. Now that he knew what Rachael's energy felt like, he could pick up traces of it near one of the benches, and here at the table.

"She likes to come here and sit and watch the water," Ellie said as if she could guess his thoughts, or perhaps his shifting gaze gave him away. "Rachael comes and borrows my dog to walk him since she doesn't have a pet of her own. Sometimes I pick up dinner, and we eat here, like a mini-picnic. It's kinda been our thing for a while."

The energy Travis picked up from the park felt contented and safe. Rachael hadn't left behind traces of turmoil, and nothing suggested any kind of tension between the two sisters. What he sought was a feel for Rachael's personality, and the hints he absorbed raised questions. Dimly, he was aware that Brent and Ellie had started talking while he tranced.

"Rachael seems like she's very sensible—good head on her shoulders," Travis said, interrupting whatever Ellie and Brent were talking about. Both of them turned to look at him, and he realized that to them, his remark came out of the blue.

Ellie nodded. "She's always been grounded. Even though she's two years younger than me. Sometimes it felt like she was the big sister because she was always planning, always thinking about what might go wrong and how to fix it if it did."

Travis pursed his lips for a second, needing to phrase his question right so he didn't lead the witness. "What about her personal life? Any enemies? Angry exes? Envious co-workers?"

"Rachael's a good kid," Ellie replied. "It's not like she was homecoming queen or anything, but she gets along well with people—even the flaming assholes. She hadn't dated anyone in a while, and the last relationship broke up pretty amicably."

Travis nodded, getting the answer he expected. "And I'm guessing the black truck murders have been in the news here."

"Oh, yeah. Can't turn on the TV without hearing about it."

"So why would someone as sensible as Rachael stop to talk to a stranger in a black pickup, even at a busy place like the truck stop?"

Ellie met his gaze. "She wouldn't have—that's what didn't make any sense to me. Rachael was a little freaked out about the whole disappearances thing. I was surprised that she decided to drive I-80 because of that, and a little shocked that she'd gone to a truck stop."

"We think the black truck is part of a bigger problem," Travis said. Even with Doug and others doing their best to keep a lid on the details, Travis knew rumors spread quickly in small towns, and that Ellie had likely heard the gossip.

"I heard someone say they thought a Satanist cult was behind all the weird stuff," Ellie said tentatively. "You know, like they used to say about gamers."

Brent rolled his eyes. "Yeah, well. Role-playing games don't really summon evil spirits. And I don't think Satanists have anything to do with this. We're trying to figure out what does."

Ellie drummed her fingers as she thought. "People have told stories about the area around Milesburg and Cooper City for a long time. They say the game lands are haunted, and that there are old mines full of dead miners whose bodies were never recovered and so their ghosts can't rest. You know, campfire stories. But they aren't new—my mom and grandma heard a lot of them all their lives."

Travis read enough of Ellie's energy to know she was open to the idea of ghosts and the unseen. He hoped she was an ally, and at this point, they needed a win badly enough that Travis was willing to risk trusting her, at least a little.

"When we leave town, we're going to go over to the truck stop and see what we can find out that the cops might have missed. But I can't shake the feeling that the spooky stories you mentioned might hold a clue. Do you think you could get people talking about the old tales and tell us what you find out? It could be important." He gave her his most trustworthy smile. "Sometimes, true things get hidden in fairytales."

"You're some kind of psychic, aren't you?" Ellie asked. She glanced at Brent. "And you're his bodyguard?"

"Close enough," Brent replied.

"I'm a medium, and sometimes I see things before they happen," Travis admitted.

Ellie's eyes went wide. "Oh, God. Is Rachael dead? Did you see her ghost?"

Travis reached out to touch her hand. "No. I expected to, but I didn't. Which might mean she's still alive. Let's keep believing that until we find proof otherwise."

Ellie sagged with relief. "Okay. All right. I can do that. And if I think about it for a bit, I can probably write up most of the stories from memory, but I'll ask around, without letting people know why," she added.

"Thank you," Travis said, standing. "It might give us the missing piece. We're going to do everything we can to find Rachael and bring her home." He hated that he couldn't add "alive," but that was too much to promise.

"I have your number," Ellie said. "I'll text you when I've gotten the stories together, and you call me if you find out anything. Deal?"

"Deal," Brent assured her as he stood.

———

"IF THERE ARE GHOULS, why isn't every TV news van already circling Bellefonte for the story of the year?" Brent asked as Travis headed through town and out the other side.

Compared to many of the other small towns in the area, Belle-fonte was doing well. The downtown boasted a number of well-main-tained Victorian homes and city buildings, and the main street had a selection of local shops and restaurants. Being close enough to Penn State to pick up overflow hotel guests on football weekends certainly helped the local economy, and many people in town either worked for the university, in the nearby town of State College, or at Rockview, the Pennsylvania State Correctional Institution less than a mile out of town.

"Because Jason's kept things bottled up, but he called me to come get a look since it's our kind of thing."

"He's one of your Night Vigil people?"

Travis nodded. "Yeah. Jason's got...talent."

"What? Telepath? Another clairvoyant? Bend spoons with his mind?" Brent asked. "Help me out—all I know about psychics I learned from Stephen King and Long Island Medium."

Travis chuckled. "Then you're in luck. Jason is a fire starter."

Brent's eyes widened. "Seriously? Like the book?"

"Like the legends—and quite a few books and old tales," Travis corrected. "It's a rare ability, and a dangerous one, but it's real."

"Shit. So he can light things on fire with his mind, and it's not magic?"

Travis shrugged. "If you define magic as hocus pocus, some power you harness from outside and channel to do your will, then no, it's not magic. If you define it as something extrasensory, supernatural, or a paranormal ability, then yes. I'm sure it would have been enough to get him killed as a witch in a past century."

"What does he do for a living?"

"He's a volunteer firefighter."

"Really?"

Travis nodded. "Yep. I kid you not. He can't put out fires with his mind, but he figured that he'd be in the safest place if he ever had a problem controlling his gift."

"Is that a possibility?"

"Apparently it's come up now and again. People got hurt, and Jason hasn't forgiven himself, so running into burning buildings is how he atones."

"Could the fire hurt him? I mean, maybe he's immune."

"I don't know. But I hope he's never in a situation to find out."

Travis drove out to Bliss Memorial Gardens, a newer cemetery at the edge of town. It was the kind of place he always thought of as a "mow-over" graveyard, where everyone had flat markers instead of headstones. While the grounds were planted with trees and flowering bushes and were well-maintained, Memorial Gardens never gave Travis the sense of peacefulness and remembrance that he felt in a traditional cemetery with monuments and gravestones.

"So where are the ghouls?"

Travis took the fork in the road that led to a large, modern mausoleum. "In there."

Rose marble slabs covered the outside of the mausoleum, which had two long slanted sides and two narrower, upright ends. From a distance, the entire building looked like a huge headstone, three stories tall. A blue Dodge pickup was parked by the main entrance, but no other cars were nearby.

"Jason's brother-in-law, Lyle, is the cemetery watchman. He saw 'strange creatures' lurking around the new graves and called Jason, thinking the two of them would go out and scare them away. They got more than they bargained for."

Brent frowned. "Fuck, why didn't we come here first?"

"Jason swore he had it under control. Said he kept one on ice for us to see, and he took care of the others. Lyle closed down the mausoleum to other visitors—said it was an electrical issue."

They parked and headed for the glass doors. Inside, the slanted walls and high ceiling gave the mausoleum a temple-like appearance. The floor was pink marble, while the etched nameplates were on gleaming white stone that glistened in the light of the frosted-glass wall sconces. Four drawers were stacked atop each other, rising twelve feet into the air, then a balcony encircled the building and another balcony above it. At the top, in the ridge of the ceiling, a stained glass window with an abstract pattern sent down multicolored rays of light.

It would have been beautiful, except for all the damn ghouls.

"Jason's good at what he does," Brent observed, stepping carefully to avoid charred bodies. At first glance, the corpses looked human, but a second look revealed longer-than-normal arms with elongated fingers. An oversized skull and clawed feet confirmed that the torched remains were not, and never had been, people.

"Thanks for coming."

Travis startled at the voice. He and Brent looked up to see a muscular man in his mid-thirties looking down at them from the second-floor balcony. Jason's brown hair was buzzed short on the sides, longer on the top, and his face and arms were streaked with soot.

"Looks like you had a hot time on the ol' town," Travis said.

"Funny. Not. I saved one for you. Come on up. Stairs are in the middle."

Brent pulled his gun, and so did Travis—just in case. Two cindered corpses sprawled on the wide marble stairs, and three more were ashy heaps at the top of the steps. A sudden growl and the snap of teeth made Travis and Brent take a step back.

"Shut the hell up." Jason raised a hand, and a bolt of fire streamed from his palm, quickly heating the handcuffs on the captured creature's wrists to red hot. The ghoul shrieked and then fell silent.

"We have an understanding," Jason remarked, never taking his eyes off the ghoul.

"That thing's even uglier with its skin on than it was fried to a crackly crunch," Brent remarked, keeping his gun in hand.

"How many, total?" Travis asked, glancing down the long corridor.

"Twelve," Jason said. "Gave me a real workout. Any more and I would have needed a flamethrower. Takes a lot out of me." Up close, he looked drained and weary, as if he'd worked hard and been up all night.

"Thanks for saving me a party favor," Travis said with a smirk and turned his attention on the remaining ghoul. Gray, leathery skin pulled tight across the enlarged skull. Black lips framed a mouth of sharp teeth. Bat-like ears, red eyes, and a tuft of scraggly gray hair on its otherwise bald head gave the ghoul a nightmarish appearance.

"I thought you might want a look at him before I finish taking out the trash," Jason said.

"What are you going to do with the bodies?" Brent asked.

"There's a crematory at the far corner of the property," Jason replied. "I've already done most of the work for them, but we'll put in what's left and fire it up. No fuss, no muss—no awkward evidence."

Travis stepped closer to the growling creature. While it looked to be barely five feet tall, its sinewy body and the talons at the end of its fingers and toes suggested that it would put up a tough fight hand-to-hand. "Where did they come from?" he asked, turning to Jason.

"Not sure. Lyle said he's had some problems with vandalism lately, and he thought there were wild dogs or some kind of digging animal. They didn't actually dig anyone up, but Lyle thinks that's because he's been staying around, keeping watch, and he started to turn on the security lights and leave them on all night."

Jason leaned back against the wall, but he also kept his gaze on the ghoul. "There's woods bordering the cemetery so they might have been hiding in there, but these sure as fuck aren't natural. Lyle and I got a glimpse of them, and so we thought we'd lure them in here, lock the doors, and call you."

"But obviously you switched up the plan." Travis looked down the hallway at the blackened bodies.

"It wasn't hard to lure them inside with some spoiled meat," Jason recounted, wrinkling his nose in revulsion. "But once they were inside, they attacked. Lyle shot a couple, but they were coming at us, fast. So I did what I do," he added with a shrug. "Lyle knows. He just hadn't seen me fire it up on quite that scale before."

"How do you think this fits in with the rest of the pattern?" Brent kept his gun trained on the ghoul as he took a step forward for a better look. The monster hissed at him, and Brent cursed at it in response.

"General emotional turmoil," Travis replied. "Having their loved ones' remains dug up and strewn across the cemetery would upset a lot of people. Can't blame them. I don't think it's about having the ghouls attack the living. All they have to do is stir up grief."

"You think there's something more behind this?" Jason looked from Travis to Brent.

Travis nodded. "Yeah, we're not sure just what, but I think we're getting close. Since it didn't feed here, it might not try again—maybe it will go somewhere else where there isn't someone like you who can easily contain it."

"I've got this hot-hands 'gift,' might as well use it for something," Jason mumbled. He'd always made it clear to Travis that while he accepted the reality of his abilities and the need to train himself in its use, it was not something he embraced or considered to be a "superpower."

"I think your talents saved this town a whole heap of trouble," Travis replied. "You did good."

"You need anything else from him, or can I toast the fucker?"

"Give me a second, and let me see what I can read." Travis widened his stance and squared his shoulders. Out of the corner of his eye, he saw Brent bring his gun up, ready to fire.

Travis took a deep breath and cleared his mind, trying to avoid thinking about the smell of charred meat and the underlying stench of rot. He forced away images of the blackened bodies in the hallway and the grimacing, snarling beast in shackles, and tried to broaden his senses, looking at and beyond the creature to the energies that surrounded it.

Ghosts. So many ghosts. They crowded in from all sides, alarmed at the assault on their sanctuary, frightened and confused. Travis sent consolation to them, doing his best to soothe and reassure. He urged them to move on, and said a very abbreviated version of the absolution and blessing, hurrying them on their way. Those that chose to remain gradually faded out, like guests in a motel who had come into the hallway after a disturbance and then returned to bed.

From the burned ghouls, Travis sensed nothing. Whatever

animated them was not the ghost of anything remotely human; rather, the energy felt tainted and twisted, like a polluted river. Hell-maggots infested the ghouls to Travis's enhanced sight, worming their way into the bodies and undulating beneath the gray skin. Fire and salt would cleanse sufficiently.

"They might be controlled, but they aren't possessed by anything worse than the hell-maggots," Travis reported. "Give me a chance to say an exorcism, and Last Rites, then you can go ahead and burn them, then salt the building. I hope we can take care of whatever's behind all this very soon, but until then, I'm afraid you and Lyle are going to need to keep up your patrols."

"Short of running an electric fence the whole way around the place, I kinda figured you were going to say so," Jason replied. "We can do that. Just let me know when you've got whatever you're doing done. I could use the extra sleep."

"You need help shoveling up what's left?" Travis asked.

Jason shook his head. "Nah. Lyle said he'd help. Between the two of us, we can handle it. Thanks for coming. I'll let you know if I see anything else."

Travis said the exorcism and final absolution, and then he and Brent headed down the wide marble stairs. Behind them, they heard the whoosh of flame, a piercing howl that was abruptly cut short, and then silence.

NEITHER MAN SAID MUCH as they drove away from the cemetery. Travis thought about Jason's dangerous and unpredictable gift and decided that glimpsing the future and talking to dead people seemed almost sedate by comparison. Brent kept his thoughts to himself, staring out the passenger window, fingers drumming on his thighs to suggest that he was mulling something over, not zoned out staring at the countryside.

"Holy shit." Travis slowed the Crown Vic as tail lights flared in front of him. Traffic on the two-lane state highway moved at a crawl, and up in the distance, Travis could see at least three sets of strobing police lights, as well as ambulances and fire trucks.

"I wonder what happened?" Brent leaned forward and turned on the radio. "News on the nines," he said with a grin.

They had barely moved more than a few car lengths when the local news update came on. "Police and emergency crews are on the site of an accident involving a minivan and a dump truck," the announcer said. "Traffic is being re-routed, and motorists are advised to avoid the area for the next several hours." He gave the route number and suggested alternatives. "We don't yet know the names of the passengers involved or the severity of injuries, but witnesses have reported seeing at least three ambulances, and we have on-the-scene footage of the van bursting into flames on our website."

Brent flicked off the radio. "Think it's related?"

"Seems like too much of a coincidence, although accidents did happen before the genius loci got fired up," Travis argued with himself over whether to poke around in town. The chance to learn something that might help them stop whatever was behind the blast zone was too tempting to pass up.

"I know how they're going to re-route us," Travis said as a uniformed cop directed them to make a U-turn and go back the way they came. "We can go to the diner in town and see what the locals are saying. There might be a reason the people in the crash were singled out."

"I hate this," Brent said, fists tightening in his lap. "I feel like whatever this energy or entity is, it's taunting us, and while we try to play catch-up, more people keep dying."

Travis turned off the road and wound their way into downtown Bellefonte. On the way, they passed several of the white and green Preston Energy trucks that seemed to be everywhere these days, thanks to the legislature opening up central PA for natural gas exploration. Some people welcomed a chance for new employment, while others warned of serious environmental damage.

"Wonder if they've driven the housing prices up here like they did in Pittsburgh?" he mused.

Brent caught on immediately. "I know. Right? Priced a bunch of people I know out of any of the downtown apartments when all the fracking headquarters came to town. Fuckin' fracking."

Travis's thoughts moved back to the hell gate. "I don't think the energy or entity is actually taunting us," he said, thinking carefully before he spoke. "I suspect it's more primal than that, more animalistic. A wolf doesn't taunt its prey. So I don't think the genius loci engineered the accident to trap us. More likely, it's like that bus crash—another way to stir up emotions, since the ghouls didn't work."

The set of Brent's mouth told Travis that his partner wasn't completely convinced, but the ex-cop didn't argue. Travis parked the Crown Vic, and they walked into a mom-and-pop restaurant called "Shelly's Place" where practically every seat was taken.

"I can seat you, but you'll have to wait a bit," a harried young woman said, flashing a tired smile that didn't reach her eyes. "You can stand over there, but don't block the door."

Travis went one way, Brent the other, edging in on the already waiting customers who clustered in the entrance. Brent clasped his hands in front of him, staring out over the busy dining room, but Travis knew the detective was listening closely to all the chatter. Travis intended to do the same.

"...out on Route 144. The Simmons family got hit by a truck—"

"...saw the ambulances go by. Van caught on fire. Heard it's already on YouTube."

"...can't imagine there'll be survivors."

The door opened behind him, and Travis had to step closer to the people bunched near him to avoid being run over. He bumped into a woman and murmured an apology.

"Travis Dominick? Is that really you after all these years?" The bottle-blonde woman in her middle years who was in front of Travis grinned. "Oh, my lands. I haven't seen you since...I don't know how long. What brings you back to Bellefonte?"

Travis felt Brent's gaze on him and knew he'd face some razzing when they got back to the car. He searched his memory for the woman's name. *Mrs. Kittering*, his mind supplied, along with the fact that she had been one of his catechism teachers and a very active member of the PTA. And, unfortunately, a friend of his mother's.

"Just passing through," Travis said, hoping he sounded sincere. Lying might be a sin, but hardly the worst he'd committed. Or, if some of the priests were right, a white lie hardly compared to the abomination of his gift. "We got caught in the traffic out on Route 144. Didn't look like we'd get through any time soon, so I figured we could come here and see if the pie is as good as it used to be."

Mrs. Kittering laughed. Her bright pink lipstick accentuated her pale skin. "Oh, the pie's awesome, like always. Which you'd know if you came home more than once in a blue moon."

Travis schooled his expression, although he flinched internally at her words. "My job keeps me pretty busy in the city," he said, and inside, he felt like a kid called to the principal's office.

"I heard you're not a priest anymore."

"I run a halfway house and recovery program. Similar work, different title." He tried to keep the defensiveness out of his voice. He wasn't entirely surprised Mrs. Kittering knew. While his mother had said she was utterly shamed by Travis's choice to leave the priesthood, she wouldn't miss the chance to get others to climb on the bandwagon against Travis.

"The good Lord works in mysterious ways," Mrs. Kittering said, patting him on the arm. Travis had no idea what she meant by that, whether she accepted his choice, or felt—like the Sinistram—that he'd eventually be forced back into the collar by circumstances beyond his control.

"The world's a very mysterious place," he replied as neutrally as possible.

"They've got a table for us," Brent said, tapping him on the shoulder. Travis didn't miss the curious look Mrs. Kittering gave Brent and wondered if his mother had asked for her friends to pray for his soul.

Travis didn't say anything until they were in the booth. "Thanks, man."

"I've got your back," Brent said with a grin. "Some enemies are scarier than others, right?"

"I prefer the ones I can shoot." Travis looked over the menu, which hadn't changed. "I imagine the cook is the same, which means everything's good—and homemade. And save room for dessert. It's worth extra time at the gym."

Travis scanned the faces at the tables around them. Some looked vaguely familiar, but he doubted he could put names to them.

"You think the genius loci knew, somehow, and decided to play with our heads?" Brent asked, startling Travis from his thoughts.

"Huh?"

Brent sat back, drinking his soda. "Benny served with me. So handling that situation wouldn't have been easy with a total stranger, but seeing him like that, knowing he—" Brent looked away. "It's rough. 'Upsetting' doesn't quite cover it. And now there's an accident that's not only going to be traumatic for the community, but it's in your hometown, and I get the feeling this isn't your favorite place anymore."

That was an understatement. "It's...uncomfortable."

"In other words, we might be off our game, exactly like the nexus wants."

Travis wanted to resist the idea that the energy had enough sentience to be conniving. Demons could certainly be crafty; after all, they served the Father of Lies—or some kind of chaotic energy. But the hell-maggots had been parasitic, and ghouls were notorious opportunists.

"I'm still trying to figure out whether the genius loci is a 'who' or a 'what,'" Travis admitted. "Forces of nature can be destructive without being malicious."

"Animals do some pretty complicated stuff that we say is 'just instinct,' but it's damn strategic," he continued. "And animals can learn. So if you've got a force with the intelligence of a wild creature that's been behind this cycle for centuries...maybe forever...it might learn a thing or two about how to lure in prey or avoid enemies. Doesn't mean it's truly sentient."

The server brought their food, and it proved to be just as delicious as Travis remembered. All conversation stopped as the two men dug in, and Travis savored the homemade meatloaf, mashed potatoes, and gravy, and Brent's pot roast and potatoes looked just as good. They polished off everything on their plates and still ordered pie—cherry for Travis, apple for Brent—when the server refilled their coffee.

Travis leaned back, feeling the knot in his shoulders loosen for the first time since they left the cemetery. All around them, conversation buzzed about the accident, the local family with four children who had been involved, and the truck driver. With first responders still at the scene, everything was conjecture, but Travis knew that tomorrow all the diners would have the scoop from friends and family who were the cops, EMTs, and firefighters. Small towns had plenty of secrets, but nothing stayed hidden for long.

"You've got nerve, coming back here."

The short, tiny woman who stood at the end of their table fairly vibrated with anger. She looked just like Travis remembered, except for more gray hair, and a few more lines around her mouth. Maria Grace Dominick shared the same green eyes and black hair as her son, but he'd gotten his height from his father.

"I didn't come because of you," Travis said, keeping his voice level and controlling his breathing. "And I didn't intend to bother you. We were just passing through."

Maria Grace glanced from Travis to Brent and back again, her lip curling. "You brought a friend here?"

Travis met her gaze levelly. "My work partner. And yes, I have friends."

"It wasn't bad enough that everyone in town knew you left Holy Orders," she hissed. Travis knew without looking that despite speaking in a stage whisper, the rest of the diner could hear every word and that the patrons had turned to watch the show. "But you bring your filth with you?"

"There's no point in having this discussion," Travis said, as he dug out his wallet to pay the check. "You didn't have to come over."

"I thought the priesthood would heal you, take away those sinful abilities," Mary Grace snarled. "Did they throw you out?"

"We've been over this before, mother." Travis raised his head and made eye contact. "They recruited me for those abilities, used them for their own purposes, and broke most of the commandments in the process. I left them, not the other way around."

"Liar! The Church hates what you are."

"Not when it finds a use for me," Travis replied.

"You shouldn't be so hard on your son," Brent said with a smile and an exaggerated drawl. "I'm a demon magnet."

Travis almost swallowed his tongue at the way Mary Grace sputtered.

"Demons killed my parents and my brother," Brent went on, as calmly as if he were discussing the weather. "I miss them every day. And here you are, hale and healthy with a living son, and you can't get your head out of your ass long enough to appreciate what you've got."

"Don't use that kind of language—"

"So saying 'ass' is bad, but hating your son isn't?" Brent's smile had turned shark-like. "Lady, your priorities are fucked up." He glanced at Travis. "Come on. We got what we came for."

CHAPTER TWELVE

"WE DON'T HAVE our information available online, I'm sorry to say," Connie Sciallo, head of the Cooper City Historical Association, said self-consciously as she opened the door to the archive. "Just hasn't been the money for that."

"That's all right," Trent assured her. "I'm used to researching the old-fashioned way."

"I thought at first, you might be either with those energy people, or one of the folks protesting," Connie said. At Travis's look of confusion, she smiled. "You know, Preston Energy? The people doing the fracking for natural gas and building the pipeline? It's been like a civil war around here, with some people focused on new jobs and others afraid for what all that's going to do to the drinking water and the mess they'll leave behind."

She sighed. "Gotta say, I'm of two minds myself. Doesn't hurt to see some good paying jobs here—although it's mostly outsiders doing them—and they spend local in the shops and diner. But I hear what the protesters are saying about earthquakes and groundwater spills and...I just don't know."

"Well, I'm not with either side," Travis assured her. "Just digging into local history."

Thanks to Father Ryan, and Brent's friend, Doug, Travis found himself with preferred access to the historical archive, which also seemed to double as the library rare book room and the newspaper morgue for the Cooper City Clarion. The room took up most of the second floor of the old courthouse, and it was obvious to Travis that whoever set up the archive knew what they were doing.

He'd expected to find a dusty attic stacked with boxes of faded, moldering boxes. Instead, floor-to-ceiling shelves were filled with color-coded binders. A microfiche reader sat to one side, and while the technology might be outdated, Travis had spent plenty of hours hunched over similar machines in Duquesne's secret libraries, accessing old documents.

"Looks like this is someone's labor of love," Travis observed. He felt certain that neither the town nor the county could pay for someone to organize and curate the archive.

Connie chuckled. "You're right. Hazel Monteleone was the powerhouse behind creating the archive. What a lady! She was a force of nature. She started the archive fifty years ago, right after the 'Bad Times,' when her husband and son were killed. Said she needed something to keep her busy, and a cause to direct her energy."

Connie leaned forward conspiratorially. "No one ever said 'no' to Hazel. She cajoled and sweet-talked—and occasionally bullied—donors and politicians into creating the archive and giving her the grant money she needed to get it off the ground."

"What was her interest?" Travis was curious.

"Hazel had been a journalist and a librarian, and she loved history. I think that's how she finagled the politicians—made them all believe this would be the guardian of their legacies," Connie explained.

Travis looked around at the oil paintings that seemed incongruous in what looked like the "stacks" of a library. A glance at the dignified old men in the portraits suggested that these were the politicos who had been hornswoggled into giving Hazel what she wanted, and the paintings were all the "legacy" they received.

"Where does the continued funding come from?" he asked, knowing enough about non-profits to follow the money.

"One of Hazel's best friends was the daughter of Wilfred Mackinaw, the president of one of the big coal mines in the area back then." Connie's eyes sparkled with the prospect of a good story.

Travis knew how much librarians and academics loved to gossip, and he'd figured Connie would be as much a trove of information as the archive itself.

"Anyhow, Isabella Mackinaw lost her father, husband, brother, and son in the Bad Times, and so when Hazel came up with the idea of preserving the history of the area, Isabella loved the notion and made sure she had start-up money and a big enough endowment to last from now until Kingdom-come."

"That's the second time you've mentioned the 'Bad Times,'" Travis said. "What do you mean?"

Connie perched on the edge of one of the solid wooden work tables, warming to the subject. "Fifty years ago this area had a real run of bad luck. There was a mine collapse, and one of the coal seams caught fire. Not as bad as over in Centralia, thank heavens, but bad enough."

Travis knew about Centralia, a now-abandoned town where the coal fires beneath were expected to burn for at least a century.

"Two big railroad trains collided and killed a lot of people—passengers, train employees, and station crew. Hazel's husband was the engineer on one of the trains, and he died in the crash. Then there was a flu outbreak, and dozens of people died—including Hazel's son and Isabella's father. A bridge collapsed, and Isabella's husband and son were in a car that was on it at the time. They died. Two whole blocks in downtown Cooper City caught fire and burned to the ground. Isabella's brother was killed when he was in a nearby building, and the heat caused a natural gas explosion." She shook her head. "It was awful. So...the Bad Times."

The timing was right for the hell gate cycle, and from what Connie shared, the energy or entity behind the calamity had created plenty of misery for its feast. "Would the documents about everything that happened during the Bad Times be here, in the Archive?" Travis asked, and found himself holding his breath. This was why he had made the trip back to Cooper City, hoping he could piece together clues from old newspapers. Hazel's involvement, together with Isabella's backing, made him hopeful that he might find even more than he'd expected.

"Oh, yes," Connie replied. "As well as Hazel's diaries."

"Diaries?" Intuition told Travis to pay attention.

Connie nodded. "Hazel said in later years that she took up keeping a diary—we'd call it 'journaling' today—to help her through her grief. She wrote some articles for the newspaper, although she wasn't officially on staff—times being what they were and all—but she certainly had a journalist's eye for news. When she died, the City Council declared her the 'official historian' of Cooper City. There's a plaque to her memory over by the courthouse. Too bad they didn't make that fuss over her while she was alive."

"I'd like to dive into the reference material, but if I have questions later, can I ask you?" As sure as Travis was that Connie would be a good resource, he knew he could ask better questions once he had more facts, and he was itching to get a look at Hazel's diaries.

"Of course! There's no gossip as good as fifty-year-old gossip," she said with a laugh. "Kind of like wine—it gets better when it ages!"

Connie showed Travis where Hazel's diaries were kept, warned him to wear cotton gloves to protect the fragile paper, and pointed him toward the section of the archive that held all the materials from the period of the "Bad Times." Then she left him alone, and Travis eyed the shelves like a hungry man with a cheeseburger.

Travis found the diaries for 1968 and settled into a chair. Soon, he was sucked into the narrative. Hazel had an engaging voice and a unique writing style that read like a novel. From her descriptions of the town and its inhabitants, it was clear that she also had a sharp mind, an eye for detail, and a historian's insight into human nature.

More than once Travis sensed another presence nearby, but when he tried to hone in with his Sight, the impression slipped away. He didn't feel threatened, merely watched, as if the spirit might be trying to figure out his motives.

"Hazel?" he said quietly. "If you're here, I'm on your side. I think there's something going on now that happened before, and I want to stop it. So I'd appreciate any help you can give me."

He felt his throat tighten as Hazel's journal reported on the disasters that claimed her loved ones, made all the more heartbreaking because of the clear-eyed, unemotional way she recounted the details. Hazel's diary went on to document the epidemic and the accidents, and other smaller, but deadly, disasters. It all seemed to come to a head in the catastrophic downtown fire that leveled much of the city, killed dozens, and left hundreds of businesses ruined and apartment-dwellers homeless.

Travis frowned as he read, and then re-read, Hazel's paragraphs after her account of the fire.

"After the fire that caused so many deaths and ruined so many lives, the calamity ended, as if someone had flipped a switch. There were many other stories confided to me by people who would never tell such things to a newspaper, for fear of becoming a laughingstock, or thought insane. I have documented those stories in my research. They are too strange for many to accept, but my fear comes from the fact that I do believe them to be true.

I do not think our misfortune was accidental, nor do I charge human malfeasance. I am not an overly religious woman, but I am convinced that an infernal power visited destruction upon our city for its own purposes, as it has done in the past. It is my intent to gather every scrap of information to document those Bad Times so that some future champion might save our descendants from the fiery trials that I believe are sure to come once more."

Travis mused over what he'd read. Hazel was a journalist, historian, and librarian. But she was also a woman, and fifty years ago, if she suspected something might be behind the Bad Times, no one was likely to listen, doubly so if the suspected cause was supernatural.

"So she did the next best thing," he speculated aloud. "She left a trail of breadcrumbs, in case it happened again, so someone else could pick up where she left off."

The longer he spent in the archive, the stronger the sense of another presence became. When it got to the point where he felt as if an invisible someone was looking over his shoulder, he set down the journal he had been reading and closed his eyes.

Hazel? Is that you? Travis asked silently. *I'm a medium. I can hear you if you have anything you want to tell me.*

The temperature in the archive plummeted, and Travis's breath misted in the cold. When he opened his eyes, he saw a transparent form slowly taking shape a few feet away from where he sat. The ghost of a woman in her late seventies grew more distinct. With her short-cropped gray hair and tailored pantsuit, Hazel looked much like the framed photograph near the room's entrance.

"You knew that something strange was behind the Bad Times, didn't you?" Travis asked out loud after realizing he was alone with the ghost.

Hazel nodded.

It didn't surprise Travis that Hazel had remained to stand watch over her precious archive, safeguarding it so that the information she compiled might prevent another cataclysm.

"Do you know where the power is the strongest?"

Near the mines. Hazel's voice sounded far away. *Go to the mines.*

Travis knew there had been mining near Cooper City, but those had been shut down long ago, perhaps even before Hazel's time. Locating old maps rose to the top of his to-do list. "I think there's a cycle that repeats every fifty years or so, and it's started again. My friends and I want to stop it—or at least, contain the damage."

It always ends in fire.

"Did you realize there was a cycle?"

Again, the ghost nodded. *Always, mines and fire.*

"Did you find a way to stop it?" The more Travis learned, the greater his desperation to find a way to prevent a catastrophe—and the stronger his fear grew that he might not be able to do so.

Can't stop it, but can starve the fuel. Hazel's appearance had grown less solid-looking, and her voice weakened. Travis knew that even a spirit with Hazel's will and purpose could only maintain contact for a short period.

"Thank you, for what you put together," Travis told the ghost. "We'll do our best not to let you down."

Hazel looked pleased as her image faded and she vanished.

"Shit," Travis muttered, turning his attention back to the stack of books in front of him. "How do you unplug the apocalypse?"

As he read Hazel's journals, Travis made notes of dates and key events, as well as the names of local people at the forefront of the disaster response efforts. Checking the binders and microfiche gave him additional information, although the most helpful resources were the first-hand accounts Hazel documented on recordings that were later transcribed. By the time Connie came to collect him because the archive was about to close, he had read enough of the transcripts to confirm that the current chaos was history repeating itself.

"You've skipped lunch, and you're late for dinner," Connie chided. "I hope you found what you were looking for."

"Hazel really was a spitfire," Travis replied admiringly. "She must have been a very special lady."

"She's always been my hero," Connie confided. "I mean, there she was, widowed and losing her son, at a time when women were just starting to get a chance to do real jobs, and she set out to do something and did it. I wish I could have met her."

"Did her interest in local history go back farther than the Bad Times?" If Helen had figured out that something supernatural lay behind the catastrophes and feared it would happen again, perhaps she had documented the previous cycle.

"Now that you mention it, she did," Connie replied. "There were tales about another period like the Bad Times that happened a long time ago, and Hazel reached out to the old-timers around here to get their stories and try to find diaries and newspapers from those years. She was working on that project when she died, so I'm not sure she ever finished her research, but what exists is in the archive."

"I have a favor to ask," Travis said, mentally crossing his fingers for luck. "The research Hazel compiled—might I be able to borrow it overnight? I'd even leave you my driver's license as collateral if you want. And I promise to have it back first thing in the morning."

Connie cleared her throat. "If you were just some yahoo who walked in off the street, the answer would be 'no.' But seeing how both Father Ryan and Doug Conroy speak so highly of you—and you went to Duquesne, like my cousin Vincent—I can let you sign it out. And I don't even need to keep your license, because Doug will track you down like a dog if you make off with it." She said that last bit with a laugh, but Travis didn't doubt her protectiveness over Hazel's legacy.

"Thank you," Travis said. "You really do have a marvelous collection." Hazel's single-minded focus—obsession—with preserving the region's history was one more reason he felt certain that her real reason aligned with his interest and the desire to save Cooper City from the fifty-year cycle of horrors.

"Out of curiosity," he asked as he stood in the hallway while Connie locked up, "where is Hazel buried?"

"Rolling Meadows Cemetery," Connie replied. "Over on the Milesburg side of town. But she really just has a headstone there. Her will demanded that she be cremated, even though that wasn't real common around here back then. So her ashes are in an urn in the archive, and we have her wedding ring and her favorite necklace in a display case with them."

That explained how Hazel was able to manifest so strongly, Travis thought and found his admiration rising for what she had accomplished. And since she believed in the appearance of supernatural creatures, she might have also wanted to guard her remains from ghouls. If she suspected a supernatural cause for the Bad Times, was putting her ashes and sentimental jewelry in the archive a way to add her ghost to the resources available to a future champion? At this point, Travis wasn't going to rule out that possibility.

He drove back to the small motel on the outskirts of town where he and Brent had taken rooms. It was the old "motor inn" style, a one-floor stretch of rooms with doors opening to the outside and parking spaces right in front. The owners had embraced the retro vibe in their vintage neon sign and the nostalgic metal chairs that sat beneath each window.

Travis juggled the take-out containers as he knocked on the door to Brent's room. Part of their deal had been that Travis would pick up dinner on his way back, while Brent researched online.

"Finally! I thought I was going to gnaw off an arm." Brent rose to help carry in the containers from the diner. He cleared away an empty pizza box from the end table. "Lunch feels like it was forever ago. I'm starving."

Travis set out their food while Brent moved his computer onto the bed while they ate. Turkey, stuffing, and mashed potatoes for him, lasagna and garlic bread for Brent, and large soft drinks for both of them. The food was as good as it smelled, and the two men dug in, leaving conversation until they had finished.

When they both pushed back from the table, Brent took a final slurp of his soda. "I spent the day going through mythology, bestiaries, and lore sites, looking for a match for creatures that abduct their prey. And I think the Silverado killer might be a spriggan."

"Cornish fey?" Travis asked, frowning.

Brent nodded. "A lot of the people who settled in this area were from Cornwall and many of the rest from Wales. Both areas have tales about that sort of creature."

"Can't say that I've heard of one that could drive a truck."

"I think the spriggan might be capable of some kind of projection to hide its true form, and that the creature was able to influence someone it used to do its dirty work—like drive," Brent said.

"I'm betting on the latter," Travis said, thinking as he spoke. "The truck is real. It showed up on video. Although if the spriggan could create hallucinations, that would explain why no one could recall the license plate or got a look at the driver."

Brent nodded. "The driver was probably its first victim. But if it's fey, then we know iron and salt will hurt it. We just have to find the damn thing."

"Hazel said to look to the mines."

"Who's Hazel?"

Travis told Brent about the archive and Hazel's ghost. "I was planning to spend the evening reading her research—we might find out more about the kinds of creatures the genius loci juices up." He paused. "Oh—if you can find a map of where all the old mines are, that could be a big help."

"Sounds good. I was going to see what else I could dig up about fighting the fey, and make a list of supplies," Brent said. "And I picked up a couple of cartons of Yuengling. Help yourself."

Since his room was next door and Travis didn't plan to drive anywhere, he went to grab them each a bottle, then helped clean up the dinner trash. He settled into the worn armchair in the corner, while Brent returned his laptop to the table and hunkered down. The longer Travis was in the old motel, the more aware he became of the vestiges of spirits who had breathed their last in the area. He went to the window and drew back the black-out drapes to look out at the parking lot.

He saw a gray figure start across the highway, then be thrown several feet from a phantom impact. After a few seconds, the figure reappeared and began its doomed trek again.

"Ghosts?" Brent asked.

Travis nodded. "Yeah. Several, but the one I can see right away is a repeater out by the road. Looks like the poor bastard got hit trying to get across, and never left."

"Can you send him on?"

"Doubtful. Repeaters aren't sentient. They're an emotional burst that's so strong it's made an impression on the surroundings, which is why some people call them 'stone tape' images. It's like a movie clip that plays over and over. Just a projection, but no soul's really there."

"How do you see this stuff and not go bonkers?" Brent asked. "I mean, for all my weirdness, I don't see demons everywhere I go, for fuck's sake.

"Maybe 'bonkers' is in the eye of the beholder," Travis replied with a bleak chuckle. "The talent has always been there, and I didn't realize everyone else didn't see them until I made the mistake of asking about it."

"Ouch," Brent said, probably remembering their run-in with Maria Grace. "So like that kid in *The Sixth Sense?*"

"Yeah, pretty much." Travis glimpsed another ghost off at the edge of the parking lot that bore what appeared to be a bullet wound. From the clothing, Travis guessed the man died back in the 1970s. Somewhere in the long row of rooms, Travis sensed a suicide's ghost and a young woman who died from an accidental overdose. For some reason, spirits clung tighter to bed and breakfasts or mom-and-pop motels than they did to big chain properties.

"How do you keep from spending all your time banishing ghosts?" Brent looked up, sincerely interested in the answer.

Travis had always struggled to explain what it felt like to have his gift to those without psychic abilities. "When you were a cop, you probably didn't bust every car on the highway that went over the speed limit, or every drunk you saw on the sidewalk."

"There wouldn't have been enough hours in the day," Brent said. "We went after the ones who posed the greatest threat, and figured we'd catch the others another day."

Travis nodded. "Same thing with ghosts. If they aren't in pain and they aren't harming anyone, I let them be. Doesn't mean they aren't still a distraction."

He returned to his chair and started to read Hazel's research journal of the Bad Times. As he read about the events, he felt sure he could match them to the people mentioned in her diaries, only now he had the additional insight into the supernatural creatures that had been part of the cataclysm.

Brent tapped away at the keyboard, and Travis hoped he was coming up with a plan to stop the spriggan. Hazel's unfinished project might not have included everything that she hoped to catalogue, but both the monsters and the locales she described were glaringly familiar.

"I really can't believe people stayed in the area," Travis said as he leaned back and set the book aside. "The same kinds of things happening now happened back then—and I bet they also happened fifty years before that. Some of the locations changed, probably because of where traffic shifted. And there were more train and bus accidents back then, where now it's been cars. But the pattern's unmistakable."

"So why didn't everyone just pack up and leave?" Brent took the opportunity to stretch and crack open a new bottle of beer. "Or, to ask it a different way—why didn't people leave after every previous cycle?"

Travis took a long pull from his Yuengling and thought for a moment before replying. "Look at everything that's happening now. No one's shouting about the area being cursed or saying that this is all some kind of supernatural attack. People just accept that there's been a run of bad luck. Conspiracy theorists aside, most folks go with the simplest answer. And even when there's clear evidence that the simple answer isn't right, people stick with the answer that least threatens their established beliefs."

"So you're saying that people would rather just see bad luck than to wrap their heads around the notion of a demonic attack," Brent recapped. "Sounds mighty familiar," he added, sarcasm dripping from his words. "Back when my folks and Danny were killed, the neighbors who had known me all my life thought it made more sense to figure I'd suddenly become a serial killer and somehow snuck back into town that night than that there could be something supernatural going on."

Travis nodded. "A lot of people have immediate family or friends affected by what's been going on, but for others, it's second or third-hand. So they might feel upset about the deaths or be frightened, but they won't have enough details to find a supernatural explanation believable."

"And the people who do have first-hand exposure are so wrapped up with their loss that they aren't going to notice the weird pieces that don't make sense, or they'll figure that it's warped by their emotions," Brent added.

Travis nodded. "Yeah. Which makes Hazel and Isabella so remarkable. Hazel realized that more was going on than met the eye, and Isabella must have also believed. She couldn't win the fight in her own era, so she left us all the information she could, hoping someone else would pick it up the next time the cycle came around."

Brent leaned from one side to the other to crack his back. "The internet is surprisingly unhelpful about how to kill a fey-creature. At least, if you want information that doesn't come from a TV show or a role-playing game. But...even those seem to agree on a few things. Salt, sugar, iron. Silver, if they're dark fey, which these might be since they're murderous little bastards. Oh, and we should wear our clothing inside-out when we go to fight them and put stale bread in our pockets."

"Seriously?"

Brent shrugged. "I don't make this stuff up. At worst, we look like we were on an all-night bender."

"I can live with that," Travis said. He slid down in his chair and gestured toward the ledger. "Hazel got everything right—the zombies, the suicides near Peale, the disappearances. Even the ghouls and some other monsters we haven't seen, but that might mean people who encountered them didn't know to connect with us."

"If they didn't call Doug or Father Ryan, they wouldn't," Brent agreed.

"Hazel told me that the mines were the key, and that 'it always ends with fire.' In her notes, she kept coming back to the Zimmer mines, specifically mines eight. I've got to think that, she didn't pick that location by accident."

"I did some poking around on local history, from a little different angle," Brent said. "I documented all the really big disasters, going back a hundred and fifty years, so three cycles. And I looked at some of the legends told about this area."

"And you're going to tell me that Peale—or Cooper City—was built on top of a Native American burial site?" Travis asked, still snarky despite how tired he felt.

"Worse. Seems like the tribes in these parts avoided this area completely. Said there were 'bad spirits' in these hills. Even their hunters stayed away, and there were stories that those who didn't— native or settler—often weren't seen again."

"Fuck." Travis finished his beer and set the empty bottle aside. "So if the evil goes back that far, maybe it got its feast from making the deer die off, or setting the forest on fire."

"Or maybe it didn't use to be as big and powerful as it is now, without a couple hundred years of stupid people living right next to it and giving it big meals." Brent looked annoyed, and Travis couldn't blame him. Human arrogance, either the denial that anything super- natural could be real, or the insistence that anything occult couldn't hurt anyone, often made his job that much harder and got lots of people killed.

"Does Hazel's journal happen to suggest how to shut the nexus down?" Brent idly turned the bottle between his fingers. "You said it was a collection of her commentary as well as the research she documented."

"I don't think we can stop a genius loci permanently," Travis replied. "Not according to everything I've read. Although maybe we can starve it down to be less powerful the next time. But Hazel seemed to think it could be shut off before it had run its course— before the big fire."

"How?"

"In her notes, she recounts an old legend about a powerful wizard who found a traitor among the legions of the dead. The 'traitor' could close the portal between the realms from the other side."

Brent's eyebrows rose. "Really? That sounds like something out of a video game. Maybe this lady missed her calling. She should have worked for one of the gaming companies."

"I don't know what resources Hazel had, or if she ever found out that anyone around her had psychic abilities," Travis replied. "I mean, I wouldn't want to go stand in the park downtown nowadays and announce what I can do with a megaphone. People are way better about those things now, but I still might get run out of town by the church crowd. It would have been worse in Hazel's time, or before."

"So we have you, and Derek, and Jason—and maybe some of your other Night Vigil friends?"

Trent nodded. "A lot of them don't have abilities that would be much use in a fight. But Derek and Jason and I have talents that could definitely help. And you, Doug, and Father Ryan can watch our backs—maybe Michael, too."

"Michael?"

"He works night security in Clarion. Used to be an Army Ranger. Had a situation kind of like the one you ran into in Mosul with Mavet, only with what was probably a nest of vampires. He was the only survivor. The Army patched him up and gave him a psych discharge. He doesn't have any special paranormal abilities, but he used to be a sniper."

"Damn. That could be handy."

"Yeah. That would make seven of us for the actual fight, and I can tap some of the other Night Vigil folks who have clairvoyance or far sight to see if they can provide intel." He grimaced. "I wish I could count on getting a vision with lots of useful information, but I can't control when those come, or what I see."

"Sounds like a better plan than anything else we've had," Brent said, finishing his drink. "How about we go toast that son of a bitch spriggan tomorrow. And at least we can bring the Silverado killings to an end." He looked pensive. "Do you think we'll find any of the people he's kidnapped still alive?"

"No idea," Travis replied. "But if they are, we'll bring them home."

CHAPTER THIRTEEN

BRENT FELL BACK ASLEEP hard after breakfast the next morning. Travis left to return Hazel's book, but Brent promised himself a little more shuteye. His dreams had been dark but fragmented, enough to keep him from sleeping well without allowing him to remember any of the images when he startled awake. Exhausted, he pulled the covers over his head and promised himself he'd get up in an hour, maybe sooner.

He was on the football field at his high school, tossing the pigskin back and forth with Danny. Brent glanced down at his right hand and saw the scar he'd gotten in the Army from a sharp piece of metal, so he knew time hadn't changed for him, but Danny remained frozen at eighteen, as young and perfect as he'd been the last time Brent had seen him alive.

The football grazed his shoulder, jarring him out of his thoughts. "Oh no, too slow!" Danny mocked with a wide grin as he strode closer. All Brent could do was stare, drinking in the sight of his brother, feeling the familiar chasm open in his heart.

"I missed you," Brent managed as Danny closed the gap.

"Looks more like you missed the ball, bro," Danny replied. His smile vanished. "And you're missing the point."

The football field vanished, leaving them in the gray antechamber Brent had experienced before. "What point, Danny? What do you know?"

"You're running out of time. Check the date. It's later than you think. I'll help you any way I can, but you've got to move fast."

"Do you know where the kidnapper stashed his victims? Can you tell me anything that'll help us shut this down?" Brent begged. Already Danny's image had started to blur, and the antechamber began to lose its definition.

"It's the deep places. Mines and wells. Gonna be fires of hell if you don't stop it. I'm here for you."

Brent thrashed awake, kicking clear of the thin motel blankets. He sat up with a gasp, then sagged with relief that Travis hadn't witnessed his breakdown. The sense of fresh loss that always followed dreams about Danny washed over him, dredging up the grief and guilt that were never buried deep.

"Fuck," Brent groaned, dropping back onto the mattress as he tried to regroup. He knew how quickly the memories of his dreams could fade, so he rolled over and grabbed for a pen and paper, scribbling notes so he could share Danny's warnings with Travis. Maybe they were just the product of his imagination. But now that he knew more about Travis's abilities as a medium, his doubts about the reality of Danny's visits lessened. He hadn't relived a remembered conversation; Danny's words sounded spot on for the situation with the hell gate and genius loci. Brent just wished the dead would learn to skip the riddles and speak plainly. *Or maybe they do, and it's us mortals who are always a step behind.*

———

BRENT TOOK the supply list and headed out. Travis had left him the keys to the Crown Vic, apparently opting to walk back to the archive. A stop at the building supply store yielded large bags of rock salt and a couple of boxes of small iron hardware. The local Walmart offered iron buckshot, lighter fluid, hairspray, sugar cookies, and powdered coffee creamer. Brent didn't care what kind of skeptical look the clerk gave him, relieved that the young man didn't seem to realize just how flammable some of the items were.

Travis was back at the motel by the time Brent returned with packages and lunch. "Find anything new?" he asked.

"I called Simon Kincaide. Told me the same thing about the fey hating iron and salt. He wasn't sure the bit about wearing our clothing wrong-side out and having bread in the pockets would help but said it wouldn't hurt. He did say that fresh cream made good bait to draw a fey out of hiding and that horseshoes over a doorway are supposed to stop them from entering. For what it's worth."

Brent thought the lore on fighting fairies sounded like something out of a Dungeons & Dragons session, but hours of searching online hadn't turned up anything better, and Simon had a friggin' Ph.D. in folklore, which ought to be good for something.

"I scanned through the information Hazel started to compile about the 1918 cataclysm," Travis said, digging into the burger Brent handed him. "The interviews she did with people who had survived that period matched up with what happened in 1968—and what's going on now. And I did find a map of the mines—took a picture of it in case you didn't find anything better."

Brent shook his head. "Everything I found is partial at best. You know what it's like around Pittsburgh—so many old mining companies got bought, went bankrupt, or had their offices catch fire that no one has an official, complete map of anything. It's just as bad here."

"Yeah, half the time no one knows there used to be a mine under a neighborhood until the street—or a house—drops into a hole," Travis replied.

Travis sent the photo of the old mine maps to Brent, who pulled them up on his laptop and did an overlay with the I-80 map showing the disappearances.

"If I draw lines like the spokes of a wheel from each place someone vanished with the black truck, the hub would be here," Brent noted, letting his mouse hover over the point of convergence.

"Zimmer Mine number eight," Trent said, looking up to meet Brent's gaze. "And here's another bit of news—there wasn't a mine number nine until later when a second access shaft was built. So when Hazel's cataclysm happened—and the 1918 event—there was only mine number eight."

"I've got the ammo," Brent said, crumpling up the wrapper for his burger and tossing it into the trash. "Let's go spriggan-hunting."

———

THE OLD ZIMMER MINE road was barely visible after decades of abandonment. Weeds and brush filled in the track, but nature had not yet obliterated the man-made gap between the older trees. Once he knew what to look for, Brent could clearly see the path. They took the Crown Vic as far as they dared, then loaded the supplies into their backpacks and began the hike.

"The weeds have been flattened," Travis pointed out.

"Yeah, your car might not be able to get through here, but a four-wheel-drive pickup could, easily," Brent replied. "I'd say we've come to the right place."

All of the disappearances had occurred at night, and everything Brent had found about the spriggan suggested it was strongest in the dark. That made daylight the best time to fight it, assuming they could lure it from its hiding place.

Tension churned in Brent's stomach, as they neared the closed mine. He'd gone back over the disappearances, committed the list of names to memory. Those that had been gone the longest, he doubted they would find alive. But the most recent victims might not be dead yet, and he clung to that thin hope.

"There it is," Travis said, pointing to where a black pickup sat in the shadows beneath a stand of trees. Nearby, the remains of the buildings that had once supported the mine could still be seen amid the overgrowth. The concrete arches of a loading area, the metal scaffolding of a tipple, and the tumble-down bricks of a small office building were almost all that remained of the once-busy mine. Not far beyond, weathered boards and a rusted steel grating blocked the entrance to a large hole carved into the side of a steep hill.

"Can you get anything with your ESP?" Brent asked.

Travis rolled his eyes. "I hate that term. Next, you'll want to know if I've heard anything on the psychic hotline." He paused, and his gaze lost focus. "There's a lot going on near here, a lot of energy, and most of it's bad. Ghosts in the mines—no surprise from all the collapses and fires Hazel documented. It's dangerous work in the best of times. Violence—maybe a strike? And over everything, it's like there's a dark film, an oily residue that's just...evil."

"The genius loci?"

Travis shrugged. "More like a side effect of it, I think. Or maybe it goes with the spriggan. Let's do the job, and see if it gets any better." He didn't have to add that the area had triggered a headache. Brent could see from the squint of his eyes and the pinch of his mouth that Travis already felt the area's effects.

The truck was empty. They checked it, careful not to touch or leave fingerprints or DNA. After they dealt with the spriggan, Brent would call Doug. Before then, the cops would only be a liability.

One by one, they eliminated the ruins and the crumbling structures as the fey's hiding places. Most were too small or offered too little shelter, and even the brick building looked like it had lain undisturbed for decades.

That left the mine, as Brent feared from the start. Going in after the spriggan would be suicidal, so he could only hope that the lore wasn't a bunch of malarkey.

In addition to turning their shirts inside-out, they had iron filings and salt in their pockets along with the bread crusts. Both men carried silver and iron knives. Travis's shotgun shells were filled with rock salt, while those in the gun Brent carried were iron pellets.

Travis covered him while Brent made a large circle with the rock salt on a bare patch of ground, leaving one part open for the trap. Inside the salt circle, Brent set a large bowl and filled it to the brim with fresh cream. Since a few of the sources also suggested that the fey had a sweet tooth, he added some cookies for good measure. Once the spriggan went inside the circle, he shouldn't be able to get out except through the gap in the salt, where Brent and Travis would be waiting.

Assuming the lore was right.

Brent dribbled some extra cream from the trap circle up to the mine entrance, dropping a few cookies as well. Then he and Travis found cover in the concrete ruins of a building's foundation and waited.

Nothing happened for long enough that Brent's patience waned. He fidgeted, checking the time, staring at the mine entrance as if he could force the spriggan from cover by sheer willpower. Travis gave him a glare that got Brent to settle but only for a short time.

After what seemed like an eternity, Travis raised his head as if he were scenting the breeze. "Something's coming."

When Brent thought of the fey, he pictured the exceptionally pretty creatures seen in movies or the equally impressive dark beings from his gaming manuals. Apparently, movie animators and game designers had never seen a real fairy.

The being that slipped cautiously from between the broken boards at the mouth of Zimmer Eight moved like a hunched ape. Its size—that of a chimp—strengthened the impression. The body was hairless, and its limbs long and thin, but the spriggan was hardly the graceful, elegant fairy from the illustrations in children's books.

Yet for all its oddities, something about the spriggan captivated his attention. Brent took a half-step toward the circle and stopped when Travis held up a hand. *Was this magic?* Brent had read enough stories where the fey tempted people away from their homes, into the marsh or elsewhere, never to be seen again.

"It's a glamor," Travis said. "Like a vampire can cast. You see the ugliness, but you don't care. It's the way it lures its victims."

Maybe the bread and wrong-side clothing helped, at least a little, or perhaps it was the iron in his pockets and the knives in his scabbards, but Brent saw the spriggan with an odd double vision. The misshapen creature, with its too-long face and frighteningly wide mouth, was overlaid with the image of a luminous being that morphed into the artist's ideal of a wood nymph the longer Brent stared at the monster.

"Look," Travis murmured, barely audible.

The spriggan paused as it followed the dollops of cream and bits of cookie, hesitating as it neared the broken circle. Travis had intentionally left the entrance wide enough that the salt would not crowd the opening, and Brent hoped that the ample break gave the creature a false sense of security.

Hunger won out over caution. The spriggan loped up to the opening and then through it, intent on claiming the large bowl of cream and the pile of cookies in the center.

Brent and Travis shared a look. *Now!*

The blast of Travis's shotgun echoed from the hills as the salt rounds hit the dirt, scattering and sealing the spriggan inside the circle. Alarmed, the fey drew itself up and screeched, a hideous, ear-piercing wail. Seconds after Travis's shot, Brent unloaded both barrels of iron pellets, hitting the fairy directly in the chest.

The creature screamed again as black streaks appeared from every place the iron pierced its milk-white skin. The glamor vanished, leaving only the fey's hideous true form, and it bared its knife-sharp teeth. The spriggan launched itself at them but drew back from the salt as if burned.

"Now what?" Brent asked. They had the creature contained, but he wasn't entirely sure how to kill the thing.

"You keep him covered, and I'll check inside the entrance to the mine for the victims," Travis said.

"You're the one with the magic."

"You're a better shot."

Brent conceded with a glare.

"I want to get the victims out before you cap him," Travis said.

"*Cap* him? Why don't I just *waste* him or *blow him away*? Did we somehow end up in a Bruce Willis movie?"

Travis shot a grin over his shoulder as he jogged toward the mine. "I'm just trying to speak the language of a hard-boiled private dick."

"Bite me," Brent replied, flipping him off for good measure.

Bleak humor in the face of danger felt familiar, a way Brent and his squadron coped when shit got real. Brent turned back to the spriggan, which paced its circle like a death row inmate, testing the warding and drawing back with a squeal each time as the salt repelled it.

"Settle down," he warned. "Your time is coming."

The image of a suitcase full of money suddenly filled his vision. Beyond the table that held the case and cash, an idyllic beach stretched toward the ocean. Brent heard music and laughter coming from nearby, as a warm breeze caressed his face. A figure on the beach waved, and he recognized Danny, healthy and whole, standing beside a beautiful woman who blew a kiss to Brent.

"Whoa!" he muttered, realizing he'd taken a step or two closer to the circle. Inside, the spriggan watched him, its golden eyes burning with an inner fire. Brent backed up, and raised his Glock, figuring that putting a silver bullet between the creature's eyes would be a first step to making it real dead.

"Try it again, and I won't wait for him to come back," Brent growled.

Had that been how the spriggan drew its victims within reach? From the knowing, crafty smile the monster gave him, Brent figured that to be true. What had it promised each of the young women it lured into the truck? Brent juggled the guns so he could close one hand around the bread crusts and iron in his pocket. Immediately, his mind cleared, and the spriggan growled as any remaining connection severed.

"Hurry!" Brent shouted as anger replaced the disorientation and allure of the fairy's trap. Money, luxury, and sex were generic bait, but somehow the monster had picked Danny's image from his mind, and that made Brent furious. Could the creature read his thoughts? Brent imagined taking the fey apart limb from limb, slowly and with a lot of salt. The spriggan hissed and jumped back, putting more distance between them.

"Fuck with me again, and I'll do it," Brent promised, leveling the Glock at the creature.

"Coming out!" Travis called. Brent did not turn, unwilling to take his attention off the spriggan for even an instant.

He heard the weeds rustle and Travis murmuring to someone else, but no other voices. After a few more minutes, the ex-priest joined him, shotgun in hand.

"Three of them were already dead, along with a man, whom I guess was the truck owner," Travis reported. "Looked drained dry, like mummies. If there were other bodies, they were farther back. I found two of them alive—the most recent ones taken. Rachael and Alicia. I got them out of the mine. They're waiting near the tunnel mouth, with the thermal blankets I packed in and some water bottles. Let's finish this, and we'll get Doug out here to clean up the mess."

"Thought you'd never ask," Brent muttered. His silver bullet hit the spriggan squarely in the forehead. The creature dropped to its knees with an unholy shriek, then threw itself in their directions, hands outstretched as if to rip them apart.

Travis's shot with an iron round caught the spriggan full in the face. Its head split open, and the rest of its body shriveled. Brent unloaded another two shotgun shells of iron into the monster, and the creature collapsed in a flash of light that caused them both to look away. When they looked back, all that remained was a cindered shell.

"Now what?" Brent asked.

"Burn the fucker," Travis said. "And chop it to bits, for good measure. Salt the remains. I saw those bodies in the mine. We need to make sure the son of a bitch stays dead."

Brent moved warily to comply, deciding this was one situation where overkill was a virtue. He hacked at the stringy body with an iron machete and sprinkled the parts with salt and iron filings. Lighter fluid set what was left of the corpse aflame. Travis stood watch for a few moments until he seemed sure the creature would not rise from the ashes, and then went back to check on the victims, who were just beginning to rouse from the glamor the spriggan had placed on them.

"We found them," Travis reported on his phone to Doug as he came back to rejoin Brent. "They're weak, and it looks like they might have been drugged, maybe in shock. But we've got two of them alive, and the bodies of some others are in the mine." He paused to listen. "Yeah, we're just leaving. Give us fifteen minutes for a head start, and we'll be long gone."

He turned to Brent. "Come on. I need to call Ellie and let her know Rachael's okay. Let's get out of here before we have to explain any of this. Neither of us would look good in orange jumpsuits."

CHAPTER FOURTEEN

"WE HAD A LESS than friendly visit from the diocese," Jon reported as Travis headed back from the archive. "They didn't *do* anything, but they made a lot of comments that could be taken as a threat."

"St. Dismas doesn't belong to the diocese," Travis snapped, then took a deep breath, remembering that his second-in-command knew that. "Sorry. I mean, the diocese doesn't have any control over us."

"No, but you know how sensitive donors are to any hint of scandal," Jon replied. "A word in the right—or wrong—ear, some vague rumors floating around, and our funding could get cut back. Donations could fall."

"Fuck," Travis muttered. No one knew how to play politics like high-level Vatican operatives; after all, they'd been doing it since the time of the Medicis. Machiavelli learned everything he knew from the cardinals; of that, Travis felt certain after his time with the Sinistram.

"Any idea of what they're fishing for?" he asked, doing his best not to take out his ire on his friend.

"You. Oh, besides that?" Jon answered. "I imagine whatever you did lately to piss off Father Liam has him trying to mark his territory and remind you who the alpha dog is."

"I'll call him. Not that he or the Sinistram have been remarkably helpful with the current fuckupedness," Travis grated.

"Can't imagine that central Pennsylvania is on their radar," Jon said. "Not big-picture enough."

"From what I can tell, it wasn't on their radar the last two times the cycle happened—and I'd bet money they didn't bother coming around before that, either." That was one of the things that always bothered Travis the most about the Sinistram, the way it picked and chose its involvement in ways that seemed more driven by internal politics than saving lives.

"Do you really want their help? Be careful what you wish for."

Travis glanced up. "No. Since they'd be about as helpful as the feds, rolling in and taking control and making everything worse." He thought of Brent doing the same dangerous dance to stay out of CHARON's reach. Ironic that they both found themselves saving the world in spite of the supernatural special ops folks, not because of them.

"I did my best to smooth things over, answered their questions, told them what they wanted to hear," Jon continued. "But it was pretty clear that they really wanted to talk to you."

"You didn't tell them where I was?"

"Hell, no! Matthew and I've got your back," Jon replied with a laugh. "But I'm sure they'll return, and they aren't going to take 'no' for an answer for long."

"If they're really as good at monitoring threat levels as they claim to be, I would have thought Father Liam could have figured it out for himself."

"Maybe he has, but he still wants you to come to him."

Travis felt sure that Jon was right; it was always a power game with Father Liam. No doubt that was part of what enabled his rise to the upper echelons of the Sinistram—that, and his ruthlessness wrapped in convenient piety.

"Travis? Are you still there?" Jon's tone told Travis that his friend had tried and failed to get his attention.

"Yeah. I'm here. What else?"

"I asked if you knew when you'd be back. If it's more than a few days, I'm gonna need to drive some paperwork out to you."

"Don't," Travis warned. "Stay clear. We'll figure out something, but stay the hell away from here. I have a feeling that it's going to come to a head soon, and when it does, you'll hear about it. Just...stay safe."

"You, too," Jon warned. "You're not expendable, Travis. I seem to need to remind you of that fact. You paid a little too much attention when they were talking about guilt and martyrdom."

Travis's laugh was bitter. "Yeah. Maybe so. Don't worry—I intend to come back, just to drive you and Matthew nuts."

"You still working with that PI, or is he dead in a ditch somewhere?"

Travis grinned. "Actually, we've got an understanding. He's okay."

"Well, whadaya know? The Lone Ranger finally found a sidekick."

Travis felt certain Brent would kick him somewhere else if he ever heard that reference. "Not exactly. But...we're good."

Jon was quiet for a moment. "I'm glad. Too risky to be doing this kind of thing all alone. Maybe it's true, what they say about 'mysterious ways' and all that."

"More like 'necessity is the mother of intervention.'"

"That's 'invention.'"

"Says you." Travis sighed. "Look, thanks for the head's up. I'll call Liam and get back as soon as I can. If you need something before then, there's always email."

"Be careful," Jon replied. "Matthew says he'll kick your ass if you don't come back in one piece."

"Duly noted." Travis ended the call, dodged a couple of white and green slow-moving Preston Energy trucks, and speed-dialed Father Liam.

"Travis. So good to—"

"Lay the fuck off my people," Travis snapped.

"I don't know what you're talking about," Liam replied, as smooth and unruffled as always.

"The hell you don't. Tell your diocese dogs to stop sniffing around St. Dismas. Threatening a halfway house is low, even for you."

"We merely want you to return to the fold."

"Sorry, I'm busy saving the sheep that aren't worth your while."

"You're meddling in things you don't understand," Liam replied, as his velvet tone turned to steel.

"I *understand* that a lot of people are going to die unless I do something to stop it."

"Every war has collateral damage. In the big scheme of things, there are much more important targets."

"Next you're going to tell me we have to destroy the village to save it."

"Sometimes, yes."

"*No.* Listen to me, you sanctimonious prick. I'm going to do my best to save some people who aren't important to your grand scheme. When that's done, I'll be back in town if you want to talk. But keep your dogs away from St. Dismas. If there are whispers of any kind that affect the Center...just remember that you're not the only one with a few well-placed friends." Travis ended the call before Liam could bluster in response.

Travis pulled into the motel parking lot just as a pizza delivery driver pulled out, giving him an idea of Brent's plans for dinner. His stomach rumbled, reminding him that he'd only had the motel's cold muffins for breakfast and a protein bar for lunch since he'd spent the day scouring Hazel's research for more clues to how to stop the cataclysm.

"Pizza again?" he asked as he walked in.

Brent grinned. "You're psychic, right?"

"No, dumbass, I passed the driver on the way in." Travis shrugged out of his backpack and headed for the cardboard box that held the pizza.

"Make any progress?" Brent snagged two pieces before Travis reached the box and dodged out of the way.

"Not as much as I'd like," Travis replied, deciding not to burden Brent with Liam's most recent shenanigans. "Validation that the 1918 cycle looked a lot like both the 1968 one and the current mess. Hazel had some bits and pieces about the 1868 cycle, and it matches, too. Although there was so much chaos after the war and such a frenzy of mining and new railroads and factories being built that big messy accidents seemed to be the rule more than the exception."

Brent nodded, his mouth too full of pizza to speak. "I have Simon looking into how to close a hell-mouth, hell gate, nexus...whatever we want to call it," he said when he swallowed. "And I heard back from Chiara Hamilton, my friend Mark's go-to researcher for hunter intel. She's got some ideas on how to stop the grief demons. Figured we'd want them out of the way before we go after the genius loci."

"Good." Travis paused to take a bite. "Because Paige called me— the pharmacist with the ghost sister?" Brent nodded to show he remembered. "She says Penny is keeping tabs on the ghosts, trying to find any who might remember the last time everything went down. She got a lot of warnings about wells, mines, and fire—and that time is running out."

"I had a dream about Danny, and he said the same things," Brent replied, sobering. "So I ran with it." He gestured toward the big white sheets of paper covered with scribbling he had taped to the wall from a flip chart, and the area map he'd pinned up beside it.

Travis plopped down in a chair, after snagging a beer and another slice of pizza. "Danny said 'it's later than you think.' You got the feeling from Hazel and Penny that the clock was ticking. I think I know what they mean."

Brent pointed to the white chart. "I tried to track down the dates for the last two events. It's hard to tell the start—sometimes an accident or a murder isn't part of a demonic apocalypse," he added with a grimace. "But it wasn't hard to find the end of each cycle because it's too big to miss. A mine collapse and fire. Burning most of the town. And before that, the 1868 event was a huge wreck with two big passenger trains colliding and exploding."

"Lovely."

Brent ignored his comment. He pointed toward the scribbles. "In each case, the event is one hundred and fifty days long. It might have an extra day or two on the front end, but the one-fifty is pretty solid. Which is where it gets tricky. Because depending on what you count as the beginning of this cycle...we have about four days left."

"Shit." Travis nearly choked on his beer. "That can't be right."

Brent nodded. "'Fraid so. Maybe a day less, depending on whether a car accident or a suspicious death counts, or was just bad timing."

Travis set the beer aside and found he had lost his appetite for the third piece of pepperoni pizza. "We're not ready."

"I don't think it cares."

Travis rose and walked over to decipher Brent's handwriting. "What's this?" he asked, flipping the page.

"I started looking at the history of Cooper City and Peale," Brent replied. "Making note of any old notable disasters. They might or might not have been part of old cycles. What I found was that while many of them were spread all around the area, one place keeps coming up over and over again."

He pointed to a spot on the map. "Bliss Memorial Gardens."

"It's not an *old* cemetery," Travis argued.

"No, but the land has been unlucky for a long time," Brent replied. "Which makes me think that it's connected. Maybe not the hell gate, or where the genius loci hangs out, but home base for the grief demons? Maybe." He took another bite of pizza. "I happened upon an article in the local paper—archived online—from when Memorial Gardens was dedicated back in the 1950s. The writer knew the area history. She mentioned that a cemetery was a suitable use for land that had been so stained with blood."

"Stained, how?" Travis moved to look at the map, noting all the red pins where bodies had been found.

Brent shrugged. "It seems to have checked off all the boxes to qualify for ground zero in a horror movie. All that's missing is a creepy overnight camp for horny teenagers. It was the site of a colonial-era settlement, which burned to the ground after its residents died from the plague. The local tribes avoided it—said it had 'bad spirits.' Over the last two hundred years, it's been the site of an orphanage, a hospital, a tuberculosis sanatorium, and a mental institution. None of them stayed open long, and all closed with tarnished reputations. Nothing fully proven, but allegations that there had been abuse, experiments, neglect, patients gone missing."

"Fuck. So maybe it wasn't strange that the ghouls picked Bliss."

"Maybe not," Brent agreed. "And the location is central between Cooper City and Peale. In fact, it's on land that was included in the original charter for Peale, and got annexed later by Cooper City after the mining town shut down."

Travis rubbed his neck, feeling his muscles tense and knowing a headache would soon follow. "You think that's where the grief demons are coming from?"

Brent nodded. "Yeah. And the whole area is honeycombed with mines. They're everywhere, and they're all abandoned—some for decades. So if there are supernatural creatures down there, they've had the run of the place since the last cataclysm. Maybe the energy from the genius loci extends into the tunnels, too."

Travis snagged another beer and returned to his seat. He flipped the cap between his fingers as he thought. "I don't think creatures like the ghouls and the spriggan and the grief demons—or that psi-vamp you killed—are actually part of the main event. I think we were right about them being the vultures on the battlefield. Doesn't mean we don't want to shut them down, but they're the symptom, not the disease. Seal up the hell gate for another fifty years, and we cut off their energy. They'll either go elsewhere to find new hunting grounds, like wolves when the deer herd gets too thin, or they'll go dormant until the next cycle."

"I think you're right. And we've taken care of a bunch of them already. But we haven't seen more come to take their place, so maybe there isn't an infinite number." Brent pointed out. "Or maybe we're too close to the main event for them to regenerate?"

"In Hazel's notes, she speculated that it might not be possible to stop the cycle, but someone could close it down early to prevent the big bang at the end," Travis said. "Getting rid of the grief demons before we go after the genius loci and the hell gate means one fewer set of enemies in the final battle."

"We don't have much time left to figure out how to win that big fight," Travis continued. "Or what it means to have an 'inside connection.' But Derek said he's willing to fight the battle with us, and if there's a traitor on the other side, a necromancer should be able to make use of it."

"Anything from your other Night Vigil folks?" Brent reached for a cold bottle, and then grabbed last congealed slice of pizza from the greasy box.

"I told you about Paige and Penny. Angie's a clairvoyant. She said she's been dreaming about green fields with white flags on them that suddenly catch on fire and burn like the sun. No idea what, where, or when, but she's been dreaming the same dream for over a week. Trece is a trucker. His far sight comes and goes, but when it hits, he sees something far away like it's happening in front of him. He called me with a warning."

"About what?"

"Green and black smoke, filling tunnels underground," Travis replied. "Sounds like demons gathering for the big finale."

"Ellie called. She said that Rachael is still in the hospital, but they expect she'll recover," Brent told him. Rachael had been one of the two Silverado killer's abductees to make it out alive. "And she didn't forget her promise to track down old stories. She typed up everything she found and sent it to me. I forwarded it to your email."

"Every needle we find in the haystack helps," Travis replied. He watched Brent drink the beer and hesitated before speaking. "You think CHARON could be any help?"

Brent sputtered a little, then cleared his throat. "No. They'd show up with their black SUVs and throw their weight around, probably get us all killed because they won't listen to anything we've figured out and want to start from scratch, only there isn't time, and we all just get our asses handed to us." He shook his head. "No. Definitely not."

Travis nodded. "I figure the same about the Sinistram. If they wanted to be part of this, they'd have beaten us to it, which means we're the cleanup crew. Us, and the Night Vigil."

"Don't forget Doug and Father Ryan," Brent reminded him.

"I'm not. Michael—that sniper I mentioned? Said he's in. And Jason, the fire starter. What about your friend Mark? He's a hunter."

"I asked. He's got a situation up by the New York border that's going nuts, and there's no one else to cover it except him. Monsters don't schedule these things to let us synchronize our calendars, I guess," Brent replied.

"Too bad. I think we're going to need all the help we can get." Travis paused to let the cold beer burn down his throat. "So...you think the place to fight the grief demons is Bliss cemetery? What did you have in mind? Because if we blow it sky high, even for a worthy cause, they'll probably haul our asses to Rockview, lock us up, and throw away the key."

"Blowing up the mausoleum won't do squat to demons," Brent replied. They had both fought enough of them to know. "I figure that with all your priest-y stuff, you know plenty of exorcism variations, and one of them might work. But there might be a ritual specific to grief demons, and if you didn't find it with your sources, maybe Chiara could find it with hers."

"The special library at Duquesne has a lot of manuscripts from the Vatican," Travis said. "What kind of resources is she using?"

Brent grinned. "Italian witches, Mafia sorcerers, Polish mystics. The Vatican isn't the only game in town, you know. Plenty of other people with powers have figured out how to handle things without involving the guys from Rome."

Brent's laptop chirped, indicating a new email. He glanced at the screen, tapped a few keys, then hunched forward, reading the message. A smile spread across his features.

"It's from Chiara," he reported. "And it's the details for the ritual."

———

"I'M NOT sure how I feel about using a synthetic ritual," Brent grumbled.

"Syncretic, not synthetic," Travis replied. "It's the difference between blending two cultural traditions, and being made out of nylon."

"I don't do the woo-woo stuff," Brent replied. "But it seems like sticking to the recipe would get the best results. Doing a mash-up sounds dangerous."

"And going up against a nest of grief demons isn't dangerous?" Travis chuckled, despite the situation.

They had spent the previous evening comparing the exorcism variations Travis had uncovered from his last trip to Duquesne's secret library with the rituals that Chiara's practitioners unearthed. Brent had admitted that it was all mumbo-jumbo to him, so he deferred to Travis to make the call.

Travis poured over the texts, dismissing some as questionable, others as outright fakes, but in the end, half a dozen litanies had both power and history in their favor. Yet none by itself seemed right to bind entities like the grief demons and send them back to the abyss or the primal darkness.

"I didn't 'mash up' the rituals," Travis replied. "More like layered the appropriate ones to reinforce and amplify each other."

"Have you ever done it before?"

Travis fixed him with a glare. "You mean, have I ever tried to bind an entire nest of demons at once? No. But I don't see how there's a choice in the matter. We've already expelled the ones we heard about, but that's not all of them. And we don't have time to hunt them down one at a time."

He knew his short temper with Brent came from his own nervousness about the unfamiliar liturgies. He had done a conference call with Chiara and Simon, and they had given him valuable insights, but he was the one who would be making the invocation. Travis had done his best to recall everything he'd learned in the Sinistram, but he could not remember the elite group taking on such a large foe.

And maybe that was why the Sinistram and CHARON weren't here doing the real work, he thought with annoyance. Maybe they cherry-picked their battles to be the ones most likely for them to win, not those with the most lives at stake. The thought only strengthened Travis's resolve to steer clear of the organizations. Although having that level of skilled help going into a situation like this would have been fucking awesome.

Sunset came early in autumn, so Travis and Brent went out to Bliss in the late afternoon. Jason and Lyle were waiting for them.

"Here. Take one of these. They'll help to deflect the demons from attacking you—or using you to attack me," Travis said as their group assembled—Father Ryan and Doug, then Derek.

He handed out protective amulets that he and Brent had made the night before for all of the participants, acting on directions and advice from Chiara and Simon. Father Ryan had given him several of the silver crucifix necklaces his church usually gave to those making First Communion, making sure to bless them and anoint them with holy water. Travis and Brent had wrapped each necklace around chunks of oak they had cut from the forest after Travis carved protective runes into the wood and added drops of blessed oil.

Travis also wore several religious medals for protection, along with a silver ring and a bracelet with silver, onyx, and agate. Brent didn't hold much with saint's medallions in general, but he wore one for St. Michael and St. George, patron saints of law enforcement.

The first step in their plan for the night was to place a warding on his helpers. Travis had worked the warding into the blessing on the amulets, and he felt the protective connection expand as each person took their charm and closed their hands around the blessed silver.

They all turned as a newcomer in a white truck drove up.

"Who's that?" Brent asked, eyes narrowing. Out of reflex, his hand fell to his gun.

A short, sandy-haired man swung down from the driver's seat and grabbed something from the back. He sauntered toward them, and between his buzzed hair and the way he carried himself, he was clearly ex-military.

"Michael. Glad you could join us." Travis welcomed him with a handshake, then introduced the sharpshooter to the others. He had to smile despite the circumstances as Michael and Brent eyed each other in a testosterone-fueled challenge.

"Save the arm wrestling for later," he remarked, and both men stepped back warily. "We're all on the same side."

Michael did a slow turn, taking in the surroundings. "I do my best work from up high," he said and pointed to the tall white bell tower not far from the mausoleum. "How about there?"

Lyle nodded. "There's a maintenance ladder that goes up the side, and a platform just beneath the clock and bell mechanism. It's not roomy, but it'll hold your weight."

Michael flashed a wide smile. "That'll do. Probably better than a lot of places I've been."

"Once I start the litany, the demons themselves should be compelled to enter the mausoleum," Travis told the group. "What we don't know is whether the energy will draw other creatures. That's where Michael, Doug, and Brent come in to make sure that nothing gets past the perimeter once we start the working." He gestured toward the line of burning pillar candles that formed a large circle around the big granite building.

"We'll make sure of it," Michael promised. Brent clenched his jaw and gave a curt nod.

"Father Ryan and I will handle the liturgy," Travis continued. "Lyle and Jason will back us up, in case the demons break the containment area I'll set up."

"And then what?" Doug asked. He had a shotgun as well as his sidearm, and Travis knew from overhearing his conversation with Brent that the man had plenty of iron and silver ammo.

"Then with luck, you have a very boring night, and all the action happens in there," Travis said, pointing. "Just make sure we don't get interrupted. I don't know what's likely to happen when we start the banishing. As far as we can tell, no one's tried before."

"Let's get to work," Brent said grimly, and the participants veered off to their places.

Travis felt a knot of nervousness. He had practiced the liturgy, and he knew the wardings that were needed. He had drawn on Wiccan and other old traditions outside of Catholicism for the amulet and elements of the warding and containment, spells more than sacrament, but he reminded himself that the Sinistram never had any qualms about using such things in the heat of the moment. The invocations would raise strong energies to counter the demons, and Travis sincerely hoped he could control that power so it would not destroy him.

"Can't say I expected to be wrangling demons when I came to Cooper City," Father Ryan remarked, jostling Travis from his thoughts.

"And people think nothing ever happens in small towns," Travis replied.

He and Ryan followed Lyle and Jason into the mausoleum.

Derek stayed outside with the shooters, where he could use his necromancy to deflect an attack by zombies or ghouls.

Travis sent the others up to the second level inside the mausoleum, while he made a circuit of the first floor, laying down a cordon of salt and iron filings at the edges of the walls, and tracing protective symbols every few feet onto the granite with blessed oil. The sigils were currently invisible to the human eye, but they would blaze brightly in the presence of demons. When he finished, he joined the others and looked down on the wide front entranceway.

"It's showtime."

The ritual's complexity lay in its many parts. The wardings were as complete as Travis could make them without creating a barrier that the demons couldn't cross, which would be counterproductive. The containment spell that he placed on the first floor of the mausoleum could be snapped shut with a word once the demons were inside. And after that—Travis stopped himself from going back over the plan. They would have to survive each step to get to the "after that."

"You're sure about this?" Father Ryan asked, coming up to stand beside Travis. Lyle and Jason kept watch from the other side of the open balcony. Travis and Lyle had guns, but if they needed them, the cause was already lost. Jason's fire starting provided some protection, but as they'd seen with the ghouls, the demands of his gift regulated his stamina.

If the ritual didn't work, they were screwed—and so was Cooper City.

"*Veni, immundus spiritus...*" Travis began the litany, which was basically a reverse exorcism. He had worked out the wording very precisely with Simon, Chiara, and Father Ryan so that he did not find himself besieged by every demon in range. Just the grief demons, and only those in the immediate area. Precision mattered when dealing with supernatural creatures. Souls had been lost over bad phrasing.

Travis shuddered as the temperature dropped. A primal sense of fear and the urge to flee slithered up his spine, and he felt the energy shift. His gift as a medium took over, giving him an odd, slightly off-kilter double vision of the living and the dead. The mausoleum's ghosts heeded the containment spell and stayed clear.

Father Ryan had a chant of his own in this ritual, and his voice rose and fell in counterpoint to Travis's, tenor and baritone, in defiance of infernal power. Travis watched the doorway and wondered how many of the grief demons remained to heed his summons.

When the first tendrils of black and green smoke oozed into the mausoleum, Travis's medium senses recoiled violently. The demons stank of sulfur and rot, and as the summoning compelled them to enter the containment area, the wards on the walls flared bright silver. Travis had no idea how many demons responded to the call, but soon the entire first floor of the building roiled with black clouds with streaks of foxfire glow.

Travis closed his hand around the silver amulet in his pocket as he chanted, not daring to hesitate. He felt the added protection of Father Ryan's litany, and he knew Jason's fire starting could drive off at least some of the demons, but he was aware of the massed evil below him and its barely constrained power and knew it could destroy them all if he lost control.

When he could sense no new demons entering the building, Travis finished the summons and spoke the word of power to snap the warding shut on the containment spell.

The demons, realizing they were trapped, howled and screeched like wretches in the depths of the Pit. Travis shifted to a liturgy of cleansing to make the stone floor and the ground beneath it less conducive for the demons. Travis knew he could not completely eliminate the ingrained old taint, but his intent lay in building a shell to isolate the demons from any energy reserves that might enable them to fight his power over them.

Outside the mausoleum, gunshots rang out. Travis recognized the crack of Michael's rifle, the blast of Doug's shotgun, and the *pop* of Brent's Glock. He dared not stop the ritual, but he sent up a silent prayer for their protection—for all of them to survive the fight.

Travis felt the demons pushing back against him, straining

against the wardings that held them in place. He forced himself to pay attention because he could not falter in his incantation. But he knew that the demons seethed at being summoned and contained, and would gleefully strip them all to the bone given any misstep. Father Ryan must have recognized the danger as well, as his chant grew louder, reinforcing the energies Travis had called and laying a second layer of binding on the malevolent spirits gathered beneath them.

An ear-piercing shriek rose from the mausoleum's lower level as the maddened demons fought their containment. The entire structure trembled, and Travis realized that if he couldn't finish the banishment quickly enough, the demons might be able to damage the solid building in a desperate bid for freedom.

Travis's head ached at his temples and sinuses. His mouth felt dry and tasted of ash. Power thrummed through his body, as his psychic abilities merged with the energies on which he called to dispel the demons. He shifted into the exorcism, relieved at the familiarity of the words, grateful to be on known territory once more.

His headache spiked, and he tasted blood in his mouth. The pushback from the demons was invisible, but unmistakable despite the containment warding. Down beneath them, the silver flare of the sigils blazed through the dark smoke like a beacon from a lighthouse, holding the separation and, Travis hoped, weakening the demons' power.

The building was as frigid as a meat locker, and Travis saw his breath. Exhaustion became euphoria as the long chant continued. Travis felt light-headed, and the tether between his soul and his body felt alarmingly loose as if he might step away from himself like shucking off a worn suit. A warm rivulet of blood trickled from his nose, and he wiped it away with the back of his hand, smearing crimson across his skin.

All of his senses, normal and extra, had heightened to the point of pain. He did not have to extend his abilities to know that the mausoleum's ghosts watched the proceedings in utter terror, or that beyond the granite building, the cemetery's restless residents had taken notice.

More gunshots, then silence. Travis couldn't allow himself to think what that might mean.

As Travis chanted the exorcism to banish the grief demons, Father Ryan continued the litanies of protection, invoking the saints and the Holy Mother, surrounding them with white light.

As the exorcism rose to a climax, Travis felt the containment spell weaken. He could not stop now, not when he was so close to the end. The demons sensed that their banishment was imminent, and fought to free themselves and destroy their tormentor with all of their waning power.

Tendrils of black and green smoke thrust up from the first floor, tearing through the fragile spellwork barrier. Father Ryan brought up a shotgun loaded with shells packed with salt and silver, blasting at the demons as they neared where Travis stood.

Behind him, Lyle shot into the hissing, roiling mass. The demons shrieked loudly enough that Travis thought his ears would bleed, but he kept on chanting. He was so cold that his numb fingers and toes no longer felt like his own. He willed his lips to continue as fear constricted his throat and made his heart thud.

Fire streamed all around him, driving back the encroaching smoke.

"I've got your back!" Jason yelled. "Now finish the hell up!"

Travis shouted the last few lines of the exorcism, straining to be heard above the shrieks and screams of the damned. He cried out the final words in triumph, and Father Ryan's voice rose to join him in the benediction.

With his inner Sight, Travis thought he glimpsed a rift opening into utter darkness. The grief demons gave a final, desolate howl before they were pulled like a maelstrom into the rift. The sigils flared once more, blindingly bright, and when the light faded, the mausoleum was empty.

Travis staggered, catching himself on the railing as Father Ryan grabbed him by the arm to steady him.

"That was...awesome," Ryan said, looking as if he had just witnessed something miraculous.

"Wasn't sure we were going to pull it off, for a few seconds there," Travis admitted. Ryan pulled a handkerchief from his pocket and Travis did his best to dab away the blood from his face.

"You look like you've been on a bender," Jason observed. "Haven't seen eyes that bloodshot since my freshman year in college."

Travis managed a weary laugh. "I might look bad, but you oughta see the other guy."

"Shit." They all turned to see Lyle, who had his hands on his hips and was glowering. "How in the hell am I going to explain all the pellet holes in the marble?"

Jason laid a hand on Lyle's shoulder. "We'll blame it on vandals. The cops will round up the usual suspects and let them go for lack of evidence. Then we'll hold a fundraiser to repair the damage."

Lyle looked barely mollified, but he nodded and let Jason steer him toward the steps.

They descended warily, but both the demons and the wardings were gone. Travis dreaded learning what had transpired outside, fearing the worst. They swung open the heavy doors to the outside, surprised that the autumn air seemed warm compared to the chill of the mausoleum.

"What the fuck?" Jason muttered behind him, as they surveyed a landscape littered with dismembered ghouls and rotting corpses.

"Sorry about the mess," Derek said, stepping out of the shadows. He had come straight from work, and his polo shirt and chinos were stained with dirt and gore. One sleeve had been clawed to shreds, and four deep gashes in his upper arm suggested a nasty fight.

"Brent? Doug?" Travis called.

Brent jogged up from one side of the mausoleum, while Doug joined them from the other. In the distance, Travis could just make out a dark form climbing down from the bell tower, which he figured was Michael.

"What happened?" Father Ryan asked, looking over the memorial gardens that had turned into a battlefield.

"It happened pretty much like Travis thought it might," Derek said. "The demons got sucked into the mausoleum. But before they went, they must have put out an S.O.S. because there were so many dead people clawing their way out of their graves, I thought it was the Second Coming."

As Brent and Doug drew closer, Travis noticed the toll the fight had taken. Brent's clothing looked like he'd been mauled by dogs, and he was bleeding from gashes on his shoulder and thigh. Doug must have taken a punch to the face since one eye had swollen closed and was darkening to bruise. He was covered with dirt and stained with grass, suggesting he'd wrestled with an attacker.

"The demons tried to take us," Brent reported. His face held the flush of the fight. "Derek's magic saved our bacon."

"I didn't know necromancy could hold off demons, at least for a short while," Derek said with a shrug. "I never thought of them as dead, but since they're not living, maybe they're 'undead'...I'll have to look into this further. But, I'm glad I could help."

"I thought I had a bird's eye view of *The Walking Dead*," Michael said, joining them. At first glance, Travis thought he had escaped unscathed in his aerie, but then he realized that the sniper's jeans were clawed to ribbons from the knees down. Michael seemed to follow his gaze.

"A couple of ghouls climbed up after me. I shot them."

Lyle looked over the carnage with a hopeless expression. "I'm not sure we can cremate this many bodies fast enough," he moaned. "And how do we explain the dug up graves?" He gripped a handful of his hair as if he was distressed enough to tear it out by the roots.

"You've still got the backhoe and the forklift, right?" Jason said, coming up beside him. Lyle nodded. "Well then. You drive the forklift, and I'll dig a hole. We'll blame the dug up graves on mutant gophers. With everything that's gone on around here, that's not even strange. Problem solved."

CHAPTER FIFTEEN

"I THINK I've found the hell gate—which means I've also probably found the genius loci." Brent didn't look up from his computer screen, but out of the corner of his eye, he saw Travis's head snap up.

"Where?"

Brent angled his laptop so Travis could see. "I've been going over the old mine maps. Mining was the first real industry in these parts, and it brought the first big settlement, so I keep coming back to thinking it helped to strengthen the dark energy. And when I made an overlay of the oldest maps and layered them, I found this."

He pointed to a deep, central shaft that was common to more than half a dozen of the oldest mines for which they had maps. "It took me a while to catch on that the mines had different names because there were branches and spurs that opened up in new locations. So instead of expanding and getting backlogged trying to bring more coal up out of a single entrance, they dug new tunnels to the surface to connect."

"But at the heart, it's one mine," Travis murmured, leaning forward for a better view.

Brent leaned back and rubbed his eyes. They were dry and

strained from too much time at the computer in the poorly lit motel room. He'd grown to hate the blue-green wallpaper and the ugly brown carpet almost as much as he disliked the strong smell of bleach when the housekeeper doused the shower with disinfectant. His apartment over the shop back in Pittsburgh looked luxurious by comparison.

"I don't think *all* of the mines are connected," Brent said. "At least based on the maps we have. But these are the oldest, and I think that might matter."

Travis stood and stretched, arching his back and flinging out his arms. They were both tall men, and the motel's chairs were not built for ergonomics. "So you think they drilled down deep enough to awaken a creature from the Pit?"

Brent shook his head. "Not exactly. But the center shaft is in the area the native tribes considered to be a bad place. So maybe whatever this energy is, having a clear shot to the surface makes it worse." He leaned to the side, cracking his neck. "Demons, I understand. This genius loci thing is fucked up."

"I've been talking with Simon and Chiara," Travis said. "Derek, too, since he has a perspective with the necromancy that might come in handy. I keep going back to what Hazel wrote in her research notes about working a ritual on this side and having someone on the other side do something to interrupt the hell gate so we can close the door, so to speak. Hazel gave very specific instructions in her journal."

"You're basing a lot on something that might really have been speculation," Brent warned.

"I know," Travis admitted. "But it's the best lead we've got. I was a priest, not a witch. *We* had fancy religious names for the magic we did," he added with a wry twitch of his lips. "But Paige had to do some dark magic to bind Penny's soul to her, and Benjamin messed with forbidden magic to raise his brother. Plus there's Aricella—"

"Who?"

"One of my Night Vigil folks. She's a baker—and a powerful

bruja. She knows how magic can go wrong. One of her spells got fucked up and killed her grandmother."

"Which is how she got to be one of your people, isn't it?" Brent asked. Travis nodded. All of Travis's Night Vigil crew seemed to have reached rock bottom because of their abilities, and saw helping out as a way to put things right, or at least atone.

"Anyhow, they know magic; I don't. So I asked them whether the ritual Hazel wrote about in her notes was real, and they all thought it sounded legit."

"Hazel was one hell of a woman," Brent said, shaking his head in admiration.

"Finding the best place to do the ritual was one of the last missing pieces," Travis said. "I spent all morning gathering the materials Hazel listed in the ledger. There weren't many, but it took a bit of searching. Now, all we need is someone to close the door."

Brent felt a chill, and he sensed Danny's presence. *No,* he thought. *Not you.* Brent shivered again. *Not gonna happen. I don't want to talk about it.*

"Something wrong?" Travis asked, and Brent wondered whether Travis could sense Danny the same way he could.

"No," Brent said a little too quickly. "What did you have in mind for the ritual?"

Travis's gaze lingered a second too long just off to Brent's right side, making him suspect that his partner did see Danny's ghost. "I want to reach out to Hazel and to the spirits of those killed by everything that's been going on, and see if we have any volunteers. They lost their lives because of the genius loci; they should have a chance to put an end to it."

That seemed fair, Brent thought, a little desperately. Let the people who died get a chance at revenge. *Danny's death didn't have anything to do with the hell gate. This isn't his fight.* Brent felt uncomfortable as if he was on the receiving end of a disapproving glare.

"When will you know?" Brent asked, hating that he sounded nervous.

"It'll have to be soon. If your date calculations are right, we only have three days. But I was trying to wait at least until this evening. What we did at the cemetery last night kicked my ass," Travis admitted.

"And we still don't know what this cycle's grand finale would be, in case we can do something besides close the hell gate to stop it," Brent pointed out.

"The trains don't run here anymore, and the mines are all closed," Travis said. "There's I-80. I guess the genius loci could undermine the road, make a bridge collapse again, or cause a huge accident—"

Brent listened, staring out the window past Travis, watching traffic on the road. Two white and green Preston Energy trucks drove by, and Brent felt a shiver go through his body.

"Wells and mines—isn't that what Hazel told you?" he asked, interrupting Travis. "Danny said something about wells, too."

"I figured they meant deep places, like the shaft you found," Travis said, obviously not following Brent's sudden conversational shift.

"You said one of your Night Vigil saw a field with green and white flags that went up in flames," Brent persisted. "Danny and Hazel both talked about fire. Gas wells," he said, words coming out in a rush. "Preston Energy. Oh, God."

He dove for his computer, typing quickly as Travis pulled up a chair beside him, watching over his shoulder. The Preston Energy website promised better living through cheap, plentiful natural gas, and downplayed concerns about fracking, their controversial extraction method.

"Look." Brent's voice was hollow with fear. A map of the county popped up, with red dots and lines that showed the expanding network of gas wells and pipelines. "They're everywhere."

Travis stared at the map and paled. "Fuck. That doesn't count the trucks that are full of who-knows-what to pump the gas out of the shale."

Brent traced the latticework of lines. "They're all around Cooper

City, over by the highway, near the power plant. If those blew, it would take out half the county. Probably fuck up the drinking water for a century, too."

Travis carded a hand back through his black hair as he stood and paced. "We're going to have to do the ritual before the hundred and fiftieth day. We've got three days."

"Maybe," Brent warned. "Remember, we weren't entirely sure what counted as Day One. There were some iffy things that happened—"

"So, tomorrow night," Travis said, practically vibrating with tension.

"Are we ready?"

"We have to be," Travis replied, looking a little shell-shocked. "If we counted wrong, and those gas wells go up—"

Brent flinched at the thought and looked away quickly. He'd had a bad night, after the fight at the mausoleum, and hoped Travis hadn't heard him cry out in his sleep through the motel's thin walls. His dreams had been a mashup of Mosul, the clusterfuck when he was with the Bureau, and the monsters in the cemetery. Only in his dreams, every time, the demons won, dragging away the soldiers in his unit, killing his FBI partner, and slaughtering them all at the mausoleum.

"Brent." Travis's voice was quiet, but with a tone that said he'd spoken more than once.

Brent jerked, eyes wide, breath shallow as he came out of his thoughts. "Sorry."

Travis brought a hand down on his shoulder, grounding him. "You're safe here, for the moment. We got out okay yesterday. Breathe."

Brent let out a defeated sigh and turned, pulling away from Travis's grip. "Maybe I'm part of the problem. Demon magnet and all. I'm too fucked up to be much good."

Travis frowned. "And I'm not?" he barked with a laugh. "Jesus, that would be funny, if it weren't fuckin' sad. Us, saving the world.

Must be scraping the bottom of the barrel." He gave a lopsided grin. "And yet...here we are. Halfway house heroes. We'll have to do because I don't see anyone else riding to the rescue."

Brent managed a wan smile in response. "I guess we'd better get to it then. Time's a wasting."

Travis put out the call to Ryan, Derek, Michael, and Aricella, while Brent asked Doug to meet him, not wanting to discuss the threat against the gas wells on the phone. When Doug pulled up, Travis finished his Coke and tossed the can in the garbage.

"I've got my folks ready to meet us tomorrow night at ten outside the main shaft," Travis said. "I'm going back to my room to pull some last pieces together, meditate a little, and call Father Pavel."

"He's your Confessor?' Brent asked, having picked up bits and pieces about Catholicism in the time he'd been traveling with Travis. Although Travis had left the priesthood and remained wary about the Church, old habits still provided comfort, Brent guessed.

"Yeah. I try to keep the slate as clean as I can, just in case," Travis admitted.

Just in case. It hit Brent then that Travis wasn't sure they'd survive the fight, and in the back of his mind, he'd known that all along. Everything they'd gone up against so far, the psi-vamp, ghouls, the spriggan, hell-maggots, and even the grief demons were—by themselves—manageable. But the energy or entity of the genius loci was old and powerful, and if not sentient in a human way, it was still able to fight with as much cunning as a wild animal. It needed the hell gate to stay open, while Travis and the rest of them were willing to risk everything to shut it down. The odds were against them succeeding, and even more so against surviving.

Brent nodded. "See you for breakfast. Shouldn't try to save the world on an empty stomach."

After Travis left, Brent tried to call Angela. He wasn't surprised to get voicemail. They had exchanged a few texts and one hurried call since he left Pittsburgh, but he couldn't share what was really going on, and he'd been too stressed and weary to chit-chat. He figured that if he survived the encounter with the hell gate, his reward would be getting dumped by his girlfriend.

"Hey, it's me," he said, feeling like he needed to say something. "It's been kinda crazy here. But I should be coming back soon. And I miss you. Take care."

Brent ended the call and stared at the phone in his hand. He hadn't wanted to worry Angela by sounding like it might be his last call, but the reality of the danger sank in a little more as he thought about the battle to come. All the battles and firefights he'd survived wouldn't hold a candle to what they were going up against.

He shook off his mood and called Doug. The police chief arrived a few minutes later, listening gravely as Brent filled him in on the plan and the threat against Preston Energy.

"Makes sense," Doug said. "Those wells and the pipeline are about the only things worth blowing up or burning down around here. I can report an anonymous tip, but I don't have the manpower to defend every site."

"This isn't like watching out for a terrorist with a backpack full of explosives. If the genius loci goes after the gas wells, it'll be an energy attack—magic, basically—and nothing security guards can do anything about. Best if there's no one around."

"Let me think how to do this then," Doug said. "I'm not sure that there's staff at most of the sites once they're active. It might be better not to report it if you don't want people in harm's way." He clapped Brent on the shoulder. "I'll take care of it. Thanks for the head's up."

After Doug left, Brent turned the TV to a sports channel to fill the silence as he looked at data for the fifty-year catastrophes. *"Two hundred and two presumed dead, 1868. Two ninety-five, 1918. Three fifty, 1968."* The records were spottier before 1868, but what he found suggested "more than one hundred dead or missing" from 1818, and a passing mention of the "great calamity" of 1768 when fever struck the village leaving "uncounted numbers" dead of disease.

All day Brent had argued with himself about whether he and his companions could handle the genius loci. He didn't have any illusions about stopping the cycle, but if they could avert the catastrophe, it would be a heroic, if unsung, accomplishment. And very likely suicidal. Not that Brent hadn't, on frequent occasions, thought about going out in a blaze of glory. But now his friends' lives were on the line, and that made a difference.

Travis had already told him that the Sinistram declined to help, that this threat wasn't "big picture" enough to warrant their involvement. But what about CHARON? Brent didn't like the idea of asking the shadowy group for anything, and he knew any favors would come with a high price, but hundreds of lives might be saved if he and the others could just get a little knowledgeable backup.

His thumb hovered over the contact on his phone, and he tapped it, squeezing his eyes shut in resignation. Shane answered on the second ring.

"Brent. Nice, but not unexpected. Have you decided to stop playing games?"

"We've got a situation, in Cooper City. An entity that rises in fifty-year cycles—"

"Oh, is it that time again? My how the decades fly."

"You know."

"Of course we know. That's what we do."

Brent's hand tightened into a fist at his side. "Then why the fuck aren't you here?"

"Because we can't be everywhere, and we're busy saving thousands or tens of thousands."

"These people here, they matter. They pay their taxes—your paycheck does come out of taxpayer dollars, doesn't it?" Brent sniped.

"Cute. Not relevant," Shane returned. "If this is why you called, I'm afraid it's a non-starter."

"How about if I said I'd consider coming in if you handle the entity?"

The pause went on so long that Brent thought the connection had dropped. Then he heard Shane sigh on the other end. "Tempting.

But, no. Unfortunately, I don't have that kind of say over where we go and what we do. But hold that thought. Come in, join us, and you can be a part of something much bigger, that really changes things."

It clicked then with Brent, the real reason for Shane's disinterest. "Because stopping a cataclysm in a Central Pennsylvania town won't make the news in a big way, will it? You need something big—stopping a plutonium smuggling ring, cracking down on a cartel, busting up a terrorist plot. That'll hijack the news cycle for days, and make sure your budget gets approved. That's the real game, isn't it? All about the money."

"I'd forgotten how tediously moral you were," Shane replied. "Let me recap: You're not joining, and we're not coming. Did I miss anything?"

"Just the big 'fuck you' at the end," Brent muttered, ending the call.

He pushed back from the computer and rubbed his eyes. Old injuries ached, but he couldn't afford to let pain meds get their claws into him. Instead, he reached for a bottle of Jack and splashed a few fingers of amber salvation into his coffee mug.

Brent moved from the hard plastic chair by the table to an armchair, which was only slightly more comfortable and held a musty scent from too many occupants and too much deodorizer. He took a swallow of his whiskey and let it burn down his throat.

Over the years more than one acquaintance had accused him of seeking "suicide by monster," or at least trying to check out in the line of duty. There was some truth to that. He remained convinced the demons that killed his family had been looking for him, that he had, somehow, brought death to their home. When his unit faced down Mavet, he took no pride in the commendations for saving most of his men, not when he felt certain that he had drawn the demon to them. The demon who killed his FBI partner had nearly said as much, straight out goading him. When he and his police team made a drug bust and found possessed narcos, Brent had been sure he was cursed.

And now here he was, partnering with Travis, and they were all probably going to die.

Demons lie. He reminded himself of that, knew that the infernal beings would say anything to gain an advantage, but he also knew that sometimes, the bald truth was worse.

If tonight turned out to be the last night of his life, Brent felt like he ought to do more than sit in a cheap motel room, drinking alone. But the thought of going out to a bar—even if there were one in walking distance, which there wasn't—and being surrounded by oblivious strangers who had no idea of the looming danger—left him cold.

He tossed back the whiskey, poured another shot and pounded it, deciding that he'd get a good night's sleep before the end of the world. Brent toed off his boots, stripped off his jeans and shirt, and fell into bed with the taste of toothpaste and Jack mingling in his mouth.

He was sitting on the back porch steps of his childhood home, shoulder to shoulder with Danny. Dream or illusion, it all felt real— the boards beneath him, the warm summer breeze with a hint of honeysuckle, the chirp and buzz of tree frogs and cicadas.

Danny turned to him, and while years had not changed him, his eyes held a sadness Brent did not ever remember seeing in life. "You know I have to go."

"It's not your fight," Brent argued, knowing they were talking about the battle with the genius loci and the ritual that required a "traitor" ghost to help shut the hell gate from inside. "You're not from here. These aren't the demons that killed you." Left unspoken was that he didn't want Danny to leave.

"Hazel's ghost is too weak. The others—the new dead—they're not very solid. It takes a while...after...to figure out what's going on," Danny said with a sad smile. "I'm the best bet. My spirit is more stable. And I've got a helluva incentive—keeping you alive."

"If you want to go on...to heaven...I'm not selfish enough to hold you back," Brent confessed. Even here, in this dream realm, he felt his hands sweat and his heart race at the prospect. Danny had been dead

for more than a decade, but their contact had been enough, over the years, that Brent hadn't felt totally alone. The thought that Danny might be gone for good made his gut clench, and his throat tighten.

"I don't know what will happen when I shut the gate," Danny admitted. "Maybe I can come back to you like this again, or I'll be stuck...somewhere. Or maybe if it ends me for good, I'll go on. But if I can come back, I will—if you want me."

"Of course I do, if you want to be here."

"Or you could make friends and meet someone special," Danny teased.

"Overrated," Brent replied. "Besides, that always gets fucked sideways when I try it."

"Keep trying," Danny said, his eyes losing their teasing glint. "For me."

"Yeah, yeah," Brent said, looking away, so Danny didn't see the tears in his eyes. "Hey, the priest and I get on okay; I mean, we haven't killed each other yet."

"He'll do," Danny said. "He and Simon can hear me. I like that. So they don't think you're crazy."

"Har, har."

"Like that time you had your earbuds in, and you were singing along to the music, and Old Man Kenner called the cops because he thought you were high?" Danny replied.

"More like the time you got stuck in the attic and yelled yourself hoarse because mom had the radio turned on loud enough to hear it over the vacuum," Brent answered, elbowing his brother in the ribs.

"Says the guy who got locked in the gym storage closet and almost had to spend the night before someone found you."

"Hey, that wasn't my fault! Cobie Harris admitted he pushed me in there and locked the door," Brent protested. It felt so nice, so normal, to banter and remember. Most of the time Brent was torn between not wanting to forget all the good times he and Danny had, and not being able to bear to recall them.

"I hope I can come back," Danny said, growing wistful. The

dreamscape around them was beginning to fade, and Brent knew their time in this place between waking and sleeping was ending. "But if I can't, some of me will be with you as long as you don't forget."

"Never," Brent swore. "And if this goes badly, I might see you on the other side sooner than you think."

"Let's hope not," Danny said. "I'd much rather come back here. Good luck, Brent. Tell Travis I'll be waiting for my cue."

With that, the dream, vision, sending—whatever it was—ended, and Brent woke tangled in the motel bedspread.

———

IT WAS like facing Mavet all over again. Different landscape—the rolling, tree-covered hills of Central Pennsylvania instead of desert and ancient ruins—but the same feeling of dread at going up against an enemy that might have existed before time itself.

Brent choked down his fear and locked away his doubts. Whether they died facing down the energy of the genius loci or got blown to Kingdom Come, their odds of living through the confrontation were slim.

Unlike the Zimmer Eight mine where they had faced down the spriggan, the mine entrance that Brent's maps showed to be closest to the central pit was long abandoned by even the monsters, nearly lost to view in a tangle of overgrowth. The Carmichael Mine was the first in the area, overshadowed years later when the larger, more industrialized Zimmer Mining Company bought up the land and forced out the owners. They had bricked up the mine mouth, relocating the heart of the operation to Zimmer One, never imagining that the old tunnel might hold the key to their descendants' salvation.

"This is Aricella," Travis said, introducing Brent to a slim, dark-haired woman dressed in a flannel shirt, down vest, jeans, and hiking boots. She looked more like a trail guide than a *bruja*. Everyone shook hands. Father Ryan didn't seem to have any qualms about working with either Derek or Aricella, and if they had reservations about collaborating with a priest, it obviously didn't keep them from putting their lives on the line.

It had taken several hours to lug all the materials in from where they had to leave their vehicles. More time had passed getting everything into position. Now, they were as ready as they would ever be.

"Everyone, listen up!" Travis said, halting the low buzz of conversation. The small team drew closer, instinctively moving away from the mine entrance.

"We've got one shot," Travis told them. "And we're not entirely sure what the genius loci is, energy or entity. So there's a ritual, but be prepared, because we can be sure it will fight back if it realizes we're trying to close the hell gate and stop it from blowing up the gas wells and drinking in all that pain and suffering."

Brent looked from one face to another. Each person nodded, jaws clenched, gazes resolute. No one had to tell them the odds. They knew, and they came anyhow. Brent had the sudden, overwhelming certainty that Danny was very proud.

"We've got a man on the inside," Travis went on. "And we have some unconventional helpers. So do what you do best, and we'll shut this muther down."

"Is this where you say, 'may the Force be with you'?" Brent asked.

"And also with you," Father Ryan replied with a gleam in his eye.

"Whatever works," Travis said, but he smiled, just a little. "All right, folks. Let's get to it!"

Aricella had already driven to all of the Preston Energy sites they could locate and placed a warding and containment spell on each. Two of the wells were close to the old Carmichael entrance, and she placed her strongest wardings on those. Maintaining the protections on the gas wells and pipelines would take all of her attention, so she had set up a salt circle between the mine and the wells, reinforced with candles and blessed herbs.

Michael had scoped out the area early in the day and built himself a sniper's roost in a nearby tree where he could have a clear view of the land around the mine mouth. Brent and Doug brought a variety of guns and types of ammunition and laid out safe areas bounded by salt and iron. Jason came armed, too, with a handgun and a shotgun to back up his fire starting.

That left Travis, Derek, and Father Ryan to work Hazel's ritual, and Danny to get into position wherever the hell gate was located so he could spring the trap.

Brent took up position in a salt circle just a few feet from Travis, while Michael did the same on the other side, near Derek. He shuddered to think that the battle might reprise the fight at the mausoleum. That had been close, maybe closer even than Travis realized. The creatures had come at them out of nowhere and kept on coming, and he had doubted for a while that they would be able to fight them all off. Then Travis had sent the grief demons packing, and the others lost their mojo.

"First, some help from our friends on the other side," Travis said. He glanced at Derek, who gave a nod. Then both the medium and the necromancer closed their eyes, and they each held out a hand as if beckoning for the spirits to join them.

The temperature dropped, going from late autumn chill to winter frigid in seconds. Brent could see his breath in front of his face, and he was glad he had dressed for the cold. A gray mist rose all around them, not the ominous black and green smoke of demons, but the fog of clustered spirits. Sometimes he could glimpse shapes or faces, and he strained to see Danny, but couldn't make out enough specifics to be sure.

Danny always wanted to play super spy. Now he gets to infiltrate the enemy location and be the hero. Go, Danny. A swell of pride filled him at his brother's bravery, and Brent refused to let himself feel the impending sorrow of their final separation. He drew on all his training as a soldier and summoned his battle calm, pushing everything extraneous from his mind, shutting down his feelings, heightening his senses. This was the kind of war he was, unfortunately, uniquely ready to fight.

As Derek and Travis called to the angry dead, enlisting their protection against whatever the genius loci might throw at them, Father Ryan started to chant. By now the rise and fall of the litany was a familiar comfort to Brent, despite not having grown up Catholic. Father Ryan sang the words of the prayers in simple Gregorian plainsong: haunting, ancient, and beautiful. Brent didn't know Latin, but Ryan had told him that the chants were for cleansing, protection against evil, fortifying the faithful, and blessing soldiers about to go to battle. That seemed entirely appropriate.

Brent had left his own faith behind in the wake of his family's deaths. God had grown ever more remote after Mosul, though demons seemed to dog his steps. Still, knowing what lay before them, he had stumbled through an awkward confession and a plea that, despite his many failings, if he fell he and Danny would be reunited. It was the best he could manage, and now he let the battle coldness settle over him, resigned to take as many of the sorry bastards down with him as he could.

CHAPTER SIXTEEN

"SOMETHING'S WAKING UP!" Derek shouted.

"Can you ground it?" Travis yelled back. Derek considered the genius loci to be "undead," and his goal was to use his power to bleed off any energy he could to weaken it.

Travis had begun Hazel's ritual. The words did not flow quite as naturally as did the Latin, but Hazel's litany was both a binding and a banishment, if not quite an exorcism. He kept one hand out, palm open and forward like a conduit for the magical and sacred powers that he called; his face rigid with concentration, eyes narrowed.

Derek murmured to the swirling mists, bidding them to rally to the cause. He roused from his trance and glanced toward Travis. "I'm trying. It's...slippery."

The mine opening was sealed, but the woods around the abandoned tunnels had grown thick over the years, a perfect hiding place for the kinds of creatures drawn to the dark energy of the hell gate and the genius loci.

Aricella maintained the invisible wardings that protected the gas wells and pipelines and secured them in case the two nearest wells went up close to the Carmichael Mine entrance. Travis felt her power like an odd shimmer of bells at the very edge of his consciousness.

Derek's magic felt earthy by comparison, like a flowing river, a force of nature. Travis wondered how his own abilities—he still wasn't comfortable thinking of them as magic—felt to them. He'd never thought to ask.

Somewhere out there Michael had a sniper's roost while Doug, Jason, and Brent were ready for a repeat of the onslaught at the mausoleum. That left Travis with the ghosts, Danny, and the hell gate, while Derek held back the genius loci.

Danny's spirit was strong, familiar. In the weeks since Travis and Brent had partnered, Danny had shown up several times, and Travis figured he was lonely for someone who could see him more easily than Brent. He hadn't felt comfortable recounting those conversations with Brent yet, but he would when the time was right. Danny was a good kid, a lot like his more care-worn brother, and their chats gave him insights into his new partner that made him more patient when Brent got prickly.

Now Danny waited for orders.

Travis had gone over the plan with Danny, answering all his questions. The toughest one, he didn't have an answer for—whether Danny would be trapped within the hell gate, free to move on, or able to come back. For all his time in seminary, any answer Travis had learned was really just theoretical when the rubber met the road. Despite the uncertainty, Danny stood firm, and so Travis had guided him toward where his clairvoyance suggested there might be a weak spot, a place where Danny might be able to slip in among the vengeful ghosts and minor demons in the sway of the genius loci's power to help Travis shut the hell gate from the inside.

Go, Travis told him. In his mind's eye, Danny gave him a jaunty salute and then vanished.

The genius loci pulsed deep within the Carmichael Mine like the heartbeat of an ancient god. No, Travis corrected himself. Not a god. Something more powerful than a man, but just another predator that had become invasive without a natural enemy. The energy felt tainted, not merely hungry, but cruel. The genius loci gorged itself on pain, death, and grief until it had taken in enough to slumber for another fifty years. Travis knew they couldn't stop the cycle, but if they kept it from its grim harvest, perhaps when it did reawaken, it would be weakened and easier to fight.

He felt the genius loci stir, a frisson of energy that sent a shiver down his spine that had nothing to do with the cold autumn air. The entity—or whatever it was—shifted, and Travis felt awareness wash over him. Their prey had noticed the arrival of the hunters and understood itself to be their target.

Game on.

Derek must have felt the shift as well. "Incoming!" he shouted, as good a term as any, Travis supposed, for the psychic wave that thundered toward them.

The wall of spirits Derek had called as an extra layer of protection rallied, and a thick, gray fog surrounded the living fighters, clammy as it slipped against their skin. Travis—and Derek, he was sure—heard voices and glimpsed forms and faces, as the ghosts held their position.

From one side, Travis heard a howl like a wolf, and from the other, the guttural groans of zombies and ghouls. He heard a shotgun blast and the crack of Michael's rifle and Brent's Glock, firing over and over again to pick off attackers. Streaks of fire burst across the night, proof that Jason was on the job. Travis could not spare his attention from the task, sending his power toward the weak point where the hell gate would form, and finding a way to shut it down.

Shots rang on every side, and Travis fought the urge to duck or run for cover. He, Derek, and Ryan stood in the middle of a war zone as their protectors fired and reloaded. The smell of gunpowder and rot was so thick it seemed palpable. Behind him, Travis heard Father Ryan saying a litany for protection against evil, but Travis feared that this time, they might be out of luck.

The ghosts moved across the land between them and the mines

like a tide, doing their best to interfere with the creatures the genius loci sent as its first wave. Derek's magic increased the spirits' strength, and the more powerful among them tore at the ragged clothing or grabbed at the dead limbs of the zombies and ghouls as they ran forward, slowing them enough to give the shooters a chance to aim, or deflecting the attackers from their targets.

Derek couldn't keep up that kind of defense for long, and Travis hoped Danny had been able to get into position. The notes in Hazel's journal speculated that an uprising of ghosts and a "traitor" who stopped the hell gate from opening could prevent the genius loci, in its full power, from emerging for its final, catastrophic feeding. All the details she provided, Travis passed on to Danny, hoping that Hazel had a solid basis for her ideas. If Hazel had decided to take up writing fiction, they were all well and truly fucked.

Travis hadn't told the others that he'd had two visions, one of them forcing the genius loci into early hibernation, emerging bloodied but victorious, and the other—in the other, there'd been fireballs and explosions, scorched earth, and charred corpses. He took that to mean that both futures remained possible and that it would come down to a choice, an action, a split-second impulse that would make all the difference.

But who might be the deciding factor, Travis didn't know.

Now. Danny's thoughts stretched across the distance, just as Travis felt the lurch of the genius loci's dark energy.

"Now!" he told Derek. Behind them, Father Ryan shifted to the Rite of Exorcism, authorized or not, Vatican be damned. Derek gave a cry, and Travis felt a push as the necromancer lent his magic to the storm of ghosts, sending them back toward the hell gate to spend their remaining vengeance helping to push the doorway closed from this side.

"It's getting through!" Travis grated. In the distance, a loud explosion echoed, and seconds later a pillar of fire rose high into the air. Aricella's protections were weakest the farther the wells were from her, and Travis was just grateful that the two nearest them hadn't gone up instead.

He'd seen a vision. He'd called the ghosts and sent Danny. Now, as Travis moved into the banishment portion of Hazel's ritual, he felt helpless. What good were the psychic abilities for which he'd been ostracized from his family and badly used by the Church if he couldn't do something truly useful with them? And as he said the words of the litany, and listened to Father Ryan's exorcism voiced with full-throated belief, something inside Travis shifted. He reached into his core self with all the resolve he possessed and *pulled*.

Hazel's ritual held real power. Travis felt the magic—this had to be magic—rise within him like fire in his blood, terrifying and powerful and barely within his control. The night was cold—frigid after the ghosts appeared—but he was sweating, drops running down his back in rivulets and plastering his hair to his forehead.

Another of the wells exploded, a little closer, and Travis set his jaw and hardened his will. His heart thudded and his head pounded, pain throbbing behind his eyes and in his temples. Travis kept on reciting the words of the banishment. But as he spoke, he fixed his focus on the place where he had sent Danny, where the legion of their ghostly protections had gone—to the hell gate between *there* and *here* that the genius loci entity needed to escape. He called to his psychic gifts and pulled from what he thought might be his life force itself, willing to give everything he had to stop the cataclysm.

The ground around them shook, and he felt the dirt slide under his feet. Brent and Doug cried out, and as Travis watched, he saw a sinkhole open between them and the blocked up mine entrance, a chasm stretching into the abyss.

He felt the touch of the genius loci, sliding over him like dirty oil, trying to latch on to use his power for itself. Travis pushed back with everything he had, roaring the final words of the ritual like a rebuke of every betrayal, of all the ways he had been manipulated by the Sinistram, and of the times he had tried and failed to save someone. This time, *this fucking time*, he would do it right, and make a difference.

Even if it killed him.

Travis tasted blood in his mouth and blinked bloody tears from his eyes. His lungs burned as he hyperventilated, and his body felt like a human torch, aflame from inside with the magic awakened by Hazel's incantation. Nothing in her notes said that the one who worked the ritual became a sacrifice, but if that was the case, Travis willingly offered himself.

His pulse thundered ever louder in his ears, blocking out Derek's chant and Father Ryan's rite, the gunshots, the screams of the monsters. Nothing mattered—nothing existed—except the magic, and Travis opened himself to the strange surge, letting it flow through him, following the channel he had opened to Danny and the other ghosts, a willing conduit.

He saw the ghosts more clearly than ever—probably a sign that he might soon be among them. The ghostly horde on this side of the hell gate pushed back to keep the genius loci from coming through. Travis sensed Derek's magic in the struggle, and together they poured all of the power that they possessed into the effort. In the distance, another muffled explosion told Travis they were losing the fight.

Hike! Danny's voice called out the football play, and suddenly, the hell gate wavered.

"This is it!" Travis shouted, though whether he said the words aloud or silently to the ghostly legion, he couldn't tell.

The ghosts swarmed forward, a tide of soul energy and the strength of memory, as the insurrection on the other side also gained momentum. The genius loci, caught between both sides, let out a psychic shriek that made Travis reel, and he fell to his knees. Derek grabbed for him, but Travis pushed him away, staggering to his feet, intent on his objective.

Bit by bit, he felt the hell gate close. The genius loci thrashed and screamed in fury, but Travis could tell it was weakening, overspent by the creatures it had sent against them and the power it expended fighting off a rebellion it never expected.

Travis's breath came in harsh, wet pants. He spat out blood, but his mouth filled with it again. A crimson haze covered everything. His body felt numb, distant, as if he could step away and leave it behind. Nothing mattered except closing the hell gate, and doing that could claim all of him, body and soul.

He lurched forward with his power, reaching deep inside and finding a final vestige of strength, adding it to the effort of the ghostly defenders, who had become nearly solid. And then, just as Travis was certain they had come so far just to fail, the last resistance yielded, and the hell gate snapped shut.

Sealing off the genius loci for another fifty years, ending the deadly cycle.

The magic he'd called up faded and his body felt burned and raw from the inside. Travis called out to Danny but got no response. *It's done*, he thought, as he fell forward. As he drifted, he felt a faint glimmer of warmth and reached out to it, because the darkness was so very cold. Perhaps it would carry him onward; maybe it would take him home. Travis didn't care. They won. The battle was over. And he was done.

CHAPTER SEVENTEEN

"IT'S about time you woke up." Brent cloaked his relief in humor as Travis groaned and opened his eyes. The bloody sclera of Travis's eyes almost made Brent look away, but he figured if Travis could endure the injuries, he could dignify them by not pretending they weren't there.

"How long?"

"Two days," Brent replied. "You're in the hospital in Bellefonte. Christ, you gave us all heart failure. Wasn't sure you were going to make it."

"Neither was I." Travis's voice was rough, and Brent held out a glass of water with a straw so he could take a sip.

"We won, right?" Travis croaked.

Brent put the glass back on the nightstand. "It was a close thing, and pretty messy, but yes. We won."

"The gas wells—"

Brent sighed. Leave it to Travis to want to talk about the failures first. "Aricella did a hero's job, but she put most of her energy into shielding the wells near us and near populated areas. The genius loci blew up four of them, and it was a very impressive fire, but there wasn't any staff on hand and no collateral damage."

Travis let out a little groan and closed his eyes. He looked a damn sight better than when the ambulance had taken him away, deathly pale, barely breathing, coughing up blood. Derek had insisted on riding with him, and while he'd told the EMTs he was a friend, Brent knew it was because the necromancer was helping keep Travis's soul in his body long enough for the doctors to resuscitate him. Even then, Derek told Brent it had been a toss-up for a while.

"I'm sorry," Travis managed. "About Danny."

Brent blew out a breath. "Yeah. Me, too. But it was his choice. And he's a hero, even if no one knows but us. Derek and I had time to talk, waiting on your sorry ass to come around. He isn't convinced that Danny or the other ghosts could be permanently trapped since he says they're a different type of energy than the genius loci, whatever that means." He rubbed his neck, trying to ease the knotted muscles. "But he did say that ghosts can be drained, and so even if Danny doesn't leave permanently, it might take him a while to charge up enough to show himself. We'll have to wait and see."

"Better than the alternatives," Travis rasped. His eyes suddenly flew open. "Shit. Bellefonte. My family—"

"Has not been given permission to see you, thanks to that health-care power of attorney you gave to Jon," Brent replied with a grin. Travis sank back into the bedding with a sigh. "Smart move. For what it's worth, your mom was pissed."

"She wasn't worried about me. She was scared the news people would find out about the psychic stuff," Travis whispered.

Brent had that impression too, but he didn't think it helped to agree.

"Considering it's a hospital, the food here isn't too bad," Brent said. "No beer, but Doug brought me a flask," he added, holding it up in a "cheers" gesture. "We tag teamed—Doug, Derek, Jason, and me— so someone would be with you. Aricella came in at the beginning, as soon as the docs were done with you, and I think she might have added a little magic to help you heal."

"Tell her thanks." Travis's voice was fading. Brent knew he had to be barely functioning.

"I wanted to ask...any chance you've got room for a new recruit with your Night Vigil?" Brent managed a lopsided, self-conscious grin. "I've got experience."

Travis didn't open his eyes, but his lips twitched in a smile. "I think we could arrange something."

"Jon was here, but he went back to mind the store," Brent continued.

"You're going to have to do that, too."

"Yeah, well. Someone had to watch your back," Brent said. "I've got my laptop. There weren't any clients that couldn't wait until next week. And I decided to bring in another PI, to give me a little more flexibility."

They fell into a comfortable silence. Brent had always been antsy with a partner at the FBI and the PD, but working with Travis—after their initial pissing matches—felt natural. And hey, they'd saved their corner of the world without the help of the Sinistram or CHARON.

"Get some sleep," Brent told Travis. "I've got your back. And— I've got my Glock."

AFTERWORD

Pittsburgh is dear to my heart, since we lived there for ten years and I'm originally from north of the city. I guess that's why we keep setting books and series there, because it's a great city with a lot of history and lore.

Many of the locations in the book are real, and others have been fudged a bit or are an amalgam of other places created to suit the story. Peale, for example, is real and really a ghost town. Cooper City is not, but people familiar with the state will recognize real places like Wylie Avenue and the South Side in Pittsburgh, Bellefonte, Miles-burg, and of course, State College. (I'm a PSU grad.)

If you liked Mark Wojcik (the mechanic/monster hunter friend in Atlantic) and Chiara Hamilton, the researcher, they have their own series, Spells, Salt, & Steel—co-written with my hubby, Larry N. Martin.

Likewise, Simon Kincaide stars in his own books written under my Morgan Brice pen name (urban fantasy male/male paranormal romance), the Badlands series. Yes, Simon is a cousin of Cassidy Kincaide, the main character in my Deadly Curiosities series, and the owner of the antique shop they mentioned that helps get rid of cursed and haunted objects. Her boss, a nearly 600-year-old vampire, writes that mysterious check to St. Dismas to help pay the Night Vigil.

Travis and Brent make a significant appearance in two of my Morgan Brice stories—*Dark Rivers* (Witchbane #2, which also is set in Pittsburgh) and *Lucky Town* (Badlands 1.5, part of which is set in Pittsburgh.)

Just a shout-out to our other Burgh-based series, *Iron & Blood* (and the related Storm & Fury collection), for those who like stories set in that neck of the woods.

It takes a village to write a book. Thanks first to hubby and frequent co-author Larry N. Martin, for all his hard work behind the scenes. Thanks also to cover artist Lyndsey Lewellen for the fantastic cover, and to Jean Rabe for excellent editing. Many thanks to Mindy Mymudes for wrangling my street team, the Shadow Alliance, and to all the wonderful Shadows for their support. Thanks also to my beta readers who help make the books the best they can be, and my launch team who help to spread the word: Amy, Andrea, Anne, Candi, Chertex, Cheryl, Chris, Darrell, Donald, Jason, Karolina, Laurie, Lynne, Mary Mac, Mike, Sharon, Shauna, Sherrie, and Susan. I appreciate all of you!

And most of all, thank you to my readers.

ABOUT THE AUTHOR

Gail Z. Martin is the author of *Vengeance*, the sequel to *Scourge* in her Darkhurst epic fantasy series, and *Assassin's Honor* in the new Assassins of Landria series. *Tangled Web* is the newest novel in the series that includes both *Deadly Curiosities* and *Vendetta* and two collections, *Trifles and Folly* and *Trifles and Folly 2*, the latest in her urban fantasy series set in Charleston, SC. *Shadow and Flame* is the fourth book in the Ascendant Kingdoms Saga and *The Shadowed Path* and *The Dark Road* are in the Jonmarc Vahanian Adventures series. Co-authored with Larry N. Martin are *Iron and Blood*, the first novel in the Jake Desmet Adventures series and the *Storm and Fury* collection; and the *Spells, Salt, & Steel: New Templars* series (Mark Wojcik, monster hunter). Under her urban fantasy M/M paranormal romance pen name of Morgan Brice, *Witchbane, Burn, Dark Rivers, Badlands*, and *Lucky Town* are the newest releases.

She is also the author of *Ice Forged, Reign of Ash*, and *War of Shadows* in The Ascendant Kingdoms Saga, The Chronicles of The Necromancer series (*The Summoner, The Blood King, Dark Haven, Dark Lady's Chosen*) and The Fallen Kings Cycle (*The Sworn, The Dread*).

Gail's work has appeared in over 35 US/UK anthologies. Newest anthologies include: *The Big Bad 2, Athena's Daughters, Heroes, Space, Contact Light, With Great Power, The Weird Wild West, The Side of Good/The Side of Evil, Alien Artifacts, Cinched: Imagination Unbound, Realms of Imagination, Clockwork Universe: Steampunk vs. Aliens, Gaslight and Grimm, Baker Street Irregulars, Journeys, Hath no Fury,* and *Afterpunk: Steampunk Tales of the Afterlife.*

Where to find me, and how to stay in touch

Find Gail at www.GailZMartin.com , on Twitter @GailZMartin on Facebook.com/WinterKingdoms, at www.DisquietingVisions.com blog, on www.Pinterest.com/Gzmartin, and on Goodreads https://www.goodreads.com/GailZMartin.

She is also the organizer of the #HoldOnToTheLight campaign www.HoldOnToTheLight.com. Never miss out on the news and new releases—newsletter signup link http://eepurl.com/dd5XLj

Support Indie Authors

When you support independent authors, you help influence what kind of books you'll see more of and what types of stories will be available, because the authors themselves decide which books to write, not a big publishing conglomerate. Independent authors are local creators, supporting their families with the books they produce. Thank you for supporting independent authors and small press fiction!

ALSO BY GAIL Z. MARTIN

Darkhurst

Scourge

Vengeance

Reckoning - *Coming in 2019*

Ascendant Kingdoms

Ice Forged

Reign of Ash

War of Shadows

Shadow and Flame

Convicts and Exiles (Prequel) - *Coming in 2019*

Chronicles of the Necromancer / Fallen Kings Cycle

The Summoner

The Blood King

Dark Haven

Dark Lady's Chosen

The Sworn

The Dread

The Shadowed Path

The Dark Road

Legacy of the Necromancer

Coming in 2019

Deadly Curiosities

Deadly Curiosities

Vendetta

Tangled Web

Trifles and Folly

Trifles and Folly 2

Assassins of Landria

Assassin's Honor

Sellsword's Oath - *Coming in 2019*

Night Vigil

Sons of Darkness

Other books by Gail Z. Martin and Larry N. Martin

Jake Desmet Adventures

Iron & Blood

Spark of Destiny - *Coming in 2019*

Storm & Fury

Spells, Salt, & Steel: New Templars

Spells, Salt, & Steel

Open Season

Deep Trouble

Close Encounters

Spells, Salt, & Steel: Season One (Collection)

Other books by Larry N. Martin

Salvage Rat